PETER CHEYNEY
YOU CAN ALWAY′

REGINALD Evelyn Peter South
born in Whitechapel in the East E
as a lieutenant during the First Wor₁
a police reporter and freelance investig.   .ound
success with his first Lemmy Caution nove   .is lifetime
Cheyney was a prolific and wildly successful author, selling, in
1946 alone, over 1.5 million copies of his books. His work was
also enormously popular in France, and inspired Jean-Luc
Godard's character of the same name in his dystopian sci-fi
film *Alphaville*. The master of British noir, in Lemmy Caution
Peter Cheyney created the blueprint for the tough-talking,
hard-drinking pulp fiction detective.

PETER CHEYNEY

YOU CAN ALWAYS DUCK

DEAN STREET PRESS

Published by Dean Street Press 2022

All Rights Reserved

First published in 1942

Cover by DSP

ISBN 978 1 915014 01 6

www.deanstreetpress.co.uk

CHAPTER ONE
FOR ME—GAYDA!

I

THE grandfather's clock half-way up the windin' staircase outside
the bar-parlour strikes twelve. Grandpop is plenty wheezy. They tell
me this clock is three hundred years old. It sounds like it has got the
bellyache. An' why not? If you was three hundred years old I reckon
you would have the bellyache too.

I lean my head against the back of the armchair an' relax. I am
thinkin' about Adolf Hitler. I am thinkin' that if it was not for this
guy I would probably be kickin' around some swell place in the U.S.
takin' things nice an' easy.

A funny guy this Adolf. Personally I think he is nuts. All over
the world guys are thinkin' what they would like to do to that baby.
Different people have got a lot of different ideas about just what they
would do. Some of the ideas are very interestin'.

This is what they call wishful thinkin'!

Anyhow, I reckon Adolf is redundant right now. So I start thinkin'
about women. This is a good habit because any time you have not
got anything else to think about you can always start thinkin' about
some dame, an' even if it don't get you any place it can be restful.

Outa the corner of my eye I can see Benzey. Benzey looks to me like
he's taken too much liquor. His head is lollin' over to one side an' he's
breathin' like somebody hit him in the stomach with a baseball bat.

I say: "Listen, you Canadian bloodhound, are you awake or are
you?"

He says: "Yeah . . . so what!"

"I was thinkin' about women just now, Benzey," I tell him. "Did
it ever strike you that the dames over in England are pretty good?
They got somethin'!"

"I know," says Benzey. "One of 'em told me."

"Yeah?" I tell him. "What else did she tell you?"

He says: "You'd be surprised." He yawns. "I been thinkin' about
dames too," he says. "I been sorta runnin' through the list of all the
mommas I tried to make an' threw out over. There was more than I
thought. It's funny how a fella can miss sometimes."

"Not you," I tell him. "You couldn't miss with a frill. You're no ordinary guy, Benzey."

I grin at him.

"Goddam funny, ain't you?" he says. "Seriously though, there was one or two of them babies I ought to have worked harder over. There was that one in Hollywood. She was cute she was. She had scarlet hair an' she usta do her toenails to match. I ought to have married that one."

"An' she wouldn't play, hey?" I ask him.

"She was all tied up," he says. He yawns. "Half the guys in Hollywood was tryin' to marry this frill." He gives a big sigh. "The other half already had," he goes on. "She was sorta popular."

"But she didn't wanta marry you, hey, Benzey?"

"I told you she was all tied up," he says. "She was married to some sound-effects guy. I wanted her to get rid of him. I told her I knew a lawyer who'd fix a divorce for her for five hundred dollars, but she didn't like it."

"Maybe she thought it was too much dough," I tell him.

He shakes his head.

"She figured she wasn't goin' to pay any five hundred bucks for a divorce. She said she could have him shot for fifty dollars. She said she even knew a guy who would do it for nothin' . . . you know—just for the ride. . . ."

"But she still wouldn't play?" I say.

"No," says Benzey. "She hated that guy too much. She told me that she disliked his innards so much that it sorta fascinated her. She said that every time she usta look at him an' realise that he was her legal husband her stomach usta turn over. I reckon she got a sort of kick outa loathin' this guy."

"Women are goddam funny," I tell him. "They're like whisky. You always want some when you haven't any around."

"Women certainly are not like whisky," says Benzey. "You can always *get* whisky."

"You *hope*," I tell him.

He says: "Look, I wanta sleep. Will you wake me up any time that somethin' is liable to happen?"

He turns his head away. In two minutes he is snorin'. He sounds like a tank.

I get around to thinkin' about this Travis dame. Me—I would like to take a look at her. There was a baby had somethin' if you like. An' did she do somethin' to that husband of hers or did she! I can remember Lolly describin' this baby to me. He says:

"Listen, Lemmy, maybe you've seen dames all over the place. An' maybe you've been plenty places, but I'm tellin' you, you ain't seen nothin'! I'm tellin' you that I have never seen so much woman done up in one packet of my life before. If Casanova hadda seen this baby he woulda give up."

I tell him that generalisations like that are no good to me.

He says: "All right. I'll give you a blue-print. She's tall, see—but she ain't too tall. An' she's slim but not that thin sorta slimness. No, sir, this baby is curved but the sorta curves that don't throw themselves at you, see? They're sorta discreet an' clever curves an' all the more attractive because they are.

"Also she is one of these supple babies. Boy, I would give two months' pay," says Lolly, "to watch that dame walkin' for about an hour on end. Because she has gotta rhythm like you have never seen before. Her feet are slender an' she has got sweet ankles. I have been lookin' at ankles all my life," says Lolly sorta ruminatively. "I have seen good ones and not so good ones. Once or twice I have seen real queen ankles, but I'm tellin' you, with my hand on my heart, that I ain't never seen any ankles until I saw this baby's."

I say: "That's fine, Lolly. Well, I reckon this frill's under-pinnin's an' foundation are pretty good. Supposin' we get to the upper stories."

He says: "O.K. I'm gonna start with her neck. She's gotta nice neck—maybe she was a swan in some previous existence—an' not only is her neck good but the way her head is set on it. An' she has got an oval face an' her skin is the colour of the milk that you skim off the top of the bottle. You know, the thick part—nice an' creamy an' soft. An' she has gotta little colour in her cheeks like you see on a peach that's been hangin' out in the sun. She has gotta nose that is perfectly straight an' sorta sensitive, delicate nostrils. Her eyes are grey an' violet an' blue—"

"Hooey!" I say. "No dame ever had eyes like that. You've been drinkin'."

"No," says Lolly. "I only took to drinkin' *after* I saw that woman. I am tellin' you that her eyes are all those colours, dependin' on how she's feelin', see?"

I say: "I see. You are hypnotisin' me. Go on, pal."

He says: "She has long beautiful eyelashes an' a nice forehead, an' her hair is brown with little lights in it." He sighs. "I have left her mouth till the last," he says. "Me—I can't properly tell you about this baby's mouth because every time I start to tell some guy about her mouth I get the jitters. I can't talk properly."

I say: "She musta had some mouth."

"Yeah," he says. "I reckon she's still got it. It's sorta small an' beautiful an' tender—an' it can be tough too—an' her teeth are like little white seed pearls. Oh boy, every time I think of her I wanna pass right out."

This is what Lolly has told me about the Travis dame. Well, he should know!

I light a cigarette. Benzey is snorin' like hell. I reckon Benzey ain't got a properly developed sense of beauty. If he had he wouldn't snore like that. I wonder how long I'm gonna stick around this dump just on the chance of somethin' happenin'. I am feelin' what the English call "browned-off." It's the sorta feelin' you get when nothin' happens, when you're bored, when you're standin' on the edge of somethin' watchin' life go past you an' nothin's happenin' to you. I have smoked half the cigarette when the door opens. The landlord sticks his neck in. He says:

"Your friend was askin' about a sergeant who comes here. He's just come in."

I say: "All right. I'll tell him."

He goes away. I dig Benzey in the ribs. He wakes up.

He says: "So what!"

"Come to," I tell him. "The landlord has just been in here an' says your pal the sergeant's around. Go an' do your stuff. An' try an' be clever if you can."

"O.K.," he says. "If I can't, I'll get some lessons from you, Sourpuss." He lumbers out.

I gotta flask in my hip pocket. I take a pull an' light another cigarette. I sit there for about twenty minutes lookin' at the ceilin'. Then
Benzey comes back. Just behind him is the sergeant. He is a nice
slim, clever-lookin' guy with a brown face.

Benzey says: "Meet a countryman of yours." He points at me.
"This guy's Pleyell—40th Marines."

The sergeant says: "Hi'ya!" He gives me a quick look-over—the
sorta look-over that all technicians in the U.S. Army give when they
see a Marine. I give him a cigarette.

Benzey says to him: "You needn't be afraid of havin' a drink, see?
We're livin' here. We're old pals, Pleyell an' me. We've gotta week's
leave, so we're spendin' it together." He puts his hand in his hip an'
brings out a flask about three times as big as mine. He gives it to the
sergeant. "Have a drink," he says.

The sergeant takes a long pull. He says:

"This is nice of you boys."

Benzey says: "Yeah. We're kind-hearted. You'd be surprised." He
turns to me. He says: "You know, the world's a funny place. Who d'ya
think's in this guy's outfit?" He points to the sergeant with his thumb.

"You tell me," I tell him. "I ain't a thought-reader."

He says: "Nobody else but Travis. He's a Lieutenant. The sergeant
here says he's a great guy."

"It's goddam funny," I say. "You see, Mrs. Travis—who I reckon
is this guy's wife—is a friend of some friends of mine. She's often
talked about him."

The sergeant grins. "I'll bet it wasn't nice," he says.

I pick it up that way. I take a chance on bein' right.

I say: "You're tellin' me. There was nothin' too bad to say about
that boyo. She was a lovely piece too, this Travis piece."

The sergeant says: "Yeah? Well, she may be, but I don't think she
was so hot. Travis is a good guy. He can be tough, but he's a good
soldier. I don't see why there should have been so much trouble
between him and her. I reckon she was one of those babies who was
too beautiful for an ordinary guy to string along with."

I nod my head. "That's how it goes," I say. "If a woman is beautiful it spells trouble."

Benzey says: "So what's trouble? I never met an ugly dame yet who didn't mean trouble if she wanted it. Whatever you do you're gonna get trouble if you play around with babies, so you might as well have beautiful ones."

I say to the sergeant: "You don't wanta take any notice of him. He took a correspondence course in philosophy." I light another cigarette. "It's funny what you've just said about Travis," I tell him, "because the people I know who knew his wife didn't make him out to be that sorta guy at all. They say he was just a bad-tempered cuss— that there was nothin' good about him. They didn't like him a bit."

The sergeant says: "Well, he's changed a lot, that's all I can say. But I'm betting that guy is a hundred per cent. He's got a nice nature. Any woman who couldn't get along with him I reckon there's got to be something wrong with her."

"It's nice to hear that," I tell him. "How long's he been over here?"

"Not long," says the sergeant. "He came to our mob with the last draft—about four officers and thirty men."

I yawn. "They said he used to drink like a thirsty shark," I go on. "I suppose that wasn't the truth either?"

"He likes a drink," says the sergeant, "but in a controlled sort of way, see? He's quiet. He's the sort of guy who never uses bars or saloons much, but that don't mean he's not tough. He's got to know nice people around here. They're plenty glad to have him. He's a social sort of cuss."

I nod my head. "He's a wise guy too," I say. "The only place you can get good liquor these days is in private houses—in any quantity, I mean. Some guys have all the luck," I go on. "I suppose the women around here are a bit stuck on him?"

He says: "Why not? He's just a nice natural sort of guy. Say, I think he's got something that women would fall for in a big way. He's got that sort of quiet approach, you know?" He grins. "There are three daughters in that big house on top of the hill," he says. "I reckon they're all a bit nutty about him. And are they jealous of each other? He just plays 'em along. He was going up there to-night to dinner. There was some sort of dance planned for afterwards. Those three girls were callin' the camp-orderly office all mornin'—each of 'em in turn—trying to date him up for to-night for the dance."

"Some guys have all the luck," I tell him. I wink at Benzey.

He gives the sergeant another pull of his flask. He says:

"I don't know about you. I'm gonna bed."

"Me too," I say.

The sergeant puts on his hat. "Well, I'll be seein' you," he says. He goes out.

Benzey lights a cigarette. He says: "You got what you wanted?"

"Maybe," I tell him. "How do I know? I got *somethin'*."

"What are you gonna do?" says Benzey.

I grin. "I'm gonna take a look at this paragon," I tell him. "I think I'll invite myself to the dance."

"All right," he says. "But don't do anything too funny, willya?" He goes upstairs.

I look at the clock. It is twenty minutes to one. I light another cigarette an' I flop in the armchair an' do a little more thinkin' about Travis. Just as if thinkin' got you any place.

II

Half-way up the hill I take a breather. I sit myself down on a tree stump on the grass edge at the side of the road. I light a cigarette an' give myself up to a little more deep thought. Way up towards the top of the hill I can see the house. The moon has come out from behind the clouds. It is almost as light as day an' the countryside around here is lookin' marvellous. Sittin' there, smokin', lookin' over the green fields, I sorta get the idea of this England—just a pint-sized green island that's been havin' wars fought over it for hundreds of years an' comes up smilin' all the time.

As I go up the hill I can see that the house is a pretty big sorta place. There are some trees behind it. Somehow it looks like a stage settin'—somethin' not quite real if you get me.

I go through the big gates an' up the semicircular carriage-drive. Everythin' is good an' dark, but somewhere inside the house some-body is playin' a piano-accordion, an' boy—can they play! Whoever is squeezin' that music-box certainly knows his bananas.

There is a bell-pull by the side of the door. I pull it an' wait. About three-four minutes afterwards the door opens just a crack. Inside is a tall guy with grey side-whiskers. I take one look at him an' see that he is the family butler. This guy mighta been playin' the part on the stage.

He says casually: "Good-evening, sir. Can I do something for you?"

"Just a little thing," I tell him. "Maybe there's a party or somethin' goin' on around here an' I don't wanta butt in, see? But I believe Lieutenant Travis of the U.S. Army is up here."

He says: "Yes, sir, he is."

"I'd like to have a word with him," I say, "just sorta quietly, you know."

He says: "And your name, sir?"

I draw on my cigarette. "Just tell him Carlos Pleyell of the U.S. Marine Corps," I tell him. "I won't keep him a minute."

He says sorta dubious: "Well, I'll try and find him, sir. . . ."

Just then some voice says over his shoulder: "What is it, Blythe?"

The butler steps back an' opens the door a little way farther. I step inta the hallway, an' I wish you monkeys coulda had a sight of the frill who is standin' just behind the butler!

She has on a black velvet frock, a string of pearls, beige silk stockin's an' high-heeled crêpe-de-chine shoes with little diamond buckles. She is a chestnut brunette an' one big curl tied with a black moire ribbon is hangin' over one shoulder. I'm tellin' you guys that if I was in a train wreck with this baby I wouldn't even pull the communication cord. I would just stick around an' sing Halleluiah until they brought the ambulance.

She says: "It's all right, Blythe."

She throws me a little quick smile. Did I tell you that this doll has a very nice line in mouth and teeth, because if I didn't she has. She says: "You want Mr. Travis?"

"That's right," I tell her. "I'd like to have a word with him."

She says: "Well . . ." She looks sorta dubious.

I take a look around the hallway. It has all the hall-marks of the old-time feudal set-up. Sam Goldwyn might have designed this dump. There are even a coupla suits of armour stuck up against the wall. May be they haven't got around to meltin' them down for tanks yet.

I say: "Of course I don't wanta be inconvenient or anythin' like that."

She says: "That's not it. I'd like you to see Mr. Travis if you want to, but . . . well, first of all he's busily engaged at the moment in a pistol-shooting competition down in the kitchens, and secondly, I think he's a little tired."

I get her. I tell her: "You mean he's too cock-eyed to talk?"

She says: "I'm not quite certain about that. Perhaps some black coffee . . ." She looks at me sorta old-fashioned. She says: "I heard you talking to Blythe. You're a U.S. Marine?"

"That's right, lady," I tell her.

She says: "I've always wanted to meet a Marine. I've seen so many films about United States Marines that I've always wanted to see one." She gives a little sigh. "You look just like I expected you'd look," she says.

"Now what do you know about that?" I tell her. "I think it's marvellous me bein' like that. I hope you're gettin' a kick out of it."

She says: "To tell you the truth I am. Do you know what I think?"

I tell her no. I also think it is a darned good thing she don't know what *I* am thinkin'.

She says: "I think you're cute!" She is standin' there with her hands clasped behind her back, a posture which believe me is very good for the figure. She looks so good that I am thinkin' I could eat her.

She says: "Look, Mr. Pleyell, would you do me a favour?"

"I'd do anythin' for you," I tell her, "even if it landed me in the brig, an' anyway if I do you a favour maybe you'll do me one an' find Travis."

She says: "Oh yes, I'll do that. I'll find him and give him a lot of black coffee and try and produce him for you."

"Fine," I tell her. "Well, what's the favour you want me to do, lady?"

She says: "Don't call me 'lady.' My name's Gayda."

"Mussolini's mouthpiece!" I tell her. An' we both laugh. Anybody would think it was a good joke. I do a bit of quick thinkin'. "My front name's Carlos," I tell her, "but my friends usually call me 'Sourpuss'!"

She says: "I shan't do that. I'll think up a nicer name for you. This is what I want to know. Can you tell me what a 'crummy bastard' is?"

"It's an old-fashioned expression used amongst American sailors," I tell her. "It can mean practically anythin'. You can translate it how you like. The word 'bastard' is either a term of affection or it means a love-child. 'Crummy' is the U.S. equivalent of your English 'lousy.' "

"I've got it," she says. "You wait here, honeylamb, and I'll come back for you. I'll get somebody working on Mr. Travis for you." She goes away.

I light myself a fresh cigarette an' I go over an' look at one of the suits of armour. It is real all right. Maybe some guy wore this at the Battle of Hastings or somethin'. Personally, I would rather be in a tank. I am also thinkin' that it looks to me like there is gonna be some redeemin' features about this Travis business.

I have burned half the cigarette when she comes back. I watch her walkin' along the passageway that leads inta the hall. She knows how to walk, this Gayda. She says:

"Look, Lollipop, he's practically unconscious, but Blythe's filling him up with black coffee. He thinks he can have him more or less right in about a quarter of an hour. Will that suit you?"

"That'll be fine," I tell her. "Did the Lieutenant look affected any when you told him I was waitin' to see him?"

She says: "He couldn't even understand what I was saying. I told him it was important and he just made a noise like a seal."

"How did you know it was important?" I ask her.

She says: "I'm only a sweet English girl and I haven't been around very much, but it is quite obvious to me that an out-size U.S. Marine doesn't come here at this time of night to ask a U.S. officer what the time is. By the way," she says, "why aren't you in uniform? I think you'd look fearfully nice in uniform."

"You're dead right," I tell her. "I heard that before some place."

She says softly: "I suppose the women fall for you like ninepins?"

"I wouldn't know," I tell her. "I've never seen a ninepin fall."

She asks me for a cigarette. I give her one, light it.

She says: "What's it like outside?"

"It's marvellous," I tell her. "You know, when we came over here they gave us a little handbook. They told us all about the English people. At least they told us what they thought they knew about the English people. They also told us about the weather over here, but I think the weather's marvellous. It's the sorta weather you could have bets on. But to-night everythin' outside looks sorta mysterious an' soft. There's a little wind blowin' through the trees. There's a moon. From this hill you can look a pretty long way over the country, an' it looks good to me."

"It looks good to me," she says. Her voice is serious. "It looks so good to me, and a lot of other people like me," she goes on, "that you just don't know how glad we are to see a whole lot of husky people like you coming over here. It means that, as you would say, we're all going places pretty soon."

"You're tellin' me!" I tell her. "An' in a very big way, I hope."

She puts her hand on my arm. Her fingers are long. Her fingernails are pretty and pearl-coloured. She says:

"Look, while they're getting Mr. Travis into a more or less conscious state, suppose you and I walk a little."

"Marvellous," I tell her. "The guy who wrote, 'I don't wanta walk without you, Baby,' musta seen you some time. I feel just like he did."

She says: "You are cute, aren't you?"

I open the door an' we go out down the steps. We turn to the left an' go round the side of the house. We go across a lawn that slopes down the side of the hill. There is a little clearin' where we can look through the trees. We stand there lookin' at the moonlight on the fields below. She sighs. She says sorta wistful:

"The moon always does something to me. I can't quite describe it, but standing here looking at this with you almost makes my heart come up into my throat."

I look at her sideways. I say: "Oh yeah!"

She says: "I mean that. Doesn't it affect you? Doesn't it make you feel as if you're drawn towards everything and that life is really rather beautiful?"

I put my arm around her waist. She lays her head on my shoulder. I take a look at her an' I forget all about business for a minute. When I tell you that I kissed that dame I mean it.

She sighs. She says: "This is quite mad, of course. If any one had told me earlier this evening that I should be standing here kissing a United States Marine I wouldn't have believed it."

"Neither would I," I tell her. "But why worry about that?" I look at my wrist-watch. "Look, Gayda," I say, "don't think I'm tryin' to interrupt anythin', but do you think the Lieutenant might be a little more conscious by now?"

She says: "Why not? You're wise, aren't you, Sourpuss? If I stay out here with you much longer I might even lose my viewpoint."

"You're tellin' me," I say. "Not to mention your reputation!"

We start walkin' back towards the house. When we're half-way across the lawn I say:

"Look, maybe it would be a good thing if I talked to him out here, see? What I've gotta say is sorta private."

She says: "Yes. Perhaps it would be. The air might do him good. I'll go and fetch him." She walks off towards the house.

I stand lookin' at her for a minute; then I walk back across the lawn an' lean up against a tree. Right then there is a pop like some-body pullin' a champagne cork only it wasn't somebody pullin' a champagne cork. I've heard that noise too often not to know what it is. I ease round the other side of the tree pretty quick. I wait a minute or two but nothin' happens. I go around the tree again, take out my pocket flash an' take a look. Just about six inches above where my head was a coupla seconds ago is a lead slug. I take it out with my penknife. It looks like a .45 pistol bullet. I put it in my pocket; light another cigarette.

After two-three minutes Gayda comes back again. She says: "He'll be out in a minute. He's much better now."

"I'm glad," I tell her. "How is the pistol-shootin' competition goin' on downstairs?"

"Not too bad," she says. "Why?"

"They're usin' silencers, aren't they?" I tell her.

She raises her eyebrows. "How did you know, Lollipop?" she says.

"Oh, nothin'," I tell her. "Only somebody musta fired outa the basement window. They put a slug inta that tree. I was leanin' against it at the time so I was sorta interested."

I take the slug outa my pocket an' show it to her.

She says: "That's the trouble with soldiers—they're careless with firearms, aren't they?"

"If that was the only thing they was careless about I wouldn't mind, precious," I tell her.

We can hear the front door openin'. After a minute a big burly guy comes across the lawn. He's not quite steady on his feet, but he looks all right.

She says: "Well, I'll leave you. If you've nothing better to do some time, or you're feeling bored, you might telephone me. You'll find the number in the book. The house is called 'Mallows.' "

"I couldn't forget it," I tell her. "So long, sweet."

"So long, honeybunch," she says very softly.

She goes away.

III

Travis leans up against the tree. He still looks as if he ain't quite certain whether it's Christmas Day or Manila. He fumbles for a cigarette-case an' takes out a cigarette. I light it for him. He draws the smoke down inta his lungs an' takes a long look at the moon. He looks at it for such a helluva long time that I reckon that any minute he might start bayin'.

Then he says: "What can I do for you? They said you were a Marine. What're you doing out of uniform?"

So the boy is beginnin' to pull himself together.

"I'm on leave, Lieutenant," I tell him. "An' I've got permission to wear civilian clothes. I thought it might be better if I wasn't in uniform when I saw you. . . ."

He says: "What is all this goddam mystery anyhow? What is it you want to see me about?"

"I wanted to have a little talk with you about Mrs. Travis, Lieutenant," I tell him. "I sorta thought it might be a good idea."

He looks at me like somebody had poleaxed him.

He says: "What the hell have *you* got to talk to me about Mrs. Travis for?"

I light a cigarette. I take a long time about it. Then I say: "Look, maybe you didn't quite get my name. I'm Carlos T. Pleyell of Wynn, Stromberg, Fidelli & Playell—they're your attorneys, ain't they? Or don't you remember?"

He gives a grunt. He says: "So you're Pleyell. Wynn handles my affairs. You're the partner I've never met. What's the trouble about anyway?"

"There's no trouble," I tell him. "The only thing is about that divorce you've been tryin' to get. When I got over here a month ago Wynn got in touch with me on the Transatlantic telephone. He was so goddam worried about you he got special permission to make the call. He told me that the boat you came over here on was torpedoed. He said that about four days before you sailed he sent you the divorce papers and the evidence that our people had got for you. He didn't know whether you'd got all that stuff. An' if you had he didn't know whether you'd lost it when your boat was sunk. He was worried sick."

Travis says: "Why was he worried sick?"

"He'd got a good reason," I tell him. "You know as well as I do that Mrs. Travis didn't want that divorce to go through. Wynn told me that she'd been leadin' such a pure life that it almost hurt—just so's you shouldn't get rid of her. He said he'd had five of the leadin' investigators on her tail tryin' to dig up evidence an' it took 'em a year to get it. Well . . . he rushed the whole goddam lot to you right away in such a hurry that his secretary didn't take any copies—there was a general mix-up about it. Wynn was worried sick that if you'd lost all the stuff in the shipwreck he'd have to start diggin' all over again an' Mrs. Travis would be sittin' on top of the heap, laughin' her head off—an' there wouldn't be any divorce."

He says: "Wynn needn't worry. I've got all the papers." He grins suddenly. "I'd rather have drowned than lose those," he says.

"Then everything's O.K.," I tell him. "An' I can stop bein' an attorney an' go back to bein' a private in the Marine Corps—which, between you an' me an' the doorstop, is a much more interestin' job."

He says: "I bet it is. You look more like a Marine than a lawyer to me."

I nod. "I've always been that way," I tell him. "Me . . . I didn't want to go into no attorney's office. I've always been stuck on the wide-open spaces—if you get me—but my old man was always stuck on me bein' a lawyer so I went through with it just to keep him sweet. Now he's dead, it don't matter, an' you won't catch me in any attorney's office when this man's war is over."

"Maybe you won't have the chance, soldier," he says. "Maybe you'll be a nice corpse and you won't have to worry about anything at all."

"Maybe not," I tell him. "I should worry anyhow. I'm here at the moment an' that's all that concerns me right now." I throw my cigarette stub away.

"O.K., Lieutenant," I say. "I'm glad we got this all fixed. I'll get permission to get a long cable off to Wynn an' tell him that you got those papers all right. Then when I've done that you better go before a notary here an' swear the papers an' get a High Court confirmation here. Then Wynn can start in an' get action in the New York Courts."

"Yes," he says. He sounds sorta doubtful. Then he goes on: "I don't know that I'm going to worry a lot about it," he says.

I look at him sorta surprised.

I say: "I don't get this at all. Wynn told me you was goin' to move heaven an' earth to get rid of that wife of yours. He told me that you hated her worse than poison; that she'd played you up hell an' devils for years; that you told him you'd cut your right hand off if you could get out from under. Now, when everything's set an' he can go ahead you say you're not goin' to worry."

"Well . . . it's different now," he says. "It's true what you say about Cara having played me up but that was in the old days. There's a war on now an' she's in America an' I'm here. First of all I might not get through this war, an' secondly, it's a helluva job tryin' to run a divorce action in America from this country. The other thing is that if she's still feeling tough she'll put every goddam obstacle in the way of a decree—and she's plenty clever—you ought to know that. But if I don't do anything and she thinks I'm not bothering, then—being a woman—maybe she'll get tired of being good and she'll fall for somebody and start things off herself."

"That's true enough," I tell him. "She's certain to fall for somebody, some time. Tell me, Lieutenant, is that one as beautiful as they all say she is?"

"You never saw anything like it," he says. "She's just as beautiful as she's bad. Any time you take a long look at Cara you forget everything."

I nod my head. "Well," I tell him, "I'll be on my way."

He says: "All right, and thanks for your trouble. You let Wynn know that I've got all the papers and I'll think things over. Where can I reach you—if I want you any time?"

"I'm with the Headquarters Staff in London," I tell him. "You can always get me."

"Right," he says. "Well . . . good-night, Oh, by the way, what was Miss Vaughan talkin' to you about?"

I ask him if that would be Gayda Vaughan. He says yes.

"Mainly," I say, "she was talkin' about the chances of gettin' you sufficiently sobered up to come out an' talk. Why?"

"Oh, nothing," he says. "Good-night."

He turns away an' goes back towards the entrance door.

I wait till I hear the door shut. Then I light myself a fresh cigarette an' start walkin' down the carriage-drive. Me—I reckon I'm happy enough. What the hell! Somehow I'm quite pleased with the situation. Travis seems a reasonable sorta guy—tough—good-lookin'. I reckon dames could fall for him when he was sober. I get to wonderin' just how often he gets cock-eyed.

I get to the big iron gates. I am passin' by a rhododendron bush when a little voice says: "Oh, darling!"

I stop an' take a look. It is Gayda Vaughan. She is standin' behind the rhododendron bush holdin' up her velvet skirt. I can see her little shoes are damp with dew.

I say: "What is this? Is this a game?"

She says: "Hush, sweet. This is a secret, see? I didn't want anybody from the house to know I'm talking to you."

"I get it," I say. "Romance, hey?"

She smiles. I believe I told you about this baby's teeth before. In the moonlight they look swell.

She says: "You *are* cute, aren't you? I bet anything you like you look good in Marine uniform."

"You're tellin' me!" I say. "When I walk down Piccadilly, all the dames get a crick in the neck through lookin' over their shoulder. Look, Gayda," I tell her, "would you mind tellin' me where this conversation is leadin'?"

She says: "Yes, I'll tell you." She looks sorta dreamy. "Where are you going to, dough-boy?"

"I'm goin' home," I tell her. "I'm stayin' at an inn down in the village, but I'm breakin' outa here in the mornin'. I'm goin' back to

London. That's where I belong, see—an' there's a war on, but perhaps they didn't tell you?"

She looks at me. Her eyes are big. There are little soft lights in 'em. I start to wonder about this Gayda.

She says: "I know all about the war, but even if there is a war on you can't soldier *all* the time, can you? What do you do in the evenings?"

"Plenty," I tell her. I grin at her.

"That's what I thought," she says. "Sourpuss, do you want to take me out?"

"Why not?" I say. "What's the big idea?"

She says: "I'll tell you. There are one or two things I want to talk to you about."

I look at her. "Are they the sort of things you have to talk to *me* about or would any soldier do?"

She says: "No, don't make any mistake, my sweet. I want to talk to *you*. First of all I want to talk to you about Lon Travis."

"I see," I tell her. "Well, I'm at your disposal. What are we gonna do about it?"

She puts her hand on my arm. "Look, honey," she says, "I'm coming up to town on the train to-morrow afternoon. I'm going to stay there to-morrow night. I'm going to have a little flutter." She wrinkles her nose at me.

I'm tellin' you that when I look at this baby standin' there in the moonlight holdin' her velvet skirt up with one white hand—the other restin' on my arm—my heart misses a coupla beats or maybe three.

"I see," I tell her. "What sort of flutter?"

She says: "If I know anything of you you're a gambler, aren't you?"

"That depends," I tell her. "That depends on what the stakes are an' who I'm playin' with."

"Well, look," she says, "it doesn't matter what the stakes are because if you want financing I can help you. I should think you'd be lucky at cards. Yes"—she puts her head on one side an' considers me for a moment—"I should think you're one of those few men who would be lucky at cards *and* lucky in love."

"Gayda," I tell her, "you're makin' my head spin. Will you say what it is you wanta say?"

"All right," she says. "Here's the thing. Let you and I have an evening out to-morrow night. Can you get the time off?"

"Sure thing," I tell her. "I can always get a late pass when I want one."

"All right," she says, "I'll be waiting for you in the Berkeley Buttery at eight o'clock. We'll have dinner; then we'll go on to a place I know and play a little. Then we can talk. How will that suit you, soldier?"

"Lady," I tell her, "it sounds to me one hundred per cent. Where are we goin' to play?"

She says: "Oh, you wouldn't know the place anyway."

"You'd be surprised," I tell her. "I probably would. I've got around since I've been over here, you know. Don't get me wrong—I'm not one of those parochial sorta guys."

She says: "I didn't think you were. Well, if you must know, there's a rather nice club—*quite* nice. The stakes are pretty high but the players are nice people—you know?"

I take a shot in the dark. "That sounds to me like the Anchor Club," I say, "that place off Knightsbridge—the place that looks like a love-nest, on the fourth floor."

"No," she says, "it's better than that. It's near Mount Street. It hasn't got a name really. We call it 'Chez Clarence.' "

"Well, I never heard of that one," I say. "But it's O.K. with me."

She says: "All right. I must go back now." She takes a long look at me. "Anybody who christened you Sourpuss must be blind," she says. "I think you've got the cutest face. I like your jaw."

"Look, sweetheart, you're not proposin' to me by any chance, are you?"

"No," she says. "If I ever feel like it I'll let you know. Good-night, honey." She puts her arms around my neck an' gives me a kiss, an' when I say gives, I mean *gives*!

Then she turns an' hurries away across the lawn back to the house. I stand behind the rhododendron bush watchin' her. I'm tellin' you she looks like a little black velvet ghost.

Some little black velvet ghost.

Yeah!

IV

It is half-past one when I get back to The Plough. I go upstairs. Benzey is asleep in his room. He has not bothered to undress. He is makin' a noise like an asthmatic bull. I give him a dig. He wakes up an' rubs his eyes.

"So you got back?" he says.

He swings his legs off the bed, sits there lookin' at me.

He says: "Did you see the boy friend?"

"Yeah," I tell him. "We had a little conversation. He's got the papers all right, but he's not so keen on the divorce now."

Benzey looks surprised. "Why not?" he asks.

"Travis figures it's gonna be a lot of trouble," I tell him, "swearin' those papers on commission, gettin' the evidence back to New York. He's sorta dubious, see? Another thing, he thinks that the war's altered things. He thinks that dear little Cara Travis is not going to go through this war without fallin' for somebody, an' he thinks that when she falls for somebody she's gonna want to get a divorce, see?"

"I get it," says Benzey. "Well, maybe the guy is right. Anyway, it sounds logical, don't it?"

I tell him yes. I ask him what he's been doin'.

"I been studyin' women," he says. "After you'd gone I had a sleep for a bit; then I went downstairs. You know, the old boy's daughter here's got somethin'. She's got nice eyes."

"Yeah?" I tell him. "I bet you told her that."

"You're tellin' me," he says. "I told her a lotta stuff. A very difficult baby to get any sorta reaction from, that one."

I sit on the bed. I pick up the bottle that Benzey has got on the floor an' take a long swig. "I bet you went through a big performance with that baby downstairs," I tell him. "I bet you told her about you at Dieppe."

"An' how!" he says. "You shoulda heard it. According to me I was the only Canadian there who mattered a damn. I practically slaughtered the whole of the German Army with one hand."

"What did she do about that?" I ask.

"Not a goddam thing," he says. "After I told her this an' a few other things I said to myself this dame don't go for heroics, so I went all soulful. I told her all about herself. I told her she was lovely."

"I bet she fell for that line," I say.

"Not a hope. She never shifted an inch. Then I thought you don't go for heroics an' you don't go for flattery, let's try somethin' else. So I told her she was intelligent, an' she said she was a goddam sight too intelligent for me." He sighs. "Life can be very hard," says Benzey. He yawns. "Where do we go from here?" he says.

I sit on the edge of the bed pullin' at my lip. I am tryin' to think this one out. After a bit I say:

"Look, this is how we play this. To-morrow I'm goin' up to London, see? I've gotta date."

"No?" says Benzey. "You been workin' fast, haven't you?"

"I didn't have to," I tell him. "There's some baby up at the big house—that place that Travis is visitin'—who knows all the answers long before anybody asks her the questions. We're havin' a night out to-morrow night. We're goin' gamblin'."

"Oh boy," says Benzey. "Are you a fast worker!"

"I didn't haveta work," I tell him.

He says: "What do I do? Do I stick around here in this god-forsaken dump?"

"Stay here for two or three days," I say. "Just long enough to break the connection with me that anybody around here might have in their mind. Then get back to town. But I tell you what you can do in the mornin'. I'm gonna slide off good an' early. About eleven o'clock get through—talk to Pardoe. Tell him there's a dump somewhere near Mount Street—a gamblin' dump. They call it 'Chez Clarence.' It is a pretty classy spot, I think. He's gotta find out where that is. If our people can't find out, the English cops'll let 'em know. But I want Pardoe to be there to-morrow night. He's gotta be there from eleven-thirty onwards, an' he's gotta play it the way I want it played."

Benzey says: "I see. An' how d'ya want it played?"

"I don't know," I tell him. "How the hell can I know? I don't know a thing myself."

Benzey says: "That's fine. That's the sorta work I like. Nobody knows nothin' about anythin'."

I put my hand in my pocket. I bring out the slug.

"Somebody was havin' a little pistol-shootin' practice up on the hill," I tell him. "They had a silencer on the gun too. Somebody put a slug in a tree about six inches from my head."

"Yeah?" says Benzey. "Well, I reckon if they'd put it through your head I'd have been saved a lot of grief. Good-night, sucker." He lies down again an' goes to sleep. Before I'm outa the room he's snorin'.

I reckon Benzey must have a quiet conscience.

I go inta my room an' I take off my coat an' shoes. Then I go back to Benzey's room an' get the bottle of hooch. It's Irish whisky an' that's a liquor that always did appeal to me. I take a long pull an' sit on the bed smokin'. I wonder how the hell I am gonna play this. I wonder why it is that I always get sucker's jobs like this one.

I sit around for about ten minutes, concentratin'; then I ease quietly downstairs. I go inta the pay-box in the passageway behind the bar-parlour. I stick around there for fifteen minutes before I get through. At last I get my contact guy at the Embassy. He sounds tired an' very bored. I take a look outa the box just to make certain that I'm alone; then I say: "This is Caution speakin'. D'ya think you could do somethin' in a hurry?"

He says: "I never knew any time when you didn't want something done in a hurry. I remember when you were over here six years ago on that Van Zelden case."

"You Embassy guys haven't got anythin' to do except grumble," I tell him. "But you gotta get me some action."

"And what is the action, Mr. Caution?" he asks. "You might remember there's a war on, will you?"

"I'm rememberin' that all the time," I tell him. "Look, some time to-morrow—I'll let you know when an' where—you've gotta produce a lady for me."

He says: "Oh yes. Are you going to be good enough to tell us who it is."

"If I told you," I say, "it wouldn't mean a thing to you. I think you'd better have a talk with the boss. He'll know what I'm talkin' about. You tell him that some time to-morrow evening I'll want to produce Mrs. Cara Travis. He'll know where to put his finger on her."

"All right," he says, "I'll tell him."

"You might ask him to let me know at the Regency Hotel some time in the afternoon where she is. I wanta know where she's stayin', see?"

He says all right, he'll do it. I hang up. I go upstairs an' I go to bed. Anyhow I have started something.

CHAPTER TWO
CHEZ CLARENCE

I

I GET inta London at eleven o'clock.

The sun is shinin' an' if I hadn't got so much on my mind I would be feelin' pretty good. As it is I have got an odd sorta feelin' that I'm standin' on the edge an' if I wait long enough somebody is gonna push me over. Maybe you've felt that way some time. Maybe it's been about some frill that you was stuck on a little more than usual; some dough that you had to have quick; or some guy that you thought was one hundred per cent on the up-an'-up an' who turns out to be just another one of them boys who is always shy in the ante—if you get me.

I check in at an hotel near Jermyn Street. I go upstairs, have one outa the flask an' I make two three phone-calls. Then I call through to Benzey. My luck's in. I get him.

"Look, Benzey," I tell him, "howya feelin'? Is your headpiece workin' this mornin'?"

He says he's feelin' fine; that he's positively brilliant.

"All right," I tell him. "Well, don't make any mistake about this. Travis is with the 16th Infantry, three-four miles outside Wilminton. You get yourself inta a suit of plain clothes, go out there an' see his Commandin' Officer. When you get there flash that F.B.I. card of yours an' your British police identification an' get Travis's C.O. to send him up to London on some business or other to-day. I don't care what it is. You got that?" He says he's got it.

"All right," I go on. "Well, when Travis goes up he's gotta leave the address he's gonna stay at. He'll probably check in at some hotel here. You find out what that address is gonna be an' ring me through. I am at the Regency Hotel on Jermyn Street, see?" He says he sees.

I light a cigarette an' do a little thinkin'. It looks to me like everything has been too vague up to date. I think we'll try a little forcin' tactics.

I take it easy for a bit an' stroll around; then I have lunch. At three o'clock I get through to Pardoe. I ask him if he knows anythin'.

He says: "Yes, it's all fixed about that dump Chez Clarence. I'm going to be there to-night. How do we play this?"

"I don't know, Pardoe," I tell him. "Stick around an' take your cue from me. I'm not quite certain myself."

He says all right—it sounds as if it might be interestin'. I tell him I think so too.

I do some more phonin'; then I go to a news reel; then I have one outa the flask. I lay on my bed an' look at the ceilin'.

About seven o'clock the messenger comes round from the Embassy. He's gotta note for me. It says:

"Mrs. Cara Travis, who arrived four days ago, is in Suite 16 at the Carlton Hotel."

So that's that!

I get back on the bed an' look at the ceilin' some more. I am feelin' good an' curious about this Mrs. Travis. I wanta take a look at that baby. I wonder if she's gonna be as good as they say she is.

I take a shower, doll myself up in a nice dark-blue suit with a pin stripe. I take a quick look in the glass an' think that if it wasn't for my face I wouldn't look so bad. Maybe I forgot to tell you I got one of those pans which is a nice change from the guys in the Russian ballet. You know what I mean—strong but subdued. I weigh two hundred pounds an' have got one of them stomachs that is conspicuous by its absence. Dames fall for me sometimes an' one of 'em once threw herself off some pier because she asked me to marry her an' I ducked. Afterwards, when she had found out that there was only three feet of water off the end of the pier she took a shot at me with a .22 pistol an' hit a travellin' salesman in the navel. So now you've got a complete picture of me an' if you don't like it you know what you can do.

I get along to the Berkeley Buttery. I buy myself a long whisky, smoke a cigarette an' look at my finger-nails.

At eight o'clock on the dot Gayda comes in. Now listen, fellas, because I don't want you monkeys to get me wrong. I've been around plenty. I have seen all sorts of women in all sorts of countries, an' while I don't profess to know very much about 'em I've learned just a thing or two maybe. So when I tell you that this Gayda does somethin' special to me, you'll understand. When you analyse her everything is good, but even when you're through with that process she's still got something that you can't quite put your finger on. You know—that little thing that every man is lookin' for an' very seldom contacts.

What this frill don't know about choosin' an' wearin' clothes could be stuck in your Aunt Eliza's reticule an' even she wouldn't be able to find it. Gayda has clothes sense *plus*, an' when she moves she puts a sort of graceful urgency into her walk that woulda made King Solomon put his skates on an' skid around like he was a one-woman man.

She is wearin' a lime-green frock that was cut by a bozo that could wield a mean pair of shears. At the neck an' wrists are cuffs an' collar of primrose. She is wearin' sheer beige silk stockin's an' dark-brown glacé leather court shoes. She has got on a little shoulder cloak of mink that just comes down to her waist an' a lime-green felt hat with a little bunch of primroses stuck in the front. I'm tellin' you that a sight of this baby would make any normal guy miss a couple of breaths an' not even worry about it. She comes over to my corner an' sits down. She asks for a sidecar an' when the waiter's brought it we sit there lookin' at each other.

I say: "So what, Gayda!"

She says, sorta serious: "I wish you'd tell me your real name—your first name, I mean. I know your second name's Pleyell."

"My first name's Carlos," I tell her.

She says: "Well, I think your mother made a mistake. You don't look a bit like Carlos to me. I think I'll have to go on calling you Sourpuss."

"That suits me," I tell her.

Nobody says anything for a minute; then she says in a casual sorta way:

"Look, what do you think of Lon Travis?"

I ask her why. I tell her that I don't think it's exactly right for a private in the Marines to be handin' out opinions of his superior officers to young women with nice teeth.

She says: "Nonsense! What do you think I mean?"

"You tell me why an' I'll tell you," I say.

She says: "All right. I've got two sisters. You haven't seen them, have you?"

"No," I tell her, "I've seen you. After that I don't wanta see anybody else."

She says: "That's very nice of you, Sourpuss. But they're just as good-looking as I am, if not better."

"All right," I say, "we'll take that as read. What's this gotta do with Travis?"

She starts pleatin' her frock with her fingers.

"I'll tell you," she says. "We three girls were all rather keen on Travis. Well"—she hesitates for a minute—"my sisters still are. . . ."

"An' you've stopped bein' keen?" I ask her.

She looks at me. She throws me a wicked little look along the edge of her eyes. She smiles at me. She says:

"Yes, I think I have—since last night."

"No?" I tell her. "What's happened to you?"

She says: "I think *you* have."

"Look, Gayda," I tell her, "what is this act you're puttin' on about me? You don't really mean that, do you?"

She says: "I'm pretty sure I mean it. But I want to know about Travis because I wouldn't like to see either of the girls make a silly of herself."

I nod my head. "I understand," I tell her. I give her a cigarette, an' light one for myself. "I don't know a lot about Travis," I say, "but what I do know you can have. The boy's record is O.K.—I think. Everybody speaks well of him. He's a good officer. He's on the technical side. The main thing about him is his wife."

"Ha!" she says. "So he has a wife."

"You're tellin' me," I say. "Some wife! They tell me that Mrs. Travis is so good for the eyes that any time you take a really long look you wanta wear blinkers in case you get dazzled."

"I see," she says softly. "Like that?"

"Like that," I tell her. "But she is also very naughty."

She leans back in her seat an' inhales cigarette smoke.

She says: "So it wasn't a happy marriage?"

"Not by a long chalk," I tell her. "Travis an' his wife didn't hit it off from the start. I know all this because when I'm not bein' a Marine I'm the junior partner in a firm of New York attorneys. We've handled the Travis business for a long time—an' his father's before him, see?"

She nods her head. "I see, Sourpuss dear," she says. "It's obvious that you know what you're talking about."

"I know what I'm talkin' about, Gayda," I tell her. "Well, anyway, Travis wants to duck outa this marriage. I don't know what the trouble was but I've got an idea that Cara Travis had a *very* rovin' eye. All the things he liked she didn't like an' all the things she wanted to do meant nothin' to him. About a year before the Japs took a run at Midway, Travis had a talk to her about divorce. She just wasn't listenin'. She didn't wanta be divorced. She wanted to go on bein' Mrs. Travis."

She says: "I can understand that. Has she got any money or has he got it?"

"They've both got money," I tell her, "enough to be comfortable and independent of each other."

She nods. "What happened then?" she asks.

"Travis played along for a bit. He sorta gave up the idea of this divorce business. Then he got to hear one or two things he didn't like. So he came to us an' asked us if we could fix things. We had some of the best firms of investigators on Mrs. Travis for a long time. An', believe me, she was good an' clever, that one. She was so goddam clever half the time she didn't even know what she was doin' herself.

"But eventually one of the smart boys on her tail produced the evidence, an' he had a lotta trouble to get it."

"So the divorce went through?" she says.

"No," I tell her. "It didn't go through. By this time America was in the war. Travis was ordered over here. The evidence came through just about the time he got his orders. My partner, who was handlin' the job, just had time to get it to him before he left. No action's been taken. Nothin's happened. He's still married."

"I see," she says. She looks like she is thinkin' somethin' out.

"That oughta put your mind at rest about Travis," I go on. "At the same time I don't think he's the sorta boy to make any trouble with your sisters. He might play around a bit, see—just in the ordinary sorta way—but I don't think he's thinkin' seriously about any woman. I think he got all he wanted the first time."

She says: "You don't believe in marriage, Sourpuss?"

"I wouldn't know," I tell her. "I've never tried it."

She sighs. "That's what I thought. . . ." She goes on: "Do you think you'll ever want to try?"

"Why not?" I ask her. "I go out to try everything once. The thing is it's one of those experiments that are liable to cause a lotta trouble if they're not carried out the right way."

"I know," she says. "Still, a man's got to take a chance some time, hasn't he?"

"A guy who gets married is takin' a chance all of the time," I tell her.

She says seriously: "You know, I'm very keen on you. You've got something that appeals to me. I don't know what it is, but you have."

"I don't know what it is either," I say. "But thanks for the compliment. Look," I go on, "what time are we goin' to this card game?"

"I thought we'd go about ten o'clock," she says. "Where shall we dine, Sourpuss?"

"Let's eat here," I tell her.

We go inta the restaurant. I order cocktails an' ask her to excuse me for a minute. I slip outside. It is nearly half-past eight. I find a telephone-booth an' call through to the Regency Hotel. I ask if there is a message for me. They say yes, a Mr. Benzey has been through an' my friend is stayin' at the Hotel Le Due in Piccadilly. I say thanks a lot. I hang up an' go back to Gayda.

I'll always remember that dinner.

II

The guy who threw this Chez Clarence dump together knew his vegetables. The whole place is grey an' black an' gold. There is a big hallway with rooms leadin' off it on each side. It looks to me like a big flat that's been converted. In the room opposite the entrance is a bar with a bar-tender in a white jacket behind it. There are a lotta bottles an' the boy is very generous havin' regard to the fact that the drinks are on the house.

On each side of this room are doors leadin' to smaller rooms. In a room on the left there are about sixteen people round a roulette table. In another corner of the room five old guys are playin' poker. I cross the big room an' go inta the room on the other side. There are quite a lotta people in here too, round a baccarat table.

An odd sorta dump, I reckon. I lean up against the wall with a whisky an' soda in my hand, wonderin' who these people are an' where they come from.

Gayda, who has been powderin' her nose, comes an' stands alongside. Her eyes are bright. She says:

"What do you want to play, Sourpuss?"

"I'm gonna stick around for a bit," I tell her. "But you go ahead. I can see you got gambler's itch."

"I have," she says. "I've got fifty pounds in my bag. I want to turn it into two hundred and fifty. I could use the money."

"Go ahead, baby," I tell her. "I'll stick around. I'll play when I feel like it."

"All right," she says. "But don't go too far away."

She goes over to the baccarat table. I take my glass back to the bar an' get it filled; then I go inta the other room an' stand on the edge of the crowd round the roulette table.

Sittin' at the top of the table, with a big pile of chips in front of him, is Pardoe. I give an internal grin when I see him. He looks as if he's just come out of a hat-box. He's wearin' a tuxedo with a soft silk shirt an' collar, a black satin tie, an' he has a carnation in his buttonhole. He gives me a vague sorta look an' goes on with the game.

I stay for five or six minutes watchin'. It is ten o'clock by now. I reckon this place hasn't started gettin' goin' yet. About midnight is the time for these dumps. I go back to the bar, have a short one, go out inta the hallway an' across inta the little room where I have checked my hat. Then I go outside inta the corridor an' ring for the elevator. After a minute it comes up. There is a thin white-faced guy in a janitor's uniform inside. I say to him:

"Have a good look at me, will you, because I wanta come back later. I'd hate to be stopped on the door."

He grins. "That's all right, sir," he says. "I never forget a face."

Out in the street I pick up a crawlin' taxi-cab. I tell the driver to go to the Hotel Le Duc. Inside the cab I sit back an' relax. I think I know how I'm gonna play this. Anyway, what can I lose?

When we get to the Le Duc I pay the cab off. I have just got through the black-out curtain inta the hallway when I see Travis on the other side. He's just got outa the elevator. He's makin' for the door when I walk across to him.

"Hallo, Lieutenant," I tell him. "I'm glad to see you again."

He looks at me. He doesn't look so pleased. He says:

"What is this? Why can't you lay off me, Pleyell?"

"I'm sorry, sir," I tell him, "but somethin's turned up that I think you oughta know about. I wanta have a little talk with you."

He says: "Well, you can't. I'm busy. I've got a lot to do."

I say: "I'm sorry, Lieutenant, but I think we oughta have this talk. Anyway, I'm *gonna* have it, see?"

He says: "So it's like that, is it?" He grins. "O.K.," he says. "If it's *that* important. Come upstairs."

We get inta the elevator. He presses the third-floor button. He says: "I don't know anything about me that can be important right now."

I grin. "There's one thing about you that's plenty important," I say. "That's Mrs. Travis."

"What about her?" he says.

"Oh, nothin'," I say. "But she's over here in London, that's all. She's checked in at the Carlton."

He makes a little hissin' sorta noise through his teeth. He leans up against the wall of the elevator. He looks good an' sick. He says: "Well, I'll be goddamed!"

I grin at him. "Life is full of surprises, ain't it?" I tell him. "But believe me, Lieutenant, you ain't any more surprised than I am."

We stop at the third floor. He gets out an' leads the way along the corridor. I follow him inta his sittin'-room. It is a big room with a communicatin' bedroom.

He says: "Would you like a drink, Pleyell?"

"Would I!" I tell him.

He goes over to the sideboard an' pours out a coupla big ones. He squirts in the soda-water an' brings them over to where I am sittin' on the arm of the settee. He says:

"Would you mind telling me what the hell all this is about?"

I nod. "That's what I'm here for," I say.

"Well, go ahead," he says, "because what with one thing and another I'm getting pretty fed up with this Mrs. Travis business. How is it important?"

"It's more than important," I tell him. "It's sorta serious. When I went to Marine Headquarters this mornin' there was a helluva cablegram from Wynn. It was so long it looked like a serial story. I took one look at it, saw my Commandin' Officer an' got leave. I rang through to your unit at Wilminton an' the Battalion Office told me you were up here in London an' you'd be stayin' here."

"All right," he says. "What's the trouble?"

"Look," I tell him, "let's get this thing right from the start. You come over here on the troopship *Arkansas*, didn't you? The day on which you sailed you got those divorce papers from Wynn?"

He nods. "Maybe I did," he says.

"All right," I tell him. "The story is that three days out you were torpedoed in the Atlantic. A few rafts got away from the *Arkansas* because she went down pretty good an' quick. But you was on one of 'em. You were picked up two days later by an American destroyer. Right?"

He says: "Yes. That's all right."

"The destroyer put you aboard another boat in an English convoy. You got here about four days later. Am I still right?"

He says: "Yeah!" His face is sorta surprised. "I don't get all this—"

"You will," I tell him. "Look," I say, "this thing is so goddam ridiculous it almost hurts. But some crazy goon has got the idea in his head that you ain't Travis at all."

He puts his glass down on the sideboard. He looks at me with his eyes poppin'.

"Well, I'll be sugared," he says. "So I'm not Travis. That's a good one. Look, do you mind tellin' me who I am then?"

"Listen, Lieutenant," I tell him. "What's the good of you gettin' sore at me? These aren't my ideas. I'm just tellin' you what Wynn is sayin' in the cablegram."

He says: "All right. Go ahead. But if I'm not Travis, who the hell am I supposed to be?"

"You're supposed to be some other guy who was aboard the *Arkansas*," I tell him. "The idea is that this other guy got rid of Travis somehow an' pinched his papers."

"Marvellous!" he says. "So I'm some other guy an' I killed Travis in order to get hold of Travis's divorce papers. Is that right?"

"That's it," I say.

"Well," he says, "it's a lot of goddam hooey."

"Of course it's a lotta goddam hooey," I tell him. "But can't you see what sort of a situation it can create. Nobody knows you over here. You've reported to Headquarters. You're Travis. You got Travis's papers. Nobody over here had seen the real Travis. Supposin' you wasn't him I mean. You can imagine what a flat spin these boys are gonna get in if they get around to thinkin' there's some strange guy kickin' around here as an American officer. That's sense, isn't it?"

"Sure it's sense," he says. "Well, what are we going to do about it?"

"That's easy," I tell him. "That's where Mrs. Travis comes in."

He says: "Yeah, I forgot about her."

"Mrs. Travis is over here," I say. "She's in suite sixteen at the Carlton. She's out right now, but she'll be back later to-night—some time after twelve. All we have to do is just go around an' see her. If she says you're Travis, that's that. There's no more argument."

He finishes his drink. He comes over to where I'm sittin', collects my glass an' pours me another one.

"That's all right by me," he says.

I take my drink, sink it an' put the glass down on the sideboard.

"All right, Lieutenant," I tell him. "If it's O.K. by you, I'll pick you up here some time after twelve. Maybe you'll be waitin' for me downstairs. We'll walk round an' see Mrs. Travis. When she's identified you everything's straight. Maybe this is a blessin' in disguise."

"Is it?" he says. "You tell me how."

"Why shouldn't it be?" I ask him. "Now she's over here maybe we can get this divorce thing straightened out. Maybe she'll be in a better sorta humour."

"That'd be just wonderful!" he says. "Any time Cara gets herself into a good humour I'd like to make a note in my diary. It'd be a nice change."

I pick up my hat. "O.K.," I tell him. "Is that a date—just after midnight downstairs in the hall?"

"I'll be there," he says.

III

When I get back to the Chez Clarence buildin', the elevator guy is talkative. While we're goin' up he says:

"You missed something by not being here, sir. The lady you came in with has taken 'em for a packet."

I cock my eyebrow at him. "No?" I say. "What's she done?"

"She won five hundred at the roulette table," he says. "Everybody else was doing bad, but she couldn't do wrong. All right, she won five hundred and she asked the boss if he'd like to cut her four times for it. He said O.K. She won four times."

I whistle. "That looks to me like eight thousand pounds," I say.

"That's about it," he says.

I get outa the elevator. I walk down the corridor an' go in the hallway. There are a lot more people here than when I was here last time—all sorts of people. But they don't make a noise—they talk nice an' quiet. You can hear a subdued hum of people talkin' like a lotta bees buzzin'.

I go inta the roulette room an' look around for Gayda, but I can't see her. I go inta the other room, but she is not there. Eventually I find her in the bar sittin' on a high stool drinkin' a brandy an' soda an' eatin' a sandwich.

"Hallo, Mrs. Rockefeller," I tell her. "I hear you been doin' things to the bank?"

"I've had marvellous luck, sweet," she says. She puts her hand on my arm. "That's because of you," she goes on. "I'm lucky because I came here with you."

"I wouldn't believe that all the time," I tell her. "You string along with me long enough an' you'll think the luck I bring you isn't quite so good."

She wrinkles up her nose at me. "Anything that happened to me while I was with you would be good," she says.

I order a whisky and soda.

"Where do we go from here?" I tell her. "Are you through for to-night or are you still goin' on chasin'?"

She says: "I think I'll play a little bit more, but not yet awhile."

I give her a cigarette an' have one myself. While I am lightin' her cigarette I ask her what time they close down.

"A bit early," she says. "The crowd starts thinning out about two. The place is very nearly empty at three. They close soon after that. I think I'll wait till about half-past two, and come in at the fag-end. Everybody's tired then and I usually find my luck's good just for the last half-hour."

"O.K.," I tell her. "Well, I might have to leave you for a little while, but you wouldn't mind that, would you? I'd come back an' see the finish of this job."

"Must you go?" she asks. She looks surprised.

"No," I tell her, "not right now. But there's a guy I wanta see while I'm around this part of the world. He's goin' off to-morrow. I got to see him to-night, so maybe I'll blow just before twelve. I oughta be back about one-thirty. How's that?"

She looks disappointed. "If you say so," she says, "that's how it's got to be."

Nobody says anything for a minute; then she says:

"You do like me, Sourpuss, don't you?"

I grin at her. "The trouble is I'm likin' you a bit too much," I tell her.

"That's impossible," she says. "You couldn't like me too much. No matter how keen you were on me, you could never be quite so keen on me as I am on you."

"That's what I'm afraid of," I tell her. "You look like one of those dames who makes up her mind very quickly." I grin. "Don't tell me you're a one-man woman," I tell her.

She nods her head. "That's just it," she says. "I am, and I've got a definite idea that you're the man. I think we'll have to have a long talk about this, honey."

"Me too," I tell her. "Otherwise we might get a little involved, hey? In the meantime will you tell me where I can make a phone call?"

She says: "Yes. On the other side of the roulette room is a little writing-room. There is a call-box in the corner."

"O.K.," I tell her. "I'll be seein' you, an' while I'm away don't do anythin' I wouldn't like."

I go inta the writin'-room on the other side of the roulette room. I go inta the call-box an' get through to the Carlton Hotel. I ask for Mrs. Travis. After a minute somebody says:

"Hallo!" An' it is some voice too, I'm tellin' you. It is low an' smooth. It's got a sorta husky note in it. You know, one of them voices.

I say: "Good-evening. Is that Mrs. Travis?"

She says: "Yes, what can I do for you. And who is that?"

"My name's Pleyell," I tell her. "Carlos T. Pleyell. I am a partner in the firm of attorneys Wynn, Stromberg, Fidelli and Pleyell that act for your husband, Mrs. Travis. That's why I'm mixed up in this business. Otherwise I'm just a private in the Marine Corps."

"I see," she says. "And what would you like me to do, Mr. Pleyell?"

"So you know all about it?" I ask her.

"Pretty well," she says. "I've got a vague idea. But I can still learn."

"All right," I say. "I saw your husband a little while ago. He's up here in London. I told him the story, an' was he burned up!"

"He would be—naturally," she says. She gives a little laugh.

"I've fixed to bring him around to the hotel," I tell her. "We oughta be there some time about half-past twelve. All I want you to do is to identify him an' say he's him. Then I can fix an affidavit to-morrow, swear it, an' we can get the Embassy here to telegraph a confirmation over to New York. That puts that right. Is that all right with you, Mrs. Travis, or is it too late?"

"Oh no," she says. "That's not too late. I'd do anything for Lon." She laughs sorta malicious.

"All right," I say. "You'll be seein' me about twelve-thirty. So long, Mrs. Travis." I hang up.

When I come outa the call-box, Pardoe is sittin' at one of the tables writin'. There's nobody else in the room. He folds up the sheet of writin'-paper, puts it in an envelope, sticks it under the corner of the blotter. He gives me a wink an' goes out.

I go over an' grab the envelope. I go back inta the call-box an' read the note. It says:

"I am Cyrus Haas, a New York stock-broker, I'm over here doing a job of work on Lease Lend administration."

I put the note in my pocket an' go back to Gayda.

She says: "Well, have you done your telephoning?"

I nod.

"I bet it was a woman," she says.

I nod again.

"Is she nice, Sourpuss?" she asks.

"I don't know," I tell her. "They tell me she looks pretty swell."

"No?" she says. "Something sensational? I wouldn't know this beauty, I suppose?"

"I don't think you would," I tell her. "But I think it's on the cards you're gonna hear something about her. You might even get to know her. Who knows?"

She says: "Look, why do you make me so curious? Who was it you were talking to?"

"I was talkin' to Travis's wife," I tell her. "Cara Travis. She's over here."

"I see," she says. "Are you going to see her?"

I nod my head. "Some old time," I tell her. "I'd like to get acquainted with her. I wanta see if she looks as good as they say she does."

"All right, Sourpuss," she says. She looks at me sideways. "You be unfaithful to me and I'll kill you. You understand that, don't you?"

I grin at her. "I understand," I tell her. "I'll be careful."

She gets up. "I'm going to have just two little stabs at the roulette table," she says. "Just two bets on red. Are you going to come and watch me, sweet?"

I shake my head. "I'm goin' to see this guy now," I tell her. "I'll be back. Don't lose all that money you made."

She smiles at me. She can put something into a smile—that one. She says:

"You be back by two o'clock. If you don't, I'll disappear and you'll never find me again."

"I'll be back," I tell her. She goes off.

I get myself another whisky an' soda. I stand there drinkin' it slowly an' wonderin' what the hell everything is about. I get that way sometimes. They tell me it's nothin' to worry about. When I have finished the whisky I light a cigarette an' get my hat an' scram.

I got an idea that the next act is goin' to be goddam funny.

CHAPTER THREE
ENTRANCE FOR CARA

I

AT THE Le Duc, Travis is sittin' on the other side of the lounge. He sees me an' gets up.

As I walk towards him I notice something different about this guy. I am not quite certain what it is but it's there all right. Maybe he looks a bit more pleased with life—or does he? Maybe it's just my fancy.

He offers me a cigarette. He says:

"Well, here we are." He grins. "You know, Pleyell," he says, "there's a funny side to all this business."

I look at him. "Is there?" I ask. "It depends on what you think funny is."

"Well, *I* think it's funny," he says. "After all the time that Cara and I have been hating each other we *have* to wait till there's a war on and then we *have* to meet in London. And then *she* has to identify me just so that Uncle Sam shall know that I really am me. If you think that's not funny I should like to know what is."

"O.K.," I tell him. "But maybe my sense of humour is wearin' thin right now. Let's go."

We get inta the taxi that I got waitin' outside the Le Duc an' we drive down to the Carlton. We go up the lift an' a bell-hop takes us along to Suite 16. He taps on the door an' scrams. We go in.

The room is a drawin'-room. Everything about it is nice. It makes a good settin' for the woman who is standin' in the middle of the floor lookin' at us.

Boy! I'm tellin' you that whoever it was said that this Cara had a helluva lot knew something. I stand there just inside the doorway lookin' at her with my mouth open, because although I have seen some beauties in my time I have never seen anybody who looks like her.

She is tall and slim but the curves are in the right places, and just like they oughta be. She is a real honest-to-goodness blonde with that sheen on her hair that never came out of a bottle and the sorta skin an' eyes that go with it. She is smilin' an' there is a devil-may-care goddam insolence about her that hits you for a home run every time you look at her. You got me? At the same time this baby is definitely dignified—she has a sorta quality that you can't quite put your finger on, but that sticks out all the time. Definitely a frill this Cara.

She is wearin' a long, white satin house-coat that wraps itself close around her at the right times an' in the right places. Down the front of this house-coat are a coupla lace panels in turquoise blue. The coat is high up at the neck, caught with an antique turquoise-blue clasp, an' there are more clasps down the front of it. The coat has got long full sleeves caught at the wrists with turquoise-blue velvet ribbons an' lace to match fallin' over her hands. Underneath the lace I can see some very nice ice sparklin' on long slim fingers. Jeez . . . is this Cara a doll or is she?

When she moves I can see she is wearin' turquoise velvet mules an' no stockin's. She has got high heels an' a high instep.

I reckon that if anybody wanted to divorce a momma like this one the guy has got to be bughouse. He *has* to be. Whatever she has done or not done it oughtn't to matter one goddam. Any female who looks as good as this one does is good enough to keep as a museum-piece. Because you ain't gonna see many more like it in one lifetime. I'm tellin' you an' I know.

She says: "Well, well, I *am* glad to see you." She smiles at us—a slow, wicked smile.

I told you about her voice before. I told you it was low an' smooth, an' it matches up with the rest of her. I give a little sigh. I reckon here is a dame that men would do a murder for. I'm wonderin' where the hell you produce a dame like that from.

She goes on: "Don't you think this ought to be a celebration? Believe it or not, I've got a bottle of champagne."

An' she has. On a little table is a bottle of champagne an' three glasses.

She says: "But why are you so surprised? Come in . . . sit down. Don't be shy, Lon! Or are you still hating me so much that you can hardly bear to look at me?"

Travis looks uncomfortable. He is almost wrigglin'. "I've never really hated you, Cara," he says. "You know that. You've just made things damned tough for me."

She opens a silver cigarette-box, offers it to me, an' to him, an' takes one herself. I light the cigarette for her. While I'm holdin' my lighter up I look inta her eyes. I can remember once some guy writin' in a book about a woman's eyes an' sayin' that they looked like limpid pools. Well, believe it or not, that's how this baby's eyes look. I'm tellin' you monkeys I could go on for hours talkin' about this babe. She does things to me.

She says: "If anybody's made things tough, Lon, you've made them tough for yourself. You're that sort of person."

He says: "Look, do we have to re-open all that? If you'd played ball everything would have been all right. The trouble with you, Cara, is you're not on the level. You can be goddam mean and ordinary if you want to."

She interrupts. She says: "Lon, you bore me. Because a woman doesn't want to do what you want her to do *all* the time; because she fails to regard you as being the last thing in men; because she doesn't hero-worship you, she's mean and ordinary."

Travis says: "You know what I mean. Anyway, one or even two men aren't enough for you."

She laughs. "Why should they be?" she says. "I'm *very* selective, that's all, and the more experience I have of men the more I want to practice. Naturally I get bored now and then and want to move on to something new and exciting. That's logical, isn't it, Mr. Pleyell?"

I say: "Mrs. Travis, anythin' that you say is logical to me. Candidly, if you was to tell me that I was standin' on one ear I think I should be inclined to believe you."

She looks at me seriously. "Now why do you say that, Mr. Pleyell?" she says. "Are *you* going to say something nasty?"

"I'm just going to tell you the truth," I tell her. "You can get away with anything with me, but then I'm a guy who has always been susceptible to beauty. I reckon you're so goddam lovely to look at that you could get away with a murder any time."

"Thank you, Mr. Pleyell," she says. "Any time I want to get away with murder I'll ask you to help me. Lon, will you open the champagne?"

Travis puts his hat on the sideboard. He starts openin' the champagne bottle. I can see his fingers are tremblin' as he tries to undo the wired cork.

I say: "Look, Mrs. Travis, before we have this little drink, I think we might as well get the formal part of this job over. Do you actually identify Lieutenant Travis here as being your husband—that is himself?"

She nods. "That's Lon all right," she says. "Mr. Pleyell, you can take it from me that there isn't anybody else like him." She makes a little grimace. She says under her breath: "Thank God!"

I say: "That's all right, Mrs. Travis, but have you any particular reason for knowin' that this is your husband—some little special mark of identification or anything like that?"

She says: "Well, there ought to be a little tiny mole just at the end of his collar-bone—about three inches under the Adam's apple—that is unless he's had it removed." She looks at me sideways wickedly. "I was always rather fond of that mole. Do you remember, Lon? I used to kiss it."

He goes as red as fire. I reckon he could kill this baby. I go over to him. "Hold up, Lieutenant," I tell him.

I undo the top buttons of his tunic an' shirt. I pull his shirt open an' look inside. Sure as a gun, just over the sternum, two three inches below his Adam's apple, is a mole.

"Well, that's O.K.," I say. "We have now established the fact that you're Travis an' nobody but."

He pours out the champagne. He hands her a glass an' gives me one.

He says sorta moodily: "I would like to know who was fool enough to start the rumour that I wasn't."

"That's easy," I tell him. "I can make a guess about that. I should think it was Wynn. Work it out for yourself, Lieutenant. You came over here with those divorce papers. You're mad keen to get this divorce goin'. When you get over here Wynn doesn't hear a thing from you. So he gets in touch with the Army authorities in U.S. an' they get in touch with headquarters over here, who tell 'em that Travis is here an' been here some little time. Well, it's natural that Wynn should think it was odd. Then the story of the ship bein' torpedoed comes out an' somebody gets wonderin', so they think they may as well check up an' find out that you are you."

He nods his head. "I suppose they've got to be careful," he says.

"You're tellin' me," I tell him. "I wonder how many fifth column an' *Hitler bund* guys there are in the United States at the present moment. They're ropin' them in in dozens. Besides, it's better to be on the safe side."

He says: "I suppose you're right."

Cara Travis makes a little gurglin' sound. She's lookin' at us over the edge of her glass. She's laughin'. She says:

"So you're going to divorce me, Lon darling. That's going to be awfully nice for you, isn't it?"

He says: "Look, Cara, that's something that I'm not going to discuss with you."

She sits down. She crosses her legs. I can see that her calves an' ankles are as good as the rest of her.

She says: "Why not? Aren't you an extraordinary person, Lon? Why you can't sit down and discuss an ordinary normal thing like divorce I don't know. Or is it that you don't think you'd do so well in the ensuing argument?"

He says: "Look, I'm not having any argument. I'm just not talking about it. If you want to talk to anybody about it you talk to Pleyell here. He's a partner in the firm of attorneys who work for me. Maybe it'd be a good thing if he did talk with you."

I say: "Yeah, maybe it would." I grin at her. "It might help things along a bit."

She says: "Well, why not? I'd love to talk to Mr. Pleyell about it. After all, I'm reasonable. I'd be the last person to stand in the way of anybody's happiness."

"Like hell you would," says Travis. "There's only one reason why you *wouldn't* stand in the way of anybody's happiness."

"And what is that, honeybunch?" she asks. She makes a little *moue* at me. God, this dame is pretty!

He scowls at her. "Jack," he says. "Dough—jake—money! That's about all you think of."

"No, darling," she says, "you've got me wrong. Money never means anything to me whilst I've got enough of it."

Travis finishes his champagne. He puts the glass down.

He says: "Well, so far as I'm concerned this séance is over. I'll be on my way."

She looks at me. "And what about you, Mr. Pleyell?" she says. "Would you like to stay and discuss this divorce thing or will you come and see me some other time?"

"I'll get in touch with you, Mrs. Travis," I say. "I think it might be a good thing if I hadda talk with you. It's gonna save an awful lot of time."

"All right," she says. "Call me, will you?"

"I'll do that," I tell her.

Travis gets his hat off the sideboard. He says:

"Good-night, Cara." He doesn't look so pleased about something. "And be damned to you!" he says.

"Good-night to you, Lon," she says cheerfully. "And be damned to *you* too. And good-night to you, Mr. Pleyell. I look forward to seeing you again."

I say good-night. We go out.

I think to myself so that's that. I feel sorta contented about things. It is dark outside. Travis says:

"Would you like to come back to the Le Duc and have a drink? Perhaps you'd like to talk over what you're going to say to her—when you see her."

"Don't worry about it," I tell him. "I'll fix it. Thanks for the offer, but right now I've gotta date." I light a cigarette. "Talkin' about that date," I tell him, "there's somethin' you might do for me at that."

"Such as?" he asks.

I say: "Look, this is how it is. I ran into Gayda Vaughan this evening—"

He says: "What do you mean—you ran into Gayda Vaughan? It was goddam funny you running into her so soon, wasn't it?"

I grin. "I didn't exactly run inta her," I tell him. "Last night when I was up at the house I sorta fixed it up with her."

"Like hell you did," he says. "You're a pretty fast worker, aren't you, Pleyell?"

"I don't know what you mean," I tell him. "Anyway, you've got me wrong. Gayda wanted to go to some place she knows an' do a little gamblin'. She asked me to go along. I went. I left her there in order to get this job done. She's lucky, that one," I tell him. "When I left she was about eight thousand pounds ahead of the market."

He whistles. "What do you know about that?" he says.

"It was nice goin'," I tell him. "I was thinkin' this way. I've gotta get back to headquarters some time, see? You've gotta remember I am workin' for Uncle Sam. I'm not a free agent—I'm a Marine. I'm only an attorney on the side now. I didn't quite like the idea of that baby runnin' around with eight thousand pounds in her bag. I thought maybe she'd be thinkin' of goin' back to her hotel some time an' I thought maybe you'd like to take her back."

"Oh," he says, "that's quite an idea, isn't it? I'll come along anyway. I'd like to see this joint. What's it like?"

"It's quite nice," I tell him, "all grey an' black an' gold. She gets around—that Gayda, hey?"

"You're telling me," he says.

We wait there on the pavement. Pretty soon a cab comes crawlin' along. We get in. I tell the driver to go to Mount Street. Inside the cab nobody says anythin'. There's one of those long pauses. I get an idea that somethin' is boilin' up in Travis's head. After a bit he says:

"You know, Pleyell, I don't think you're a bad guy."

I throw my cigarette stub outa the window.

"Thanks a lot," I tell him. "But why?"

"I don't know," he says, "but you're taking a lot of trouble over this Cara thing. I reckon if anybody can straighten that job out it's going to be you."

I nod my head in the darkness.

"So you wanta go through with that divorce?" I say.

"I'm not quite sure, but I think so," says Travis. He gives a little laugh. "Every time I see Cara I weaken," he says.

"I sympathise," I say. "She's certainly a looker. Even if she's bad she's still good."

"Anyhow," he says, "it's not going to do any harm for you to have a talk with her."

"That's what I thought," I say. "I'll just have a nice friendly conversation an' see what's in the back of her head; if she wants this divorce to go through. All right, let's play it anyhow. We can't do any harm in findin' out."

He says: "Yes." He don't say anythin' for a bit; then: "Some time—maybe to-morrow—you might call through to the Le Duc," he says. "I'd like to have a little talk with you myself. Maybe if you're not on duty you can manage it."

"Sure," I tell him. "Somethin' worryin' you?"

"Well, not exactly worrying," he says. "But there's something I'd like to talk over with you."

"I get it," I tell him. "Just one of those things where you think two heads would be better than one?"

"Something like that," he says. "And anyway, you're a lawyer. You've been trained to think, I haven't."

"I'll come along," I tell him. "I'll give you a call some time to-morrow afternoon. Maybe by that time I'll have had a talk with Cara too."

He says: "All right. Do that. I'll be grateful. I shan't forget all you're doing, Pleyell."

I think to myself like hell you won't!

II

Goin' up in the elevator at the Chez Clarence I lean back against the wall an' relax. But outa the corner of my eye I am watchin' Travis. Something is worryin' that guy. All the while he seems to be concentratin' on something an' now an' again he throws a quick look at me just as if he can't make up his mind.

I give a little grin inside me. I reckon if I was Travis I wouldn't be able to make up my mind either. The guy has got a certain amount of nerve but not so much that he's got any to spare. Right now I reckon he's on the top line—if you get me. Right now he is wonderin' just how he can play this thing an' still come out the way he wants to. But he can't see it. He can't see how he's gonna do it, an' he's goddam right because it would take a cleverer guy than Travis to walk out of this Cara Travis set-up. I reckon that in a minute the big palooka is gonna wonder just what's hit him.

Maybe I'm bored with Travis. I wouldn't know. Me—I am a guy who likes followin' his own nose an' just bitin' off enough to chew over before I take any more mouthfuls. You can do two things with any given situation or set of circumstances. You can either try to play the situation along or you can just sit in the corner an' let it play you along. I'm for the last idea. All my life—ever since I started workin' for Uncle Sam anyway—I've been sittin' in the corner an' lettin' things happen.

An' when something good an' goddam big comes along that is the time I come out.

Napoleon or Wellington, or whoever the baby was who said that the good soldier always lights where *he* wants and when *he* wants, definitely knew the bill of fare, an' what is good enough for Wellington is certainly good enough for Mister Caution—even if I am only an enlisted man with a distorted vision due to tryin' to concentrate on the matter in hand and also to take a passin' peek at any doll with nice ankles who happens to be in the vicinity.

Just for a change I look at the janitor who is workin' the elevator. He has got a thin white face an' he has got red rims around his eyes. He looks as if he's been up all night for a week. I look at his uniform. It's a well-made, well-fittin' uniform but they left a lotta space when they was measurin' the collar. His neck, which is thin, sticks outa the collar of the uniform coat like a duck's. He looks plenty intelligent. We get outa the lift an' walk along the passage.

"You check your hat in the cloakroom," I tell Travis, "an' then come over an' meet me in the bar."

He says: "You want to tell Gayda I'm here?"

"That's right," I tell him. "I don't want her to get annoyed, see? She might think you was musclin' in."

I walk across the hallway an' go inta the bar. There is nobody else in the bar except Gayda. She is sittin' along at the end nibblin' a cocktail biscuit.

She says: "So you got back?"

I tell her yes. I ask her how she's been doin'.

"All right," she says. "I won a little more. I've won about eight thousand five hundred pounds to-night. What do you think of that, Sourpuss?"

"I think it's pretty good," I tell her, "An' I've got a big surprise for you."

She asks what.

"Lon Travis is here," I tell her. "I met him, so I brought him along. I thought he might be useful. With all that dough you've got you'll need an escort, won't you?"

She looks at me sideways. "I thought I had one," she says.

I grin at her.

"Meanin' me? You know, Gayda," I tell her, "you forget I'm in the Marines. I have to do duty *some* of the time. When I leave here I gotta get back quick."

"I see," she says. "So it was lucky you met Lon Travis, otherwise I suppose I should have had to go back to my hotel on my own. Is that it?"

I say: "Look, do you have to be difficult?"

She shakes her head. "No," she says. "Neither do you. In your own vernacular, I think you're a goddam heel, Sourpuss."

"Look, honey," I tell her, "don't get that way. Just relax an' take it easy."

She makes a petulant little movement with her shoulder. Travis comes inta the bar. He is grinnin'. He looks plenty pleased about somethin'.

He says: "Hallo, Gayda. This is a pleasant surprise. I hear you've been winning a lot of money to-night. Can I have a little drink on that?"

She says: "Of course you can—what you want. Ask the barman. I'll have one too."

The guy behind the bar starts fixin' the drinks. Gayda turns her back on me. Pretty soon she an' Travis get inta a close sorta conversation. I light a cigarette.

After a minute or two I ease away inta the roulette room. There is nobody there at all. I go inta the writin'-room an' take a piece of paper outa the stationery rack. I write on it:

"Work the old show-down act. You're only pretending to be Haas. You're Capelli that I knocked off in '34 in a bank heist. You can be a little high if you like and tough. But make it good."

I fold this note up as small as I can. I put it in the palm of my hand. I walk across the hallway an' inta the other room. There are three guys talkin' around the baccarat table. One of 'em is Pardoe. The guy at the top of the table is a tall, well-dressed fella in a tuxedo. He's got a thin, good-lookin' sorta face with a little black moustache. He looks a pleasant sorta guy.

I say to Pardoe: "It's a funny thing, you know, but I reckon I've met you before some place."

He says: "Yes? Well, I'm afraid I don't remember you."

I take my cigarette-case out, take a cigarette; then I offer the case to Pardoe. Underneath it I have got the note between my fingers. He takes a cigarette an' the note at the same time.

He says: "I've just been commiserating with Clemensky here. They've lost a lot of money to-night. Miss Vaughan—I believe she came with you—seems to have done very well."

I look at Clemensky. I say to him: "Too bad. But I expect you'll get it back all right. The odds are always on the bank, aren't they?"

Pardoe goes away.

Clemensky says, speakin' in very good English: "I'm not worrying. Some nights we have bad nights, so-ome nights we have good nights. At the end of the quarter we find we've made a leetle money and we ha-ave the pleasure of kno-owing that our clients have been satisfied."

I nod my head. "That's a nice thought," I tell him. "It's not so simple runnin' a joint like this. No gamin'-house is an easy proposition."

He says: "That depends—" He shrugs his shoulders. "Some places have a bad clientele so-o there's trouble. We pick our customers very, very carefully." He smiles. "So-o we don't have any trouble."

The other guy looks at Clemensky. He is a big guy with square shoulders. His tuxedo looks as if it wasn't cut in England.

He says: "You're dead right. We don't have any trouble and we don't want any."

Outside I can hear Gayda talkin'. I go back inta the bar. Travis an' Gayda are at the far end laughin' their heads off at some crack she has just made. At this end Pardoe is drinkin' a big whisky and soda.

His shoulders are hunched up over the drink. He looks unpleasant. I reckon he's gettin' ready for the act. I stub my cigarette out an' light a fresh one. I say to Pardoe sorta casually as I go past him:

"I hope you didn't *mind* my mistakin' you for somebody else, mister."

He says just nothin' at all.

Gayda says: "Well, Sourpuss, it looks as if the fun's over. Where do we go from here, my handsome Marine."

Pardoe is standin' just behind my shoulder. He says:

"Marine—hooey! Is this goddam heel tellin' you he's a Marine?"

Gayda an' Travis look at him. They are plenty surprised.

I say to him: "Look, pal, maybe you've been drinkin' a little too much. Take it easy."

He says: "Nuts to you. Why the hell can't you lay offa me. This is England, not U.S. What the hell d'ya want to come stickin' your long neck out for, telling me who I am?"

"Look," I tell him, "take it easy. I'm not startin' anythin'."

"I'll take good goddam care you don't. You're startin' nothing with me. I suppose you wanta advertise the fact that I'm Willie Capelli an' that you are the clever guy who pulled me in in 1934 for that Oklahoma Bank heist."

"Oh, can that," I tell him. "That's not necessary."

"Like hell it isn't." He says to Travis: "This guy's a flatfoot—one of Mr. Ploover's little boys—a Special Agent of the Federal Bureau of Investigation. Maybe he's sold you the idea he's a Marine. You'd better watch your step. Anything this guy sticks his nose into turns bad."

I say: "Look, Capelli—if you want it that way—supposin' you shut your trap. You're beginnin' to bore me, see?"

He says: "I'm goin' to do more than bore you, you bastard!"

He swings one at my face. I block it with my left hand. I step in an' I make out I hit him a helluva welt in the stomach. Pardoe is definitely good. He makes a retchin' sorta noise an' falls over backwards with his hands around his guts.

Gayda says: "Oh dear! I believe you hurt him, Sourpuss."

"Don't bother," I tell her. "It wouldn't be the first time he's been hurt."

Clemensky comes inta the bar. He says:

"Is anything wro-ong?" He looks at Pardoe lyin' on the floor.

I say: "No—this boyo got a little bit fresh. Look, Clemensky, I don't wanta start anything but I'm givin' you a tip off. You don't want heels like this kickin' around. This boyo sold you the idea that his name is Haas; that he is over here on Lease Lend. Don't you believe it. The guy is Willie Capelli. His speciality is heistin' banks. He's bad medicine, see?"

Clemensky says: "Thank you ver' much. It is nice of you to give me the tip, Mr.—"

"The name's Pleyell," I tell him.

Gayda's voice says very softly behind me: "Is it. Handsome?"

I say to her over my shoulder: "You lay off." I grin at her.

Pardoe gets up. Clemensky helps him towards the cloakroom. I watch the pair of 'em. I am thinkin' that Pardoe is a nice worker.

Gayda says: "I want another drink."

I tell the bar-tender. I tell him that I'll have one too.

He gives us two large whiskies. This bar-tender is an interestin' sorta guy. A dead pan. Nothin' seems to worry him.

Gayda says: "You're a very interesting person, aren't you, Sour-puss? So you're a Federal Agent? In a minute I'll believe you're Santa Claus."

I say: "Look, honey, you don't haveta believe everything you hear."

'She says: "No, and I don't have to disbelieve everything either. I think you're *awfully* cute, Sourpuss." She picks up her glass.

I wonder where Travis has got to. It strikes me that maybe he hasn't liked this show-down with Pardoe.

I say to Gayda: "Me—I'm gonna scram. I don't like bein' mixed up in these rough houses. It's not good for my reputation. I think I'll blow."

She nods her head. "When am I going to see you again, Sourpuss?" she asks. "Why don't you come down to the house one evening? One of these days I want to have a really long heart-to-heart talk with you."

"I'd like that too," I tell her. I give her a cigarette. "I'll be with you in a minute," I say.

I go outside to the check-room. Clemensky an' the elevator guy are persuadin' Pardoe inta the elevator. He's bein' a little bit trucu-lent. When he sees me he calls me a rude name.

I get my hat an', carryin' it in my hand, I walk across the hallway an' look inta the roulette room. There is nobody 'there. The door of the writin'-room on the other side is half-closed. Last time I saw it it was open.

I go across, push the door open an' look in. There's nobody there, but a cigarette stub is burnin' on the carpet on the other side of the room. I go over, pick it up, squash it out in an ashtray. Then I walk over an' open the door of the telephone-booth.

Travis is lyin' in the bottom of the booth. His knees are hunched up. There is a big black stain on the front of his khaki tunic. I kneel down an' take a look at him. I can't see very much because the light is bad, so I get out my lighter an' snap it on. Travis is dead all right. Somebody has shot him two or three times through the chest an' stomach.

I get up an' put the lighter back in my pocket. It seems to me pretty tough that, when there are so many places in this world that a guy can get shot in these days, he has to be shot in a telephone-booth in a gamin'-dump off Mount Street.

I close the door of the booth, an' light myself a fresh cigarette. I go back inta the bar. Clemensky is talkin' with Gayda. They are both smilin' about somethin'.

I pick up my drink which is where I left it an' swallow it. I say to Gayda:

"Look, Travis is more of a sport than I thought."

She says: "No? Tell me?"

"He didn't like bein' gooseberry," I tell her. "He left a message in the check-room. He's scrammed."

She smiles. "I always thought Lon was intelligent," she says. "Well, where do we go from here. Handsome?"

"I'll take you back to your hotel, Gayda," I tell her. "I gotta report back to-night."

She gets up. She says: "If you say so, but I think you're positively lousy. I really do, Sourpuss. You were supposed to spend an evening with me and most of the time you've been away from me. It's not fair."

"I know," I tell her. "I do that to women, but they still keep on tailin' after me. It must be my fatal beauty."

She says good-night to Clemensky. He gives us a smile an' a nod. We go out.

We get a cab outside. While we are goin' down Piccadilly towards Knightsbridge Gayda turns towards me. She puts her arms around my neck. She gives me a helluva kiss. She says: "I think you're fascinatin'—fascinatin' but crummy!"

I grin at her. "You're gettin' your terms mixed," I tell her. "A guy can't be fascinatin' an' crummy."

"That's just it," she says. "You are, Sourpuss. I warn you, I'm falling for you—falling hard."

I say: "Yeah?" But I am thinkin' of something else.

I am thinkin' of Travis.

CHAPTER FOUR
POST-MORTEM

I

I SAY good-night to Gayda on the steps of her hotel in Knightsbridge. The moon has come out. It is a nice night. I tell her that September in England, when the weather's good, is pretty swell.

She says: "You are a scream, aren't you, Sourpuss? You do and say the oddest things. That remark about the weather just now for instance. Why did you say that? Did you really mean it or were you just making conversation while you thought of something else?"

She is standin' two steps above me. She is lookin' down at me. She looks sorta queenly.

I say: "What the hell! I wonder why it is you are always takin' me up the wrong way. I made that crack about the weather because I believe it. It is a lovely night. I saw a picture some time. It was called 'September Morn.' You remind me of that picture."

She raises her eyebrows. "Really!" she says. "If I remember rightly the young woman in 'September Mom' had no clothes on."

I grin at her. "Why worry about a little thing like that?" I say. "What are clothes between friends anyway?"

She says: "Give me a cigarette, Sourpuss."

I give her one. She draws the smoke down inta her lungs. Then she gives a little sigh an' lets it all out again.

She says: "I want to see you soon. Don't forget, Sourpuss." She gives a little whimsical smile. "The trouble is you won't take me seriously," she says.

"I'm takin' you plenty seriously," I tell her.

"All right," she says. "When are you coming down to Mallows again?"

"I'll come down as soon as I can," I say. "Maybe one day this week. But I gotta lot to do."

She says: "Yes, I expect you have. Well, good-night, Sourpuss."

She goes up the steps an' through the black-out curtain.

I start walkin' down Knightsbridge towards Piccadilly. It is three o'clock. I turn up Down Street by the side of the Green Park Hotel, across the intersection at the top. After a bit I find the place I am lookin' for—Leavenworth Mews. No. 4 is a garage with some livin' accommodation over the top.

I ring the bell an' wait. After two-three minutes the door opens. By the half light inside the hallway I can see it is Pardoe. He says:

"Hallo, Lemmy, I'm glad to see you. How did it go?"

"You played it fine, Carl," I tell him.

He says: "O.K. I did the best I could. I couldn't quite get the idea so I chanced it."

"Don't worry," I tell him. "Everything was a hundred per cent."

We go upstairs. The livin'-room at the top is comfortable. On one wall Pardoe's Marine uniform is hangin'. It has just been pressed. A snappy dresser, Pardoe.

I give him a grin. I say: "You're takin' a lotta trouble with that uniform, aren't you?"

He says: "Why not? Me—I like wearin' a white hat. The only trouble is if somebody tells me to 'right turn.' I don't know how to do it." He grins. "Is it funny or is it?" he says.

"What's funny?" I ask.

"Us bein' Marines," he says. "Like hell! I wonder what the commandin' officer really thinks about us."

"He don't think a thing," I tell him. "He don't haveta think. What happened after they showed you off the premises?"

"The guy Clemensky, the big shot around at that Club, an' the elevator guy, took me downstairs," he says. "When we got on the ground-floor they asked me if I was all right. I said yes. I was still puttin' on a drunk act. I said some nice things about you too. You oughta heard me. It was a treat."

"Did they fall for it?" I ask him.

"They fell for it all right." He goes over to the desk an' gets a cigarette-box. He gives me one. "They're goin' to try something," says Pardoe.

I take the cigarette. I sit down in the big armchair an' put my feet on the mantelpiece.

"Yeah, Carl?" I say. "What're they gonna try?"

"Well," he says, "when I get out in the street I stagger around a bit, see? You know, the cold night air hittin' a guy fulla spirits. I slip up an' do a realistic fall. Clemensky came out an' helped me up. He asked if I'd like a cab. I told him no I was going to walk round for a bit to get my head clear. I leaned up against the wall an' looked dizzy. So then he asks me about you. He pretends to be interested in a casual sort of way. He asked if it was right that you were a Federal Bureau Agent. I give a coupla hiccups an' tell him I don't know whether you are *now* but that you was an' that your name was Lemmy Caution. I told him I got in a bit of trouble in Oklahoma over a bank heist in 1934 an' that you an' a coupla other F.B.I. guys pulled me in for it."

"How does he take that?" I ask.

"He takes it pretty good," says Carl. "He takes out a gold cigarette-case an' gives himself one. He gives me one. He asks me what I am doin'. I tell him I left the U.S. early in 1939; that I got outa the Big House on parole; that I skipped an' came over here; that I had a little dough an' I've been livin' on it, but that now I'm fiddlin' around.

"He asks me if the U.S. authorities over here have got on to me yet in the check-up they're havin' on United States nationals in England. I tell him no they haven't an' ask him what the hell it is to him anyway. He says it's not a thing to him. Then he says he'll walk me down the end of the road. He put his hand under my left arm, sorta givin' me a hand, see? But what he's really doin' is feelin' to see if I've got a gun under my shoulder."

He grins. "It was lucky," he says, "I had one. I was sorta pleased with that. Feelin' that gun made up his mind for him. He says look, maybe I'd like to go around an' see him some time to-morrow; he might be able to put a little business in my way. He told me where to go. He lives at some dump called Mayfield House on Mount Street. I fixed to see him some time round three o'clock. Then he went back."

"Nice work, Carl," I tell him. "Go an' see what the boyo wants. It might be interestin'. You know where to get at me, don't you?"

He says: "Yeah, same address, I suppose."

I tell him yes, the Regency in Jermyn Street, an' that if he can't contact me there for any reason to get in direct touch with Marine Headquarters—they'll put him on to me. He says O.K. He brings out a bottle an' we have a short one. I say good-night an' scram.

A good guy, Carl—a reliable guy.

II

It is four o'clock when I get back to the Regency. The hall porter, who is an ancient guy, is dozin' in his office on one side of the hall. On the other side, sittin' in a big chair in battle-dress with Commando flashes up, is Benzey.

Benzey is asleep—as usual. I go over to him. I give him a jerk under the jaw. He wakes up. He says:

"Why is it you always have to be rough with me?"

"Sorry," I tell him. "Was you havin' a nice dream?"

"Lovely," he says. "I was dreamin' about Dieppe. I was just killin' that German again."

"I reckon you killed that German about six hundred times already. It's about time you killed another one. What do you want? I thought I told you to stay around Wilminton."

"That's right," says Benzey. "But I got a phone-call to-night from the big boy. He said he'd got an idea that things was poppin'. He told me to get outa Wilminton nice an' quiet, come up here an' contact you. He said he thought you might need me."

"Did he now?" I say. "Any time I've got you around I get scared. Why did he think I wanted you?"

Benzey yawns. "He told me you'd asked for Mrs. Travis's address," he says. "He thought things might be gettin' interesting. Say, listen, I didn't know she was over here. I thought that dame was in America."

"So did I," I tell him.

I lead the way over to the elevator. We go up to my room. We have a drink. He says: "Did you get Travis all right? I phoned the address through here but you was out."

"Yeah, I got him," I say. "It's a bit odd about Travis."

Benzey puts his leg over the side of the chair. He lights a cigarette. Lookin' at him I think he looks more like a bullock than ever.

"What's so odd about him?" he says.

"He's dead," I tell him.

Benzey lifts his eyebrows. "You don't say?" he says sorta curious. "That ain't so good, is it? What did he die of?"

I shrug my shoulders. "He was knocked off in a telephone-box in some gamin' club. Somebody let him have two through the stomach an' one through the pump. Well, he looked plenty relaxed, which is more than he did when he was alive."

Benzey says: "Look, don't tell me anything, will you? I just like wanderin' around not knowing anything about anything. It helps."

"The trouble with you is, Benzey," I tell him, "you can never put two an' two together without makin' sixteen of it."

"The trouble with me is," he says, "I don't haveta put two and two together. Me—I am just an ordinary guy. You're the brains trust in this outfit. All I have to do is to stick around an' stooge—with an occasional drink an' some sleep when I can get it."

"*Some* stooge," I tell him. "Well, look, Travis *wasn't* Travis, see?"

"No?" says Benzey. "That's swell. Who was he?"

"I don't know," I tell him. "I was pretty certain that he wasn't Travis from the start. That's why I fixed for Mrs. Travis to identify him."

"I get it," says Benzey. "So she threw him down. She said he wasn't Travis?"

"No," I tell him. "She said he *was*."

Benzey says: "You tell me something. Are you nuts or am I?"

"Take it easy, Benzey," I tell him. "Get this straight. The dame who identified him *wasn't* Mrs. Travis, see? She was somebody we put in—a nice frill too! God—is that dame pretty!"

Benzey leans forward. He throws his cigarette stub in the fireplace. He says: "You know, I'm gettin' sorta interested. Go on, Sourpuss, tell me some more."

"I got the idea that Travis wasn't Travis," I say, "so I got through to the big boy an' told him to dig me up a Mrs. Cara Travis. I took a chance on his understandin' what I wanted. He understood all right. Anyway, the real Mrs. Travis was supposed to be in America, wasn't she? So he couldn't dig her up. All right. So he finds this honey blonde, plants her in Suite 16 at the Carlton, sends me a message that Mrs. Cara Travis has arrived an' is there, see?

"O.K. Then I pull one on Travis. I go around to him an' I tell him there is some doubt about his identity. I tell him that Wynn, the senior partner in his firm of attorneys, has got the idea that somethin' screwy is goin' on, that he's got this idea because he hasn't heard anything from Travis an' he knew the boat was torpedoed.

"Then I tell Travis that his wife is here in Suite 16 at the Carlton, an' I tell him that I'll call back for him later; take him around so she can identify him. Well, what can he say? He says O.K. Then I leave him to think it over."

Benzey says: "I think you're just too too wonderful. Ain't you the clever little bastard?"

"Maybe yes, maybe no," I say. "We'll know the answer to that one before long. Anyhow, some time after twelve o'clock to-night I go round an' pick him up at the Le Duc. He is waitin' there in the hallway an' he looks plenty pleased with himself. This tells me something."

"Yeah?" says Benzey. "What does it tell you, Sherlock?"

"Use your nod," I tell him. "If he's lookin' pleased when the time has come for him to go around an' be identified, it tells me he has done what I thought he'd do. Directly I left him he's gone rushin' around to the Carlton, seen the phoney Mrs. Travis, told her some story an' got her to agree to identify him as her husband."

Benzey says: "The mug, hey? By doin' that he kills himself. He advertises once an' for all that he's not Travis. He don't even *know* that she's not his wife."

"Right," I tell him. "Naturally the girl friend, playin' him along, agrees to do exactly what he says. He tells her he's gotta mole on the top of his breast-bone. So when we get around there an' I ask her to identify him, she says yes he's Travis; that he oughta have a mole on the top of his breast-bone. I look an' I find it, so there you are."

Benzey says: "Say, this frill who is playin' at bein' Mrs. Travis is sorta clever, isn't she?"

"She's pretty good," I tell him. "An' is she a looker! Boy, I've never seen anything like it in my life."

"I know," says Benzey. "That's the trouble with you. Any time I have to work with a dame on any of these acts we do she has a face like last Wednesday's cold cuts. You always draw all the ace janes. I wonder why."

"I wouldn't know," I tell him. "Maybe it's my personality."

He says: "So then what happens, Lemmy?"

"After this identification séance is over," I say, "we scram. I tell him I'm with Gayda. I tell him she's won a lotta jack at this club; that I've gotta go on duty; that maybe she wants somebody to see her home. He says O.K. an' he goes along there with me. On the way he makes a date to see me. He wants to tell me something. He says he thinks I'm a good guy."

"Yeah?" says Benzey. "Maybe this boy was gonna put his head on your shoulder an' tell you somethin' that really mattered—a little confession, hey?"

"Something like that," I say, "something that he decided to spill as a result of the phoney Mrs. Travis sayin' he was Travis, an' something which he wanted to spill to me because he thought I was a member of Travis's firm of attorneys."

Benzey says: "I see."

"All right," I say. "We get along back to this club, Chez Clarence. There aren't many people there—just the boss, a guy called Clemensky; a big fella who looks like a muscle-man, Gayda an' Pardoe. Pardoe is pretendin' to be a big Lease Lend shot, all dressed up in a tuxedo an' a red carnation. I slip Pardoe a note an' tell him to work the old show-down act. I think maybe we'll get a reaction somehow that way. So he does. I tell him I know who he is an' after a minute he busts out an' blows that I'm Caution—a Federal Bureau Agent; that I knocked him off in '34 for a bank heist in Oklahoma. Pardoe is supposed to be tight an' is playin' the part pretty good."

"I get it," says Benzey. He scratches his nose. "One of these days you oughta get a job on the films," he says. "So what happens then?"

"All this takes place in the bar," I tell him. "Pardoe acts all funny, see? He takes a swipe at me an' I pretend to dig him in the stomach. He falls over an' Clemensky an' some other guy get him away."

Benzey says: "Nice work. An' then?"

"An' then I miss Travis," I say. "Nobody's seen him in the excitement. I wander around an' I find him stuck in the telephone pay-box in the writin'-room on the other side of the roulette room."

"I get it," says Benzey. "So what does Mister Caution do then?"

"I don't do a goddam thing," I say. "I think it's gonna be a good idea to leave him there an' just see what happens."

He says: "Yeah, but what about Gayda? She knew he was there; didn't she miss him?"

"I took care of that," I tell him. "I went back to her an' told her I'd been told by the guy in the cloakroom that he'd left a message that he wasn't feelin' so good; that he'd gone."

"I get it," says Benzey. "So then you take Gayda home, hey? I bet you kissed that dame in the cab."

"You mind your own business," I tell him.

He says: "Well, it looks as if you've had quite an evenin', doesn't it?"

I say: "Yeah!"

He don't say anythin' for a few minutes. He is deep in thought. The guy is concentratin'. Any time Benzey concentrates he puts on an expression like he was bein' tortured to death by Apache Indians an' not likin' it much.

Then he says: "Well, where the hell is the real Travis? Where is that guy?"

"At the bottom of the drink," I tell him. "It is my bet that the honest-to-goodness Lon Travis is washin' around somewhere at the bottom of the Atlantic."

"Yeah," says Benzey. "An' that means that this is the guy—"

"Who was in the boat with him," I say. "The set-up looks to me like this. They knew all about Travis from the start. They knew what he was carryin'. They was gonna have those papers if they hadta tear everything wide open to get 'em. All right . . . they know the boat he is sailin' on an' they got somebody on that boat waitin' for him— somebody who looks like him. That's easy, ain't it? With the number of boats sailin' outa American harbours an' the general set-up an' schlmozzle of gettin' drafts an' stuff over here on Lease Lend, it's goddam easy to have a guy on the boat. You got that?"

He says he's got it.

"Right," I go on. "Well, things break for this guy, see? Some sub sinks the boat an' there is one helluva run-around. If you remember, that boat sunk in about twenty minutes. Well, this guy who is waitin' for Travis gets his chance an' takes it. He makes a certainty of Travis. He gives it to him an' pushes him in the drink after he's grabbed his papers off him. He probably stuck around an' gave Travis time to get 'em because that is the one thing that the real Travis woulda done. Then this boyo gets himself on to a collapsible raft an' floats off. You remember about that?"

"I remember," says Benzey.

"Well . . . now he's all set," I say. "He opens up Travis's document case an' finds that he's got two sets of papers inside. First of all the Government stuff that Travis was supposed to deliver, and secondly the divorce papers and investigator's reports on Mrs. Travis. Well . . . he chances it. He lands here an' reports to the U.S. Army authorities. But there is one thing he don't know. He don't know what the real Travis was supposed to do about the papers. He reckons that there will be somebody over here to take 'em off him an' he is stickin' around waitin' for his own pals to show up an' fix where he is to go an' what he is to do. But nothin' happens. An' that is something that puzzled me for a bit but it don't puzzle me now. I reckon I can guess that one."

Benzey says: "Yeah . . . I can't. But you always was a swell guesser. Go on, Brilliance!"

"Well . . . then I turn up an' pull this one on him about bein' Pleyell an' he falls for that one. Then . . . just to make certain, we pull the phoney Mrs. Travis on him an' he falls for that one too. Then just at the moment when we don't want him to get bumped he gets bumped—which is not so good. But even that don't worry me so much as one thing."

Benzey says: "You don't mean to say that *somethin's* worryin' you. It ain't possible!"

"What's worryin' me is this," I tell him. "When this dead guy went bustin' around to see the dame that he thought was Mrs. Travis he musta been pretty certain of himself, musn't he? He musta known that he was takin' a helluva chance in askin' a dame to say that he was her husband. You got me?"

"Yeah," says Benzey, "I get you. That's certainly a point."

"It's a helluva point," I tell him. "It shows that although he hadn't ever met the real Mrs. Travis he'd got somethin' on her—somethin' that was good enough for him to be able to push her into identifyin' him—even if she didn't want to."

Benzey says: "Yeah . . . I wonder what that was?"

"So do I," I tell him. "I wanta know what that was, an' the other thing I wanta know is what that guy did with those goddam papers . . . because I'm gonna bet all the tea in China that when we go over his dump an' his quarters at the camp we aren't gonna find 'em. The hell with it."

He says: "Yeah. . . . It looks like you've had quite an evenin', doesn't it?"

I grin. I reckon he don't know how right he is.

III

It is eleven o'clock when I get up. I go over an' stand lookin' outa the window. But I ain't takin' a great deal of interest in what is goin' on outside. I am doin' some very heavy thinkin'—an' I mean heavy.

After I have dressed I call through to the Carlton. I ask 'em to put me through to Mrs. Travis. After a minute or two I hear that smooth cute voice of hers on the line. I say:

"Hallo, Cara. This is that Marine speakin'."

She says: "Oh yes! And who do I have to be this morning?"

"You don't have to be anybody else but you," I tell her. "Can I come round an' see you?"

She says yes she'd like nothin' better.

I light a cigarette, go out an' take a walk down to the Carlton. On the way I am thinkin' about this frill. I am thinkin' that she has got intelligence as well as bein' somebody that is easy on the eyes an' also she can hand out a nice line in actin'. I reckon that act she put on with Travis an' the phoney stuff she handed out to him was definitely the berries.

An' I wonder what she will look like by daylight an' whether she'll be as good. Plenty dames don't look so good in the day. They need soft lights an' soft music an' all the rest of that stuff. I'm curious to see just how this baby is gonna stand up to the cold, hard searchin' light of half-past eleven in the mornin'—that witchin' hour when old man hangover is at his worst as Shakespeare or Confucius or some other of them old-time script-writers usta say.

But I need not have worried. When I take one quick look at her I know that she is even better than she was last night. I'm tellin' you monkeys that when they was servin' out allure somebody marked this baby's race-card for her because anything she hasn't got just is not worth havin—if you get me.

She is wearin' a midnight-blue velvet coat an' skirt, beige coloured silk stockin's an' blue glacé kid court shoes. Her hair is tied with a blue ribbon. So you can think the picture out for yourselves. She is one of those frills that make you wonder, when you see 'em for the first time, how you coulda ever thought that that last dame you was stuck on was pretty.

She says: "I am just going to have some coffee. Would you like some?"

She gives me a cup; then she says: "Look, you're Mr. Caution, aren't you? Mr. Lemuel H. Caution—*the* Mr. Caution."

"You wouldn't make me blush, would you?" I tell her. "Incidentally, who are you?"

She throws me a smile. "Oh, a little thing like that wouldn't really matter to you," she says. "My name's Pearl Mallory."

I ask her: "How did you come in on this. Pearl?"

She passes me a cigarette-box. She says: "Well, it seems that somebody at the Embassy wanted a Mrs. Cara Travis in a hurry. I gather you'd asked for one and it seems that, for some reason, they think you matter. It also seems that it didn't matter particularly what this lady looked like, which *I* thought was rather odd at the time. Anyway, I've been doing some work at the Embassy ever since the war started—just an unimportant job, driving a car. They asked me if I'd be Mrs. Travis for you. Naturally I said yes. Then they told me something about Mrs. Travis so that my imitation shouldn't be too bad, and there you are. But I would like to know something about it."

"You were marvellous," I tell her. "As for knowin' something about it, it was just a frame. I knew when I told Travis that his wife was over here that he'd think it was *Travis's* wife; that if he *wasn't* Travis he probably wouldn't know her; that he'd come rushin' around her to make a deal with you. That's what he did, wasn't it?"

"That's right," she says. "He rang up here last night at eleven and asked if he could come round. He said it was urgent. I said he might. Then I rang through to my boss at the Embassy, asked them what I should do. They told me to listen to what he had to say and to agree to anything within reason."

"Nice work," I tell her. "What did he say when he got around here?"

"His attitude was rather odd," she says. "He took it for granted that I was Mrs. Travis and he also took it for granted that I was going to do what he wanted; that I was going to identify him as being Lon Travis. He seems to have something on Mrs. Travis. He said I'd better do what he wanted or else, if he was going to fall in the cart, he was going to make it his business to see that I fell with him. He said that he'd had a talk with you; that you were Pleyell, a junior partner in Travis's attorneys—he'd fallen for that line all right—that you were going to bring him round to be identified. He said you'd probably ask one or two cunning questions. Then he told me about that mole just below his Adam's apple and said that if I was asked about an identification mark I could give that. Altogether he seemed very sure of himself. Does all this mean anything to you?"

"Yes," I tell her, "it means something all right, but it's gonna take a lot of guessin' to find out what."

She says: "Well, don't say that I've finished. Don't say that I'm to go back to my car driving; that I'm not to have any more excitement."

I grin at her. "You're not tryin' to tell me that you wanta go on bein' Mrs. Travis, are you?" I ask her.

She says: "Why not? If it'd help."

I think for a minute. "Maybe it would," I tell her. "But it might not be so good for you. It might be a little bit dangerous."

She says: "Well, so what! These are dangerous times, aren't they?"

I say: "Maybe, but even in dangerous times it is a good thing to go on livin' as long as possible. Some of these boys might not be so nice, you know."

She says: "I've gathered that, Mr. Caution, but I still like the idea." She smiles. "I don't think I should ever be really frightened of Lon Travis, in spite of his blustering. I think he was a little bit scared himself."

I nod my head. "He was plenty scared," I tell her. "But even bein' scared didn't get him any place. Anyway, he's not scared any more."

She raises her eyebrows. "What happened?" she asks.

"Somebody decided to crease Travis," I tell her. "He was shot last night."

She clicks her little teeth together. "You don't say?" she says.

"Yeah," I tell her, "I do. It just shows you, doesn't it?"

She says: "Yes, it does. Do you know who did it?"

"I've got an idea," I tell her. "But ideas can be wrong." I stub my cigarette out, light another one. "Pearl," I say, "it looks like you're feelin' good an' bored. You want a little excitement, is that it? In other words, you'd like to go on bein' Mrs. Travis. You'd like to play this thing out an' see what happens?"

She nods. "That'd be wonderful," she says.

"All right," I tell her. "You go on just for a bit, but you just do what you're told an' don't take any unnecessary chances."

"I won't," she says. "What am I to do?"

"Just go on stayin' here," I tell her. "Just go on bein' Mrs. Cara Travis. When I want you to do something I'll let you know."

She says: "O.K. I'll take a chance on you."

We give each other another grin, an' I go out. I sorta like this Pearl dame.

I walk around for a bit; then I give myself some lunch an' take in a news reel. I come out at two-thirty. I walk to Piccadilly Circus, go down in the subway an' ring the big boy.

He asks me how I am an' if I know what I'm doin' yet.

"I got an idea," I tell him, "but I'm still anglin' around tryin' to find out something definite. There are one or two things that happened though that might interest you."

I tell him about Travis. I tell him that I am good an' fed-up with Travis bein' knocked off like that just when I was gettin' next to that boyo. He says that is as maybe but Travis bein' put out of business has gotta be a help one way or another; that just because Travis *is* out

of business somebody will haveta show their hand in a minute. I say
that is maybe so but the thing that interests me is just *how* they're
goin' to show their hand. He says well that's my headache; that I've
had everything I've asked for includin' a phoney Mrs. Cara Travis,
an' that I've got to make it the best way I can.

I say O.K. Then I ask him about this Pearl baby.

"You certainly gave me something there," I tell him. "I haven't
seen a jane like this Pearl bundle in years. I could look at her picture
every mornin' an' swoon away. Who is this frill?"

"You be careful of her," he says. "She wants to do something
for Uncle Sam. She's got a father who's an Admiral and a few other
relations in the Army and Air Corps. She's feeling very patriotic but
if anything happens to her you're going to feel a draught. Anyhow,"
he says, "you're through with her now. She can come back here and
go on driving a car."

"No, sir," I tell him. "No dice. That dame has started bein' Mrs.
Cara Travis an' she's goin' on bein' Mrs. Travis. I got work for her."

He says all right but he wouldn't like to be me if anything happens
to Pearl. He asks me if I want anything or anybody else.

I tell him no. I tell him that Benzey—who is supposed to be a
Canadian servin' with one of the Canadian Commandos—an' Carl
Pardoe and the rest of the phoney Marines I got over here will do
all right.

I also tell him that I think I oughta have a contact at Scotland Yard
because it looks to me like something is gonna pop at any minute.
He says have I got anybody in mind? I say no, not particularly, but
if I could have a choice I would like to have Herrick who is a Chief
Detective-Inspector an' who I know pretty well, havin' worked with
him before on the Julia Wayles case. He says all right. He will do his
best to fix things through the Embassy.

I hang up, go up outa the subway an' start walkin' down Piccadilly. The sun has come out an' it is a nice sorta day. Somehow I don't
mind life when the weather's good. I reckon it is one of those days
when I would like to be out in the country some place with nothin'
to do but sit on a stile an' look at one of those English cows grazin'
in a field. I think that would be very nice an' it would be nicer still if
Gayda was with me. That baby sorta fascinates me.

I look at my watch. It's just on three o'clock. I go back to the Regency, lay on my bed, smoke an' look at the ceilin'. I got an idea in my head that Carl will be comin' through.

I am dead right. At half-past three the telephone jangles. He says: "I'm callin' you from a pay-box. I just left Clemensky. I think that guy is going to be very interestin'."

"Yeah?" I tell him. "What's he doin'?"

"I wouldn't know," says Carl. "But he's had a long talk with me. He asked me all about myself. I told him plenty. After you left yesterday I got through to the big boy and got a Transatlantic telephone-call through early this morning. I got all the dope on this guy Capelli that you say I am. It was lucky I did too. Clemensky seems to have found out something about that one."

"Has he now?" I say. I think for a minute. This tells me somethin'. "What else happened?" I ask him.

"Not a lot," says Carl. "Clemensky sort of played around with the situation. I made out I was strapped for dough; that I wanted to get my hooks on some; that I wasn't goin' to be too particular how I got it. That seemed to suit him O.K. He said all right—for me to stay around—that maybe he could put some very nice pickin's in my way. Then he got generous. He gave me a hundred pounds English money. He said that was just so's I shouldn't get playin' around after any chicken-feed and get myself into trouble at a time when he might be wantin' me."

"Nice work," I tell him. "So you made yourself four hundred dollars for nothing."

"I wouldn't like to say that," says Carl. "There're strings on this dough. Anyhow, he asked me where he could get in touch with me, so I gave him an address I got—my phoney address—the Wilber Hotel. That's a small-time dump near Russell Square. He said he'd call me through. I said O.K. I was just goin' to scram. When I get to the door he says, as if he's just remembered it, that maybe it would be a good thing if I went around an' saw a friend of his—some guy by the name of Clansing. This guy has got an address on Shepherd Market. Clemensky said it might be a good thing if I went round an' saw this boyo at nine o'clock; that it might do some good if we got acquainted."

"That's O.K.," I tell him. "You do that, Carl. It might be interestin'."

He says: "That's what I thought."

I ask him what this guy Clansing's address is. He gives me the number. I say I'll be seein' him an' hang up.

I get back on the bed, light another cigarette an' look at the ceilin' some more. I reckon I have got the angles on this guy Clansing all right.

Work it out for yourself. Clemensky fell like a load of coke for that show-down stuff that Carl Pardoe pulled. He believes that Pardoe is Capelli. He knows that I am Caution. He knows what I'm doin' over here. He reckons he can use a tough egg like Capelli but he's not takin' any chances. So he asks Carl a lotta questions to try an' catch him out an' then he fixes up for him to meet up with this guy Clansing for a final check-over. I reckon that this Clansing is gonna turn out to be a tough boyo as well; that maybe Clansing an' Carl are supposed to get acquainted because they're gonna do some work together. Havin' regard to the fact that the real Capelli is a very hard proposition indeed, it don't take a lot of guessin' as to what sorta work these boys are goin' to do.

The mugs are always the same. They start off by tryin' to be clever an' end up by havin' to be tough.

The afternoon sun is comin' through the window-curtains an' makin' patterns on the carpet. I don't know whether I told you monkeys, but I am a poetic sorta guy. I am one of those bozos who oughta have been a big poet or somethin' like that, instead of which I get myself hooked into a game like I am now on. All of which proves that this mug Confucius, who said that ninety per cent of the guys in the world are all doin' something else but what they oughta be doin', certainly knew his raspberries.

IV

I wake up an' look at my watch. It is a quarter-past eight. I draw the black-out curtain, snap the light on an' give myself a shower an' a shot of rye.

I dress an' grab the telephone. I ask the girl in the reception if she can get me the number of "Mallows" near Wilminton. Five minutes afterwards I'm on the line talkin' to the butler. I ask if Miss Gayda Vaughan's in. He says he'll go an' get her. After a bit she comes on the line. I get a kick outa hearin' this baby's voice. There's somethin' in it—somethin' fresh an' amusin' an' laughin'. While she is talkin' I get to comparin' her with Pearl Mallory. I reckon between 'em these two honeypots have got all the beauty in the world with just a little bit left over, an' the poetical guy who said how happy he could be with either if the other dame was somewhere else was just a mug. I reckon that any guy who had both these dames trailin' around would be equipped for anything. All he would haveta do would be to watch the speedometer an' check his oil every two hundred miles.

She says: "I'm awfully glad you telephoned, Sourpuss. Do you want something?"

"Plenty," I tell her. "But nothin' I can get right now. I was feelin' sorta lonely—if you get me. I thought I'd like to talk to you."

She says: "That was nice of you, sweet. I hate you being lonely. Can I help? Would it amuse you if I were to tell you the story of my life?"

"It would amuse me plenty," I tell her. "But I'm scared. You might want to start writin' the next chapter an' put me in it."

She says: "Don't you worry on that score. I'm going to begin writing that chapter very shortly and I've cast you for a leading role."

"That's what I was scared of," I tell her. "I don't like leadin' roles. I like bein' in the background an' havin' fun."

"I know," she says. "You're the original invisible man. But I'm not having it that way. When are you coming to see me, Sourpuss?"

"I don't know," I tell her. "I'm wonderin' what sort of a welcome I should get."

"That's easily answered," she says. "Two open arms and not the slightest resistance. Can't you come down to-day—or to-morrow?"

"I don't know," I say. "Maybe I can get away some time around this week-end." I make my voice serious. "I wanta talk to you, Gayda," I tell her, "something important."

She says: "Yes, and I want to talk to *you* too, and that's important as well. I've been thinking about you."

"Tell me some more, sweetness," I tell her.

There is a pause; then she says: "Well, I've been thinking very, very seriously about us, Sourpuss, and I think we *ought* to be married."

I don't say anything. But my mouth is hangin' wide open like a codfish on a slab. This Gayda is a one-woman wave of destruction.

I'm tellin' you. Here is a dame that I have known on an' off for about seven hours an' she has come to the conclusion that we *ought* to get married. Also I have got the idea that when she says a thing like that she means it. I have already told you that this Gayda is a determined doll an' if any of you monkeys have ever met up with a jane like this you will know what I mean. Also you will not have to explain why you are usin' hair restorer every mornin' an' got circles under your eyes an' a worried look.

I pulled myself together. "You don't say so, Gayda," I tell her.

She says: "But I do, Sourpuss. I think we were made for each other."

I don't say anything for a minute. I am thinkin' maybe I agree with her. After a bit I say:

"O.K. Well, we'll talk about it when I come down. I suppose it's O.K. if I show up?"

She says: "You come just when you want to. You needn't even bother to telephone. I shall be here for some days."

I fish out a cigarette with one hand; get out my lighter an' light it. While I am wrestlin' with this proposition there is a silence. Then she says:

"What are you doing in London. I believe you've got some woman there. Are you going out to-night?"

I grin. "I never go out at night, honeypot," I tell her.

"I don't believe you," she says. "You never acquired that interesting dissipated look during the daytime, I'll bet." Her voice changes. It gets all low an' urgent an' thrillin'. She says: "Please come down soon, Sourpuss. I *do* want to see you so much. And Papa wants to see you too."

I say: "Oh yeah! Have you been tellin' him about me?"

She says: "Have I! He's so interested in you he can hardly wait."

I grin. "I hope he won't be disappointed," I say. "Look, Gayda, I've got to go now. I'm sorta busy, see?"

"I'll bet you are," she says. "I know you, Sourpuss. You're going to meet some woman and she'll run her fingers through that nice crinkly hair of yours and you'll tell her all sorts of nonsense and she'll believe you and—"

"Then she'll trust me an' give me her all," I tell her. "Me . . . I am not that sorta guy, Gayda."

"No?" she says. "Well, if you're not, then I'd like to know just what sort of a guy you are. I wouldn't trust you out of my sight."

"Well, you got to trust me now," I tell her, "because I'm scrammin'. So long, Gayda."

She says so long. She makes a little kissin' noise through the receiver.

I hang up. Any time I talk to this baby I have to wait for a minute to get my breath. After a bit I grab the telephone an' call through to Benzey.

"Look, Repulsive," I tell him. "I've been talkin' to the power behind the throne this afternoon. I've got everything more or less like I want it. You're gonna work with me from now on."

"What does that mean?" he asks. "Do I have to give up wearin' this Commando battle-dress?"

"Not for the moment," I tell him. "Why?"

He says: "Why! You don't know what it means to me. I only gotta look at a baby once with these Commando flashes on an' she falls."

"That's too bad," I tell him, "because where you're goin' to I don't think there are too many babies—at least not the sort you like."

He says: "Where am I goin' to?"

"Get down to Wilminton," I tell him, "an' play it easy. Find out everything you can about Travis. Find out where he used to go; find out what sorta bozo he was—if he knew any people down there beside the Vaughan's. You'd better stay at that inn. Then I'll know where to find you."

He says: "O.K. When shall I get in touch with you?"

"Don't bother," I tell him. "I'll be around there pretty soon myself. Anything that's goin' you can tell me then."

He says O.K.

I give myself a short one outa the flask, light a cigarette an' get my hat. I go out. It has started to rain a little bit but beyond that it's a nice evenin'. I am feelin' pretty good. Maybe it ain't such a bad world after all.

I start walkin' toward Shepherd Market.

It is about five an' twenty minutes to nine when I get to this dump. The house is a little old three-story affair sandwiched in between a coupla little lock-up shops, lyin' at the end of a passage off Shepherd Market.

The front door is open. I go in an' start easin' up the stairs to the second floor. I go quietly. There is so much dust around I could sneeze. The place smells. Not a very classy dump, I think.

There is only one door on the second-floor landin' so this has gotta be the Clansing hang-out. I listen for a minute but I can't hear anything. The whole house is quiet. I wait another minute; then I knock on the door. Nothing happens. I take out my flash an' take a look at the door. It's one of those old-fashioned things with a set-in lock. I put the blade of my penknife behind the ward of the lock an' give the door a bang. It opens.

I go in, find the light switch an' put it on. I shut the door behind me, light a cigarette an' take a look around. It's a bum sorta sittin'-room. The furniture is old-fashioned. Everything is dusty except the writin'-desk in the corner. In the right-hand wall there is another door. I go over an' push it open. This is a bedroom. It is as untidy as the first room an' the bed is not made up. Altogether this place looks like the sorta dump where a woman comes in once a day an' cleans around an' if you're not up by then everything has to wait till the day after. Maybe this Clansing guy is a late riser.

I ease outa the bedroom inta the sittin'-room an' take a look over the desk. I find nothin' at all. Anyway, I didn't expect to find anything. Then I sit down in an armchair that is inclined to give way under me an' smoke a cigarette.

Five minutes go by an' then I hear some footsteps on the stairs. The footsteps stop suddenly when they get to the landin'. I reckon this is Mister Clansing an' I reckon he's just seen the crack of light under the door. Maybe he's curious an' waitin' a minute to think things out.

A few seconds go past; then I hear a key in the door. The door opens an' a guy comes in. He is an odd-lookin' guy. His clothes aren't so bad, but his shoes are patent an' too pointed. He is wearin' an overcoat with a bit too much waist on it an' padded shoulders, an' a slate-grey fedora that never came out of an English shop.

He stands in the doorway lookin' at me. He has got a nasty thin sorta mouth an' dark eyes in a thin face. I start grinnin' inside. I think this is goddam funny.

I say: "Come in an' shut the door. You're Clansing, hey?"

He says: "Yeah! Wanta make something of it? Say, what the hell—"

"You can can that stuff, Clansing," I tell him. "You wouldn't know who I was, would you?"

He says: "I wouldn't know an' I don't wanta know. You get outa here."

"Nuts," I tell him. "Just relax. I wanta talk to you. An' take it easy, pal, because you remind me of a nice fat fly who has just walked himself into a spider's web."

He gives a nasty sorta grin. "Oh yeah?" he says. "So you're the spider, hey? One of these smart spiders."

"That's right," I tell him. "Some spider! My name's Caution—Lemuel H. Caution. An' believe it or not inside my coat I gotta Federal Bureau Identification Card. Does that mean anything to you?"

"It don't mean a thing—not a goddam thing," he says. But he don't look so good. He puts his hand in the right-hand pocket of his overcoat; then he takes it out.

"I'm glad you thought better of that." I grin at him. "It wouldn't do you any good to start any gun-play around here. An' Clemensky wouldn't like it either."

He says: "No? You know an awful lot, don't you?"

"I know plenty," I tell him. "But I got the drop on you. I'll tell you why. In my business we're trained to remember faces. Every month we take a look at a lotta little pictures—the Line-Up of the month's crooks. I saw yours two three years ago. Your name's Rudy Schrinkler, an' if I remember rightly you done two terms in Leavenworth. Does that mean anything to you?"

He says: "So what! Listen, what is this?"

I stub out my cigarette butt, throw it in the grate an' light a fresh one.

"Look, Clansing," I tell him, "first of all you're in a spot. It can be tough or it can be very tough. You can have it which way you like. First of all I'd like to know how you got out of America, an' don't tell me you came out on a legitimate passport because I don't believe you.

The U.S. Government aren't issuin' passports to heels like you these days. I got that on you. If I wanta play that I can play it. I can have you knocked off here, shipped back to the U.S. an' you get another term. That's the *best* thing I can do for you."

He opens his coat. He takes out a flash cigarette-case an' lights one. He looks to me like he's relaxin' a little.

He says: "So that's the best you can do, is it, Caution? That's the best thing. Go on. You interest me. What's the worst thing—you sweet bastard?"

"Accessory to murder," I tell him. "You can have it that way if you like."

He leans up against the sideboard. He says: "You're a lousy liar, Caution. I heard about you. They told me you were always a big-time bluffer. You can't hang any murder rap on me, an' you know it."

"That's where you're wrong," I tell him. "Maybe you don't know anything about the murder but that don't mean to say I can't hang the rap on you. In a minute you'll tell me you're not workin' for Clemensky."

He says: "You know an awful lot, don't you—or maybe you're just guessin'?"

"I know you're workin' for Clemensky," I tell him. "I also happen to know that a United States Army officer was knocked off in a joint of his off Mount Street last night. There were three guys in that business. Anyhow, that's my story."

He don't look so good. His face is a sorta pasty colour.

He says: "Ain't you funny? Perhaps you know who the three guys was?"

"I know," I tell him. "Clemensky, a guy called Willie Capelli an' you. Clemensky is the brains an' you two are just the two stooges that play around an' do the dirty work."

He says: "Look, I don't know anything about any murder. Anyhow, I wasn't there."

"That's what you say," I tell him. "Anyhow, that's the rap an' I think I can make it stick. Unless you wanta play?"

He says: "I don't get this, an' I don't like it."

"You'll get it in a minute," I tell him. "An' you'll like it. Look, I'm gonna do a little more guessin'. Clemensky got you over here. He got some work for you to do. Maybe he thought he needed a little extra assistance. So he got this guy Capelli in on the job too. I suppose you're gonna tell me you haven't got a date with Capelli to-night; that he's not due round here at nine o'clock—in a few minutes. You can have it that way if you want to an' I'll stick around here an' pinch the pair of you."

He says: "Say, listen . . . this is England—"

"Nuts," I tell him. "This is England all right. But there's a war on an' the United States an' the English are in it together. Use your brains. D'you think the cops over here are gonna do what I want them to do about you or not, you dumb cluck? Or maybe you haven't got a date with Capelli? Maybe he's not comin' here?"

He says: "Well, you're right there. He's comin' here. But I don't know anything about this. I was told to meet this guy an' take a look at him. All I gotta do is to talk to Capelli an' see what sort of a fella he is."

"An' then?" I ask him.

"I don't know," he says. "What happens after that I don't know, an' even if some racket is on I don't know a goddam thing about it. So I can't be pinched for it, can I?"

"No," I tell him, "you can't be. All you can be pulled in for is the murder rap I just told you about. Look, Schrinkler," I tell him, "what are you gonna do? Are you gonna play ball, or aren't you?"

He thinks for a minute; then he says: "Look, supposin' I play it your way, what do I get outa this?"

"You don't get anything," I tell him. "All you get is that some time or other you get shipped back to the States. I let you get by, see? That's all. If you don't play it my way, I'm gonna hang that accessory to murder rap on you an' somehow I'm gonna make it stick. Now you do what you like."

He says: "Goddam you, Caution, you're a tough egg. What do you want me to do?"

"Not very much," I say. "I wouldn't trust a heel like you to do much except double-cross somebody."

He says: "Who do I have to cross up?"

"Capelli," I tell him. "Look, Clemensky is putting in Capelli to do something. Clemensky has put you in to have a talk with Capelli. He wants you guys to get to know each other. He wants you to work with each other, so he's made, this date for Capelli to come round here an' get acquainted with you. Well, you're nothin' in this business. You're just chicken-feed. I'm not worryin' about you. I wanta get my hooks on Capelli an' Clemensky, see?"

"I get it," he says. "An' if you get them you give me a break?"

"Right," I say. "If I get them I'll give you a break."

"An' how is this thing to be played?" he says.

"I'm gonna get outa here," I tell him. "When Capelli comes you talk to him. Listen to what he's gotta say. Be nice an' friendly. When he's gone an' Clemensky asks you what sorta guy Capelli is an' if you like workin' with him, all you gotta say is yes. All right, from there you go ahead. Do what Clemensky tells you. Maybe he won't give you instructions. Maybe he'll give 'em to Capelli. I'm not sure about that. Maybe he *might* give you the instructions. He might make you the head man. In any event you gotta let me know what's happening. You gotta let me know what Clemensky's doin'. You got that?"

"I got it," he says. "Where do I get you?"

"You get me at the Regency Hotel on Jermyn Street," I tell him. "An' watch your step. One dumb move outa you, Schrinkler, an' I'll get you roped in so fast you'll wonder what's hit you. You got that?"

He says he's got it.

I get up. I throw my cigarette stub in the grate an' I go out. I leave him there lookin' outa the window. He don't look so pleased about something.

Outside in the street I look at my watch. It is five minutes to nine. I walk down the narrow turnin' a little way an' stand in a doorway. Two three minutes afterwards Carl turns down the alleyway. He comes towards me. As he goes past I say:

"Pull up, Carl, an' light a cigarette. This is Lemmy."

He says outa the side of his mouth: "I got it." He takes out his cigarette-case an' makes out he is havin' trouble in gettin' his lighter to work.

I say: "I just left Clansing. He's not Clansing. He's frontin' under that name. He's a guy called Schrinkler, a tough crook with a record—a killer. I've pulled a fast one on him. I've told him I'm after Capelli— that's you, Carl—an' if I can get Capelli an' Clemensky I'll give him a run."

"I get it," he says. "The old double-double-cross act?"

"That's right," I tell him. "He's waitin' on ice for you. He's all set. Go to it, pal."

He lights his cigarette. He goes down the street. I wait five minutes. Then I scram.

Maybe this isn't gonna be so hard after all.

I turn inta Piccadilly. I walk east an' go down in the subway at the Green Park Station. I ring through to Scotland Yard an' ask to speak to Chief Detective-Inspector Herrick.

When he comes on the line I say: "Hallo, is that you, Herrick? Maybe you remember my voice?"

He laughs. "I could never forget it," he says. "What are you doin' over here, Lemmy?"

"Look, Herrick," I tell him, "don't tell anybody, but I'm a Marine."

"I bet you are," he says. "What have the U.S. Marine Corps ever done to deserve anybody like you? Anyhow, I'm glad you've called through. I was just thinkin' about you."

"Fine," I tell him. "Maybe somebody telephoned you?"

"That's right," he says. "The U.S. Embassy were on to the Commissioner. He gave me a ring a few minutes ago. He says I'm to co-operate with you on this Travis business." He sighs. "Well," he says, "I suppose I've got to do it."

"Don't you worry, Herrick," I tell him. "I'm gonna play this very nicely. No fireworks."

"Well, there's one thing," he says. "For Heaven's sake, Lemmy, remember—"

"This is England," I tell him. "You've been tellin' me that for years. I'll remember."

"Just take it easy," he says.

"You'd be surprised," I tell him. "I'll take it so easy you'll never notice. If I come along right now will you be in?"

"I'll be here," he says. "I can hardly wait."

I hang up. I go outa the station an' grab a cab. I tell the driver to go to Scotland Yard.

Chapter Five
MATRIMONIAL STUFF

I

I GET to Wilminton at nine o'clock. I walk round to The Plough, thinkin' to myself an' tryin' to put two an' two together without makin' a hundred out of it, which is not always such an easy job.

It is a nice night. Pretty soon there is gonna be a moon, I think. I grin to myself as I wonder if I shall be makin' any use of it. When I get near the inn I start havin' bets with myself as to what Benzey will be doin' if he's there. I reckon it's an even chance that he's either makin' a play for the frill behind the bar—the one with the pompadour—or else he's upstairs asleep, breathin' like a guy with apoplexy an' with his big feet hangin' over the bed-rail. These are the only two things that interest Benzey, an' if he could do 'em both at the same time would he be pleased!

When I get there I fix a room, dump my suitcase, walk along the corridor an' push open the door of Benzey's room. He is asleep. He is makin' a noise like a seventy-ton tank in reverse. One hand is hangin' down by the side of the bed next a bottle of whisky. It looks like the boy has been relaxin'.

I give him a dig. He wakes up, yawns, rubs his eyes an' sits up.

He says: "So what! So now you've come down here ridin' me again. Directly I get a little bit of peace you come around."

"There's no peace for guys like you," I tell him. "You tell me something. What have you been doin' since you've been back here besides makin' a play for that blonde baby downstairs?" I throw him a cigarette; light one for myself.

He says: "Believe me, that blonde frill is a mine of information. If I've been workin' on her it's only because I've been tryin' to find something out. I'm a martyr to duty."

"That's what I was afraid of," I tell him. "The sorta thing that you try an' find out from a dame doesn't get me any place."

He says: "Look, Lemmy, you got me wrong." He gives another yawn an' picks up the bottle. He takes a long swig, passes it to me. He says: "That girl downstairs is terrible. I can't get any place with her. She's got a great failin', that baby."

"Such as?" I ask him.

Benzey says: "It's this way: When she was young she never thought of anythin' but boys. But she's grown outa that. All she thinks of now is men. My trouble is," says Benzey, "she's not interested in *me*."

"What else did you get beside that?" I say. "I wish you'd understand I'm not particularly interested in your love-life."

"Don't worry," says Benzey. "I've found out a lot. This dump is the place for findin' out things. That honey downstairs gets everything. All you gotta do is to lead her on to talk."

I sit down. I reckon maybe in a year or two he'll come to it.

He goes on: "First of all about Travis, or the guy who was supposed to be Travis. He was posted to the Unit down here. Everybody seems to think he was a nice sorta guy. He was popular. At the same time he was a reserved sorta cuss. He didn't make any friends, see? Nice to everybody, but they never got any place with him. I got an idea about that."

"What's the big idea?" I ask him.

"Travis was a guy who went for frills," says Benzey. "He was one of those boys who wasn't interested in men. He liked to get around with dames. All the people around here liked him. Naturally they was trying to give U.S. officers the best time they could an' they invited him an' the other boys up to their houses."

I nod my head. "I see. That's how he got to know the Vaughans?"

"That's right," says Benzey. "Old man Vaughan is a good guy. He's a Canadian but he's had this house here for a long time. I understand he usta spend his holidays in England every year. He liked Travis. I got an idea that he didn't know Travis was married. I got an idea that he thought that Travis might marry Gayda. I think he liked that idea."

"You don't say," I tell him. "The idea bein' that Vaughan wanted to get Gayda off his hands."

"Not so much that," says Benzey, "but I think he *wanted* that baby to be married. I think Vaughan's a little scared of Gayda. I think he believes she's inclined to be a bit wild, see? He thought maybe that marriage would quieten her down a bit."

I nod again. "So that's it," I say. "Well, it looks as if Gayda intends to quieten herself down. Her new idea is that she wantsta get hitched up to me."

Benzey says: "For cryin' out loud! What has that poor dame done to deserve a fate worse than death?"

"She might do worse," I tell him, "except for one thing. Me—I take a serious view of marriage."

"Like hell you do," says Benzey. "So do I. So does everybody else—only they *get* married. Then after a bit they ain't so serious. It's like havin' stomach-ache. You get used to it. I reckon that marriage is like a job. You're mad keen to get it. You think it's swell. When you've got it, an' have worked a bit of overtime, you think of nothin' else but gettin' time off."

"Ain't you the little philosopher?" I tell him. "All right. What else did you find out?"

"That's all," he says. "What else is there to find out? The guy was down here on service. He's got around a bit. He's had a few drinks in houses. He's been one or two places. Most week-ends he went up to town on week-end pass. Anythin' else there is to know I reckon you know."

"Maybe you're right," I say. "An' maybe you don't know how right you are. You better get a little more sleep, Benzey."

"That suits me," he says. "Listen, will you tell me how long I haveta stick around this cock-eyed place. This dump is gettin' me down. I get sorta enervated. I'm drinkin' myself to death."

"Impossible," I tell him. I go out. When I get to the doorway I see his big fin reachin' down for the bottle.

II

When I get to Mallows the butler gives me a smile reserved for old friends of the family. He looks more like Act Three than ever. He says:

"I wasn't able to give your telephone message to Miss Vaughan, Mr. Pleyell. She hasn't come in yet."

"Too bad," I tell him. "Do you expect her in soon?"

"Any minute, sir," he says. "In the meantime Mr. Vaughan would very much like to see you."

I leave my service-cap in the hallway an' go after the butler. He takes me through a long oak passage an' inta a room at the end. It's a swell room—a library—a real one with books in it an' oak tables an' what-have-you-got. This place has got atmosphere. On the other side of the room are big curtains drawn over french windows that I reckon lead out to the back lawn. On the right-hand side is an old-time fireplace with a big fire burnin'.

Vaughan comes across the room an' shakes hands with me. I like the look of this guy. He's big an' rangy with iron-grey hair an' a good jaw. He shakes hands as if he meant it.

He says: "I'm glad to meet you." He gives me a long look-over. "I wanted to see you particularly because I wanted to find out just what sort of man it was who could make Gayda be serious for more than five minutes."

I grin at him. "You don't mean to say she's been serious for as long as that," I say.

He grins. "It's a fact," he says. "Sit down. Have you had dinner?" I tell him no.

He says: "All right. We'll fix that up later. In the meantime have a drink."

I tell him I'd like a whisky an' soda. He goes over to a sideboard an' pours me out a long one. He fixes himself a drink too. He brings it back to where I'm standin' in front of the fire.

He says: "Would it be a good idea if you and I got things straightened out?"

I grin at him. "I think it would be a hell of an idea," I say. "Who's gonna start, you or me?"

He says: "I think I will. You understand that Gayda means a lot to me. I don't know why, but she's my eldest girl and somehow I think a lot more of her than I do of the other two—a marvellous child, Gayda."

I nod my head.

"I've always let her have her own way," he goes oh, "and I've always found it paid me. I trust Gayda. She's got a sense of adventure. She likes to get around but she's got her head screwed on the right way and she's never gotten into any trouble—well, nothing that you could call serious. Now she's talking about marriage."

I don't say anything.

He goes back to the sideboard; brings over a box of cigars. He offers me one, but I say no. He lights one himself, takin' a long time over the job. I reckon this Vaughan guy is a clever sorta cuss—the strong-man type. He's got brains too. He knows what he wants an' how he's gonna get it. He puts the box back an' brings a cigarette-box over. I take one an' light it.

He says: "When Gayda came back the other night from London she told me some story about you being an F.B.I. man. She also told me she wanted to marry you." He grins. "She went so far," he goes on, "as to say that if she doesn't marry you she's not marrying anybody else."

I laugh. "I must *have* somethin'," I tell him.

He looks me up an' down. "Candidly, between you and me and the gate-post," he says, "*I* think you've got something. But first of all what about this F.B.I. business? I suppose that's just nonsense?"

I shake my head. "No, Mr. Vaughan," I tell him, "that's the truth."

He raises his eyebrows.

"I don't haveta go inta details," I tell him, "but I'm what you might call a phoney Marine. It just happens to suit the U.S. Government to have me in a Marine uniform at the present moment. There are quite a few U.S. Marines over here, see. It's an easy way of gettin' about an' it don't attract too much attention."

He says: "I see. Well, that makes it better than ever."

I ask him why.

He says: "Well, if you're a special agent of the Federal Bureau of Investigation, you're a pretty good fellow. They don't have nit-wits in that game."

"That's as maybe," I tell him, "but at the same time I don't know whether the F.B.I. is a good class for a girl like Gayda to marry into."

He draws on his cigar. "I see what you mean," he-says. "You mean it's a job that might be dangerous."

I nod. "That's right," I tell him. "I wouldn't like her to be a widow too early." I finish my whisky an' soda; put the glass on the mantelpiece behind me.

He says: "Well, that's a chance that every woman's got to take, especially these days when there's a war on. And fate's a funny thing. There are lots of people get through a war safely and get themselves knocked down and killed by a motor-bus when it's all over. Another thing, I don't think Gayda would be concerned about a little thing like your being in the F.B.I. It'd probably make you a really romantic figure in her eyes."

I say: "This is fine. And of course it's a terrific compliment, Mr. Vaughan. But nobody seems to worry very much about *my* ideas on the subject."

He looks at me with his eyes poppin'. He says:

"You don't mean to tell me that you wouldn't be mad keen to marry Gayda if you could."

"How do I know?" I ask him. "What do I know about her? I've seen her two or three times." I throw my cigarette stub away. "You see, the trouble with me is," I go on, "I'm inclined to be a bit romantic too an' I'd like you to know here an' now that I'm stuck on Gayda. But I think we oughta know a little bit more about each other before we think about anythin' serious like an engagement, don't you?"

He says: "Yes, that's sensible. Well, you'll have lots of opportunities. We'd like to see as much of you as is possible." He gives me a smile. He says: "You know, you haven't got a chance to get out of this. Gayda's made up her mind about you an' once she makes up her mind about a thing believe me she always gets it."

I don't say anything.

I think to myself you're tellin' me!

III

I am sittin' on a tree stump on the lawn at the back of the house lookin' down over the hillside. The moon is even better than it was when I was here before. Away down in the valley I can see the fields and hedges almost like it was daylight. Me—I think life is all right. I also think that Vaughan knows his cigars because the one that he has given me that I am smokin' right now is one hundred per cent an' never came out of no Christmas cracker.

I reckon I have got that feelin' of well-bein' that comes to a guy when he has had a good meal, a drink, an' knows that there is some baby in the offin' that is fallin' for him in a big way.

Somebody says just behind me: "Well, Sourpuss. . . ."

I turn around on the tree-stump. It is Gayda. I'm tellin' you monkeys that she looks a picture standin' there in the moonlight.

I give her a long look-over. She is wearin' blue serge slacks that fit like they ought to fit, a loose three-quarter length coat in some red wool stuff, a blue jumper with a red neck edgin' an' her hair is tied up in a red an' blue scarf.

"Good-evenin'," I tell her. "So you gone all Brigade of Guards on me, Gayda—scarlet an' blue, hey? Me . . . I'm hurt."

"I bet you are," she says. "Anyhow, if you'll tell me what the U.S. Marine Corps colours are I'll see what I can do about it."

"Why bother, honey," I tell her. "After all, I'm not certain about you. Maybe you're only a passin' fancy. Just one of them babies that I leave behind me. . . ."

"Like hell," she says. "You try leaving me behind you and see what I do to you."

"Think nothin' of it," I say. "Take no notice. I was just talkin' to myself."

"Well, you must find yourself a bore sometimes," she says. "Just move over, please."

I move over on the tree-stump. She comes an' sits down beside me. She puts her arms around my neck an' gives me a kiss. Then she says:

"So you've been talking to Papa. So you've been telling him that you're not quite certain that you want to marry me; that you want to know a little bit more about me. Who do you think you are? I suppose the idea is to make me even more keen on you?"

"Look, Gayda," I tell her, "don't get me wrong. I'm not puttin' on any look-me-over-kid-I'm-hard-to-get act, but this marriage is a serious proposition."

"Very likely," she says, "but you're not the type of man to run away from a serious proposition."

I grin at her. "You'd be surprised," I tell her. "I have spent most of my life runnin' away from serious propositions—"

"In the shape of pretty women, I expect," says Gayda. "Anyway, what's the idea in waiting. Why don't we be engaged and then get married in two or three months' time." She nestles up close to me. "You know, Sourpuss," she says, "believe it or not I'm crazy about you."

"I like believing it," I tell her. "But there's more to this than just gettin' married. What the hell do you know about me, Gayda?"

"Not very much," she says. "Incidentally, Papa tells me that you *are* an Agent of the Federal Bureau. How thrilling! So that odd man at Chez Clarence was telling the truth?"

"That's right," I tell her, "he was. An' that's the thing that's worryin' me. I've got an idea in my head that I'm gonna be too busy to think about anything else but my job."

She says: "I see." Her voice is serious. "You know if you want to talk you can. You know you can trust me, don't you? If on the other hand you'd rather say nothing I shall understand."

I put my arm around her. I give her a squeeze.

"Look," I tell her, "I trust you all right. I gotta trust somebody. Another thing is maybe I'll want you to give me a hand. That's what I've come down here for. I wanted to have a talk with you."

"Oh dear," she says. "I thought it was going to be romantic and it turns out its going to be business."

"An' how!" I tell her. "Big business!"

"All right," she says. "Let's get the business settled and then perhaps we can get back to the question of our getting married. How long is this business going to take?"

"I wouldn't know," I say. "But it's gonna take some weeks if not months."

"All right, Sourpuss," she says. "You can give me a cigarette and tell me what you want to tell me. The sooner you get it over the better."

"Well," I tell her, "my name's Caution—Lemuel H. Caution—Lemmy to you. I'm only frontin' as bein' in the U.S. Marines over here. That's convenient, see? It gives me a background an' it enables me to get about without folks bein' too curious."

She says: "How wonderful. How long have you been in the F.B.I., Sourpuss?"

"Quite a long time," I say. "Long enough to know better."

She says: "Is this work you're doing dangerous?"

"It could be," I tell her. "The sorta boyos that we play around with in this man's war are not noted for their sweet natures. But I think I'd like to start at the beginnin', because you come inta this."

She looks at me. Her eyes are wide.

"*I* come into it," she says. "How?"

"You knew Travis," I tell her. "I don't suppose you knew Travis very well because I reckon that you an' your Pa an' your sisters have just been nice to him in the same way as English people would be nice to any U.S. officer who was over here. But he was stuck on you. I know that. So maybe he's talked a little. An' there's another thing—"

"Yes?" she says. "What, Sourpuss?"

"This Chez Clarence dump," I tell her. "I'll take a shade of odds that you got to know about that place through Travis."

She says: "Yes, of course I did." She draws on her cigarette. "One day we were talking about gambling here at dinner, and he told us about Chez Clarence. Some friends of his in London had taken him there. I went there with him for the first time two or three days later. I lost a little money. I've been there several times since. Sometimes I won—sometimes I lost. But it was amusing, and there is so little to do in London at night. But what's Chez Clarence got to do with Travis?"

"This is a long story," I tell her. "The point is that Travis was not Travis."

She looks at me, her eyes poppin'.

"Not Travis!" she says. "Then who was he?"

I shake my head. "I wouldn't know," I tell her. "I don't know *who* he was but I know what he was."

She says: "This is terribly thrillin'. What was he, Sourpuss?"

"The phoney Travis was a German agent," I tell her. "Look, I'm gonna start this business at the beginnin'. In the United States there was an officer in one of the technical branches. His name was Travis. He was a good guy. Everybody thought a lot of him. He was a good soldier with a good record. More than that this Travis had a lotta big ideas. He was a specialist in mechanised warfare an' he put up a whole bunch of ideas to the High Command that they felt was pretty good.

"Well, this guy Travis—the *real* Travis I mean—was due to come over here. He was goin' to bring over a lot of information an' details to do with the new mechanised units in the U.S. Fighting Forces over here—up-to-the-minute stuff, see? He was bringin' 'em because he knew all about 'em an' was due to instruct our people an' the British in this new stuff.

"Well, before the time came that Travis was due to leave he started havin' trouble with his wife, Cara. I oughta tell you about this baby. She is a one that one. She is beautiful an' bad. She'd given Travis a lotta trouble for a long time an' he wanted to divorce her. But she was a cute baby. For some reason or other she didn't wanta be divorced from Travis. So she just played it so that he couldn't get a divorce. Travis got plenty annoyed about this. He went to his attorneys, Wynn, Stromberg, Fidelli & Pleyell—an' got them to keep a close check on her—to have her tailed wherever she went—in the hopes that he might get some evidence that would enable him to get his divorce.

"Well, just when the time came for Travis to sail one of the private dicks who'd been watchin' Mrs. Travis weighed in with the divorce evidence, an' Wynn—Travis's attorney—had just time to rush the reports down to Travis when he was gettin' on the boat for England.

"Well, that boat never got to England. It was sunk. A coupla days later a British destroyer picks up a collapsible raft with a guy on it. This guy has got a cask of water an' some grub an' a document case. He says he is Travis. He's got Travis's papers an' he's got Travis's documents. Also he looks like Travis.

"All right. He comes to England. He reports to Headquarters. Now get this—nobody except the High Army Authorities in U.S. know about the documents that Travis has got. The instructions he had as to what he had to do with them when he got here were secret. Only he knew an' the people over here who were to receive them. But they haven't received 'em."

Gayda says: "I see. What's happened to them?"

"That's the point," I tell her. "When Travis gets here he reports to U.S. High Command an' says that the mechanisation papers have disappeared. He says that when he opened the document case there was nothin' inside but the divorce papers. Well, he's got to say somethin' like that, hasn't he? He's got rid of those papers, see? . . . an' he had to have a story, an' that one was as good as anything else because nobody can say it ain't true. Understand?"

She nods. "I understand, Sourpuss," she says.

"Now," I go on, "I came inta this this way: I was one of half a dozen F.B.I. Agents who were over here with the Marines. That was just a front, see? We were doin' other work. All right, when the phoney Travis gets here with this story one or two people in U.S. get suspicious. I get orders to check up on him.

"Now Travis had never met the junior partner in his firm of attorneys named Pleyell an' by a bit of luck this guy Pleyell had joined the Marines. That's why I introduced myself to him as Pleyell—junior partner in his own firm of attorneys—an' he fell for it. I played a line with him that I was tryin' to fix up the divorce; that the firm had heard that his boat had been sunk an' we wondered if the divorce papers had been lost. He fell for that too.

"Everything was goin' pretty good. I hoped to get next to Travis. I hoped to find out what he'd done with those papers—the Government documents—but I've come up against a stone wall an' I don't see any way out."

She says: "What's the stone wall, Sourpuss?"

"Travis has disappeared," I tell her. "You remember that night when we were at Chez Clarence, when you an' I were talkin' at the bar, when there was the show-down with that guy Capelli? All right. Well, you remember that Travis was standin' just behind us. After that spot of bother was over he'd disappeared. Nobody's ever seen him since."

"But," she says, "you said he'd left a message with the cloakroom, didn't you, Sourpuss?"

"I made that up," I tell her. "I didn't want you to worry. But the fact of the matter is that from the time we last saw Travis in the bar at Chez Clarence up to now no one's seen him."

She says: "What do you think's happened?"

"I don't know," I tell her. "But I could make a guess, although it might be a bad one. Here it is: Travis knew about Chez Clarence didn't he? This place is run by the boy called Clemensky. He's got one or two tough eggs workin' for him—men who've come over from the States. Well, it looks as if the phoney Travis was workin' in with that bunch. It might easily be that they were the people who took those plans over from him, because he wasn't the brains in that job. He was just a messenger; just a guy put in on that boat to get next to Travis an' somehow grab those papers off him. Clemensky an' his bunch were the people who were gonna do a deal with them an' get 'em outa this country to the Germans somehow. I don't *know*. I'm only guessin'.

"If this is right, it would be on the cards that Travis would take you or any other people he knew up to Chez Clarence just to make out it was the sorta place he went to, an' took his friends to, to do a little card playin', see?"

"I see," she says. "But would that account for his disappearance, Sourpuss?"

"Why not?" I tell her. "Work it out for yourself. The phoney Travis thinks I'm Pleyell—a partner in his firm of attorneys. I start talkin' to him about this divorce. I start tellin' him that he oughta do something about it. I ask him if he's got the papers all right. Well, this worries him, see? He gets scared so he thinks the time has come when he's gotta blow. He has already handed those papers over to Clemensky. He probably handed the document case over with both sets of papers—the Government plans an' the divorce reports. He was gettin' worried in case I asked him for the divorce papers. He hadn't got 'em. So he thinks it's time to blow. He knows that the other guys will see that the papers are delivered somehow an' he gets out of it."

Gayda says: "That sounds logical. But tell me something. Supposing you're right, Sourpuss. Supposing Clemensky and his friends have got those papers, how are they going to get them out of this country?"

"I wouldn't know," I tell her. "That's somethin' I've gotta find out."

She says: "Give me another cigarette, please."

I give her a cigarette, light it for her. We sit there on the tree-stump with our arms around each other's waists lookin' over the moonlit fields.

After a while she says: "It's the devil of a mess, isn't it? But I expect you'll straighten it out, Sourpuss. You know, I'm beginning to think you're really rather clever."

"You don't say," I tell her. "Have you only just found that out? But look, Gayda, I'm plenty worried about this business because—I'll tell you somethin'—I'm not half so goddam clever as a lotta people think, an' I think that these guys have maybe got a little bit more brains than I have."

She gives a little laugh. "I don't believe it," she says. She looks at me sideways. "Now I understand something that worried me at the time."

"Such as?" I ask her.

"That woman you telephoned to whilst we were at Chez Clarence—that was Mrs. Cara Travis—and now I remember that when you came back to Clemensky's place you brought Travis with you. Now I understand—"

"You got it, baby," I tell her. "I had a phoney Travis on my hands, so I thought I'd produce a phoney Cara Travis just to see what he'd do."

She makes a little noise. "So that wasn't the *real* Mrs. Travis?"

"Not on your life," I tell her. "I borrowed a good-lookin' dame from the U.S. Embassy—a blonde honey. I put her up as Mrs. Cara Travis. Then I told him that I was gonna take him around there to be identified by her. I wanted to see what he'd do."

"How exciting," she says. "What happened?"

"He fell for it, sweet," I tell her. "Directly I leave him he goes rushin' around an' sees this dame an' pulls a fast one on her. He tells her that she's gotta identify him as Travis. Well, she's clever so she says O.K. an' she does it."

Gayda says: "But I still don't understand. Wasn't he taking an awful chance in going round and asking her to do that?"

I shake my head. "He wasn't chancin' anything," I say "because although he didn't know the real Cara Travis, what he did know was that the guys he was workin' for had got something on her. So when he went around there he said she'd got to identify him or else—"

"I see," she says. "I see. . . . They *are* clever, aren't they, Sourpuss?" She gives a sigh. "Some girls have all the luck," she says. "I never get jobs like that to do. Tell me, what's this woman like—the one who's been helping you?"

"Sweetheart," I tell her, "she's nearly as good-lookin' as you are. Believe me that baby's got something. A blonde and what a blonde! She drives a car for the U.S. Embassy normally—sorta war-service, see? She was glad to come in on this an' I expect she gotta kick out of it."

Gayda says: "I'll bet she did. I expect it won't be such fun driving a car now."

"Don't you worry your head, baby," I tell her. "She's not goin' back to the Embassy. I can still use that baby. She's goin' on frontin' as Mrs. Cara Travis. Maybe I'll find some more work for her to do."

She says: "I see. Won't you be putting her into danger, Lemmy? After all, these people seem very tough and very clever."

I nod my head. "That's the way it is," I tell her. "But Pearl Mallory's a good American, an' she doesn't mind takin' a chance. Besides, there's a war on—or didn't they tell you? We've all gotta take chances these days—men an' women."

She says: "Yes, I suppose we have." There is another pause; then she says: "When are you going to see her again, Sourpuss?"

"Pretty soon," I tell her. "There are one or two things I wanta ask that baby. Look," I go on, "I told you just now when Travis went round to see her he showed that these boys had got something on Mrs. Travis and because of that she'd got to identify him. O.K. Well, I haven't had much of a chance to talk to her yet. I wanta find out exactly what he said. Maybe I'll piece together what they had on this dame. Maybe it's gonna bring me a little closer to the solution."

She says in a very low voice: "But I think it's a great pity—"

"What's a pity?" I ask her.

"I think it's a great pity that you have to have such good-looking women to help you in these jobs, Sourpuss," she says. "I think you ought to let me help you. After all, I'm practically your wife."

"Like hell you are," I tell her. "Look, Gayda, if I were to bring you inta this business your Pa would tear me wide open. You just stay put."

She gives a sigh. She says: "So I'm merely to be the relaxation of the warrior. You'll come and see me when there's nothing exciting doing. Is that it?"

"Somethin' like that," I tell her.

She gets up. After a bit we begin to walk back towards the house.

"I think I ought to meet this Pearl Mallory," she says.

"Why not?" I say. "She's a hundred per cent. She'd fall for you like a ton of coke."

"Would she?" she says. "She might not. She might be a little bit keen on you herself."

"No dice," I tell her. "You got the idea in your head that every woman I meet falls for me, Gayda. You're wrong."

"I don't think so," she says. "I know my sex. Anyway, I'd like to meet Miss Mallory just so she could see that I regard you as my property."

"I get it," I tell her. "Sorta 'keep off the grass,' hey? Well, maybe I'll fix that. I'd like you two babies to meet. It oughta be fun."

She says: "Yes," but she sounds sorta dubious.

By now we have come to the front porch. She says:

"When am I going to see you again, Lemmy? I always seem to be saying good-bye to you."

"That's O.K.," I tell her. "There'll always be another time. Maybe you'll be comin' up to town?"

"I'll give you a ring," she says. "Shall I do that?" She puts her arms around my neck an' gives me a kiss. Then she turns an' goes straight back inta the house.

I stand there for a minute lookin' after her; then I turn around an' begin to walk along the carriage-drive, down the hill. I am beginning to think this Gayda is really stuck on me, an' I'm tellin' you monkeys it frightens me a bit because when a dame falls for me I don't like her to fall too hard because dames who fall hard can make trouble.

Or maybe you've found that out yourself.

CHAPTER SIX
SUPPER PARTY

I

I WAKE up an' look at the ceilin'. The bedroom in this inn has got a funny sorta ceilin'. Once on a time it was white. Now there are brown spots all over it. When I first took a look I thought it was my liver.

I put my hands behind my head an' do a little quiet thinkin' an' it will not take you monkeys a lotta guesses to know that I am thinkin' about Gayda, because one way an' another it looks to me as if this baby is gonna be troublesome before I know where I am.

First of all she is a frill who knows her own mind. But definitely! She knows what she wants an' she goes out to get it. She does the same thing even if she only *thinks* she wants it. My trouble at the moment is that the thing that Gayda thinks she wants right now is me.

Any guy who knows his biblical onions will know that the original trouble in the world was started by that hundred-percent baby operatin' around the Garden of Eden named Eve. Well, when that jane snapped inta action the trouble started an' it's been goin' on ever since. That's O.K. by me so long as I don't get the backwash.

I get up an' go along to the bathroom. There is a notice stuck on the wall that says that if I wanta have a bath I can only have five inches of water. The notice says that the Fuel Controller says so. I turn on the taps an' cannot even get half an inch of water, after which I say something about the Fuel Controller an' skip it.

When I have dressed I go along to Benzey's room. He is sittin' on the edge of the bed smokin' a cigarette. He looks pained. He says:

"Look, I'm fed up with this dump. I wanta go places. My temperament is getting me down."

"Like hell," I tell him. I sit down in the armchair. "You needn't worry, Benzey," I say, "you're gonna have a good time."

"Yeah?" he says. "What am I gonna do now?"

"You're gonna get yourself inta that Commando suit of yours," I tell him, "an' snap outa here. You get up to London an' fix yourself with a pass for a week's leave."

He says: "I see! So I'm goin' on leave. Who do I haveta kill this time?"

"Nobody," I tell him. "You're gonna have a good time. When you've fixed the leave business get around to the Carlton Hotel an' introduce yourself to Miss Pearl Mallory, otherwise Mrs. Cara Travis, an' don't forget that she *is* Mrs. Cara Travis. Get in the habit of thinkin' of her that way."

Benzey says: "You don't say! This is the good-lookin' dame, ain't it? Am I gettin' a break or is this some sorta catch. What do I do then?"

"Just stick around," I tell him. "Maybe you might like to take her out to lunch on the expense account."

He says: "That's all right." He thinks for a moment; then he says: "What is this?"

"Listen, Benzey," I tell him. "I had a talk with Gayda last night. She put an idea inta my head an' maybe it's right. Maybe it's not gonna be so nice for Pearl now she's supposed to be Mrs. Cara Travis. Maybe somebody ain't gonna like her very much, see?"

"You don't say?" says Benzey. "You think some of these boys might wanta take a crack at her?"

"That's right," I tell him.

"I get it," he says. "I'm a sorta watch-dog."

"Right," I say. "Just get up there; stick around."

He says: "Do I haveta stick around all the time?"

"Don't worry," I tell him. "I'll be in touch with you some time this afternoon or this evening. Just get a move on an' get outa here, will you?"

He says O.K. I go downstairs, give myself some breakfast an' one little shot outa the flask. Then I go inta the pay-box an' call through to the Carlton Hotel.

After two three minutes she comes on the line.

"Look, Pearl," I tell her, "this is Lemmy Caution speakin'. How are you?"

"I'm very well. How are you?"

"All right," I tell her. "Just a little bit perturbed but that's nothin'. Look, I'm sendin' a Canadian guy up to introduce himself to you to-day. His name's Wilberforce Benzey, but don't call him Wilberforce otherwise he'll have a fit. Everybody calls him Benzey, see?"

"I see," she says sorta casually. This dame takes everythin' in her stride. Nothin' surprises her. After a bit she says: "All right. When I've met him what do I do with him?"

"You don't do anything," I say. "He'll take you to lunch. I want you two to get acquainted. He'll stick around for a bit."

"I see," she says. "You mean he's going to act as a bodyguard?"

"Well, I wouldn't go so far as to say that," I tell her. "But you don't haveta worry."

"Lemmy," she says, "I think it's very nice of you to take the trouble but I've had no delusions about being Mrs. Cara Travis. I had an idea from the start that it might be just a little bit dangerous."

"Well, maybe just a *little* bit," I tell her. "But don't worry, Pearl. We'll look after you. Say, what are you doin' to-night?"

"I'm at your disposal," she says. "I haven't arranged anything."

"All right," I tell her. "Will you keep the evening free, because maybe I'll be able to come through a little later an' fix-up a rather amusin' supper party? I think it's about time we all relaxed an' took our hair down, see?"

She says she'd like that. I make a few more cracks an' then I hang up. I come outa the pay-box, walk up an' down the passage for a few minutes; then I get my hat, walk down to the station an' jump the nine-forty-five train for London.

II

I'm just finishin' my lunch when the guy from the reception comes in an' tells me that there's a Mr. Clansing on the telephone wantsta speak to me. I go outside in the booth an' take the call.

I say: "Hallo, Schrinkler, so you got something?"

He says: "Yeah! Look, you know I'm takin' a chance on you, don't you, Caution?"

"How do you make that out?" I ask him.

"For chrissake!" he says. "What do you mean how do I make that out? What d'you think this bunch is gonna do to me if they know I'm shootin' my mouth off to you all the time."

"Well, you haven't shot your mouth yet," I tell him. "An' I hope you got something good. What is it?"

He says: "Listen to this one. Just after you left the other night this guy Capelli arrives. A tough egg, see? That guy's gotta record as long as my arm. He's a three-time killer."

"Yeah?" I say. "Why don't you tell me somethin' I don't know? I know all about Capelli."

"All right," says Schrinkler. He goes on: "Clemensky's on something big. I don't know what it is but I don't like it. This guy Capelli's over here on the run. He's in a tough spot. He's more or less gotta do what he's told. It looks like he was strapped for dough before Clemensky gave him a hundred pounds English to kick around, see? Well, there's only one thing that guys retain Capelli for, ain't there?"

"What are you tryin' to tell me?" I say. "Are you tryin' to tell me that Clemensky's got somebody spotted?"

"It's stickin' out like the Coney Island pier," he says. "Clemensky's got somebody for the spot an' Capelli an' me are the boys who are gonna put the finger on this guy."

"Well, what do you care?" I tell him. "Clemensky's payin' you, isn't he?" I get an idea. "I suppose I wouldn't be the guy that's gonna have the finger put on him?" I say.

Schrinkler says: "You ain't come inta this yet. Nobody's even mentioned you."

I say: "That's swell! Well, all right. An' what was the big conference between you an' Capelli about?"

"We was just supposed to meet, that's all. Clemensky wanted us to get to know each other. About half an hour after Capelli had gone Clemensky called through to me, asked me what I knew about Capelli. I told him. I said Capelli was a plenty tough egg who was wanted in the States. He's got an outstandin' rap against him there that would get him sent up for about twenty years. Clemensky says fine. That news seemed to please him. He says maybe he'll be able to let either me or Capelli have some instructions within the next two-three days."

"That's all right," I say. "An' what did you say to that?"

He says: "I told him I didn't like it. Me—I ain't a guy who's tryin' to keep his nose *too* clean but I said this business was beginnin' to smell a bit. I wanted to know what I'd got to do."

"How did he take that?" I ask him.

"He just got tough," he says. "This Clemensky is a bastard. Another thing," he goes on, "for a guy who's not supposed to have been in the States he knows plenty. He told me if I didn't play ball he could make things pretty tough for me. The heel's got something on me, see? Something he can use."

"I get it," I say. "An' you haven't got anything on him, hey? He's got a clean sheet?"

"That's the worst of it," he says. "I don't know anything about him. I got nothing against the guy. But he has got me where the hair is short."

"It looks to me like you're in a spot, Schrinkler, don't it?" I tell him. "Clemensky's got you where he wants you an' I've got you where I want you. Your only hope is to play along nice an' quiet with both of us until somethin' happens. What else do you know?"

"Not much," he says, "except that he's told me to go along to the Chez Clarence place soon after ten o'clock to-night. Maybe he's gonna shoot the works."

"Maybe," I say. "Is Capelli gonna be there?"

"I don't know," says Schrinkler. "He didn't tell me."

"Well, what're you worryin' about?" I ask him. "You go along an' keep the date. Then you can let me know what happens. If anything pops late to-night at Chez Clarence you can reach me at the Berkeley Restaurant. You got that?"

"O.K.," he says, "I got it. If I could find a way outa this business I'd take a powder on the whole goddam lot of you, see? I don't like you an' I don't like Clemensky."

"I'm sorry about that," I tell him. "It just shows you, don't it? You shoulda been a good boy when you was young an' gone to Sunday-school. You guys get yourselves in spots because you're lousy heels an' then you howl because you can't get out of 'em."

He says: "You're a nice lousy comfortin' sorta crummy bastard, ain't you?"

"It's not my business to hand out comfort, honeymouth," I tell him. "I've gotta job to do an' you're gonna help. You go along to-night an' see what Clemensky wants an' then come through an' let me know."

He says O.K. He hangs up.

I lean up against the wall of the telephone-booth an' give myself a cigarette. Maybe I'm not doin' so bad. Maybe I've got things turnin' over. Maybe, with a bit of luck in a day or two, I'm gonna know what I am goin' to do.

I get out a sixpence an' some coppers an' ask for the Mallows number. While I am waitin' I blow smoke-rings. Three minutes after that Gayda comes on the line.

"Aren't you amusing?" she says. "You're a will-o'-the-wisp, Sour-puss. One minute you're in Wilminton an' the next minute you're in London. What do you want?"

"I daren't tell you," I tell her, "otherwise they might cut me off. But the thing is this. I've got an idea. I think it's time we all had a little relaxation. I wondered if you'd like to come up to-night an' have supper with me."

She says: "Sourpuss, I'd like nothing better."

"The only thing is," I say, "this is gonna be a party. I think you'd like to meet Mrs. Cara Travis."

"Would I?" she says. "I believe you've got ideas about that woman. If you have I'll scratch her eyes out."

"Don't you worry, honey," I tell her. "There's only one woman I was ever keen on an' she fell offa pier."

She says: "I see. So you don't care for me at all?"

"I'm bustin' with love for you," I tell her, "but I haven't got a lotta time to talk about that right now, see? You come up to-night an' get yourself inta a swell frock. I'll pick you up. Where are you gonna stay?"

"At the same place," she says. "The place you dropped me at before, in Knightsbridge."

"O.K.," I tell her. "I'll pick you up round about half-past nine."

"All right, Sourpuss," she says. "But there's only one thing I have to tell you, and that is I expect you to stay with me this evening and not go running off to see odd people all the time. Are you going to be good?"

"I'm givin' no guarantees," I tell her. "But maybe I'll stick around. We'll see. So long, honey."

I hang up. I go up to my room, flop down on the bed an' put my feet on the bed-rail at the bottom. Anyhow, I reckon life is gonna be interestin'.

III

When we get outa the cab at the Berkeley, Gayda says: "You wait for me in the Buttery Lounge, Sourpuss. I want to powder my nose."

"O.K.," I tell her. "But don't be too long. I'm hungry."

I pay off the cab an' go inta the Buttery. I can see Benzey sittin' on the other side with a big whisky an' soda in front of him. He's on his own. I grin to myself. Ain't these dames wonderful! Here's both of 'em—Pearl an' Gayda—gone off to arrange their hair-set an' powder their noses, both thinkin' they can make a star entrance on their own. Too bad they both thought of the same thing at the same time!

I go over an' sit down by Benzey. He signals the waiter an' orders a large whisky an' soda for me.

He says: "Where's Gayda?"

"In the ladies' room," I tell him. "I reckon that she an' Pearl are lookin' each other over like a pair of cats."

He says: "Women are funny things, ain't they?"

I nod my head. "How long since you found that out?" I ask him.

"Quite a while," he says. "Say, this Pearl's the berries! D'you realise that that dame is beautiful? An' she has class too!"

"So you found something else out," I say. "Look, take it easy with that baby, won't you. Don't try any of those Commando tactics of yours."

He shakes his head. "It wouldn't be any use," he says. "That Pearl jane is a very cool, calm an' collected piece of woman. Nobody's givin' *her* the bum's rush!"

I look at him. "You astonish me, Benzey," I tell him. "You know, I'm beginnin' to think you're developin' a little bit of sense in your old age."

"Yeah?" he says. "But don't get me wrong. Don't kid yourself that I haven't gotta chance with Pearl. It takes a long time for a woman to realise my good points."

"Like hell it does," I tell him. "A coupla hundred years at least I should think. I suppose you told her what you did at Dieppe?"

"Why not?" he says. "Anyway, I *was* at Dieppe. An' she reacted! Maybe she thinks I'm a hero."

"Either that or a heel," I tell him. "But she'll be able to check on that."

He digs my arm. He says: "For God's sake, Lemmy! Will you take a look! Have you ever seen anything in your life like that?"

I look up. Both of 'em—Pearl an' Gayda—are standin' in the doorway.

I take a very long look. I hear Benzey give a sigh that sounds like his breathin' apparatus has gone back on him. An' is he right!

I have told you mugs before that I am a poetic sorta cuss. Me—I have poetry in my blood. If I had not spent so many years workin' for Uncle Sam, pullin' in thugs an' generally spoilin' the purity of my language, maybe I coulda made Lord Byron look like last Saturday's cold cuts. Then I mighta been able to do justice to these two babies. As it is I gotta just *tell* you. . . .

They are standin' in the entrance, framed by the doorway. Pearl is on the left an' Gayda is on the right. Here are a coupla dolls that would make a guy with low blood-pressure bust the top off the thermometer tryin' to catch up with himself.

These babies coulda made history. If Henry the Eighth hadda taken one look at these honeypots he would have sent a message to the public executioner to get good an' busy sharpenin' up the old battle-axe so as to make room for the new season's goods. If Richard Cœur de Lion had even heard about this duo he woulda signed off the Crusades, hocked his mace an' started off for home like he had a coupla snakes rushin' around inside his chain mail. Charles the Second woulda put Sweet Nell of old Drury on the pension list, an' the Pretender woulda thrown pretence on one side an' had the crown of Scotland melted down for spendin' money. Yes, sir!

Pearl is wearin' a black dinner-frock with a string of pearls an' a mink coat that looks like a million dollars. She has on a light shade in silk stockin's an' black georgette shoes with little diamond buckles that make her feet look like somethin' you could eat. Her hair is dressed with a curl comin' over one shoulder tied with a black moire ribbon.

Gayda makes a contrast. She has got on a brown cord velvet coat an' skirt, beige stockin's, brown court shoes an' a beaver coat. She is wearin' a smart little beaver hat to match an' at her throat I can see a flash of pink lace cravat or somethin' that gives just the right tone to her face.

Boy . . . what a pair!

Benzey says: "Ain't it wonderful. Ain't it good to be alive. Boy . . . I could *eat* those dames."

I don't say anything. I am thinkin' that if beauty spells trouble— like old man Confucius said—then there is enough trouble here to make Adolf Hitler look like the guy who puts the paper labels on schnitzel cans—if you get me.

They come over to us. We get up while the waiter fixes chairs. I order some cocktails. Pearl an' Gayda are lookin' at each other outa the corner of their eyes. I introduce 'em.

Benzey says: "Well, I'm only a poor Canadian soldier, an' before that I was just a hick from the backwoods, but I'd like to tell you ladies that to sit around with a pair of lookers like you makes every-thin' worth while. From now on I've got somethin' worth fightin' for."

Gayda says: "Now I think that's very sweet of you. That's the sort of thing *you* should learn to say, Sourpuss."

I grin at her. "Maybe I'll take some lessons off Benzey," I say. "I reckon that he's had plenty experience in sayin' things like that. But why not? He's been a romantic guy all his life—at least until his wife found out."

Benzey says: "What the hell! I ain't gotta wife. What the heck are you talkin' about, Lemmy?"

"Sorry," I tell him. "I wasn't to know that you didn't marry that dame, was I? Why don't you be more open with me."

Pearl says: "Never mind, Benzey. I think you're sweet. I think your friend's a little jealous."

"Yeah," says Benzey. "That's right. I reckon he's a bit steamed up over my allure. . . ."

"No!" I tell him. "So you got that *too*. Where d'you keep it these days?"

Benzey gives a big sigh. "Look, Lemmy," he says, "you lay offa me to-night. Otherwise maybe I'm goin' to tell Gayda an' Pearl one or two little incidents from your past career. Such as, for instance, that baby who took a shot at you with a fowlin'-gun in Florida or that blonde half-caste momma who stuck a corkscrew inta you for—"

"You don't wanta take a lot of notice of Benzey," I say. "He just gets that way at this time of night. Let's eat."

We go inta the restaurant. It's nice an' quiet an' the *maître d'hôtel* fixes us with a table in the corner. I have just ordered supper when the page-boys, comes over. He says:

"Are you Mr. Caution, sir? If you are, you're wanted on the phone outside."

"O.K., son," I tell him. "I'll be right there."

Gayda says: "So you're not being Carlos Pleyell any more, Lemmy?"

"Only when it suits me," I tell her. "Besides, I'm tired of bein' Carlos. Anyway, all you people know who I am."

She says: "It looks as if somebody else knows who you are too." She smiles at Pearl. "Perhaps this is another mysterious woman."

Pearl says in that soft low voice of hers: "Does he go in for mysterious women, Miss Vaughan?"

Gayda says: "As he would say, 'And how!'. The last time he took me out he spent the whole time running away talking to ladies on the telephone, and I imagine they must all have been beautiful. I don't think Sourpuss knows any women who aren't."

"Look," I tell her, "do you mind leavin' some of these cracks until I get back so's I can defend myself."

Benzey says: "Don't worry, you go an' have your phone-call. By the time you get back I'll have fixed you good an' proper around here."

I tell him just what I think he is; then I follow the page-boy to the call-box. I go inside, shut the door. I lean up against the side of the call-box with the receiver stuck on my ear an' with a cigarette hangin' outa the corner of my mouth.

After a minute Schrinkler says: "Is that you?"

"Nobody else but," I tell him. "Well, what d'you know?"

He says: "I know this—I don't like this business."

"That's redundant," I tell him. "You told me that when you called through earlier this afternoon. What the hell do I care what you like or what you don't like. Now, come on—give . . ."

He says: "All right. But you don't haveta be so goddam tough about everything."

"Look who's talkin'," I tell him. "What's the matter with you, Schrinkler? Are you gettin' soft in your old age? Are you that same bozo who was pulled in for that backwoods job in Oklahoma in '36? You remember what you did to that old boy in that cabin. That was *tough* now, wasn't it? But maybe old age is creepin' over you. All right. So you don't like it. Well, what is it?"

"I came along here to-night an' met up with Clemensky, like I told you," he says. "All right. Now listen, do you know some dame named Vaughan?"

I draw the cigarette smoke down inta my lungs. Life can be surprisin', can't it? What the hell is gonna pop now?

I say: "Yeah, I know a dame named Vaughan. What about her?"

He says: "Well, Clemensky's got it in for this baby somehow. I'm not certain but I think the idea is this: Clemensky's got an idea in his head that Travis got scared an' shot off his mouth to you. Not only does he think that, but he thinks this Vaughan baby is workin' in with you. He thinks that because she took you along to Chez Clarence, see? I think he's gonna try a clean-up. . . ."

"Meanin' what?" I tell him.

"Look," he says, "I'm not certain but it looks to me like Clemensky has fixed for Capelli to rub that dame out."

"Well," I say, "what's the matter with that? If Clemensky thinks that Gayda Vaughan is playin' in with me he's naturally gonna try an' rub her out. He's naturally gonna try an' rub me out too. Go on."

He says: "I don't say it's a rub-out but it's somethin' like it. The idea is this: Clemensky knows that this Vaughan baby is stayin' at an hotel in Knightsbridge, see? He reckons she's gonna stay the night there. Well, she's out right now. When she gets back she's gonna find a telegram sayin' her father has been taken very ill an' she's to go back at once. So what does she do? She hasn't got a car an' she won't be able to get one at this time of night. You can't get a hired job under the regulations. So what does she do? She goes back by train, see? There's a train out about one forty-five. This train stops at Clapham Junction; then it goes right through to Wilminton. O.K. Well, it'll be a corridor train, see? Capelli gets in at Clapham Junction. He just wanders along that train till he finds the carriage the Vaughan dame is in. There ain't many passengers on these late trains.

"All right. About fifteen twenty miles out there's a gradient an' the train slows down to almost nothing. Capelli's job is to get the dame out of the train there somehow. I got to be waitin' there with a car. I gotta back him up."

"Nice work." I tell him. "Clemensky must think he's a big guy to introduce kidnappin' in this country. All right. When you've picked her up where are you gonna take her?"

"I don't know," he says. "Clemensky hasn't told me yet, but I think he's got a place somewhere around there."

"I got it," I tell him. "Look, Schrinkler," I say, "what's the big idea in all this? You said just now that Clemensky wanted to bump this dame. If he wantsa bump her why don't he get Capelli to do it when he gets her outa the train. Everywhere's so goddam dark these days you could kill anybody anywhere."

He says: "That's so, an' I've got an idea he's gonna rub her out all right, but he wants to find out something first."

"I get it," I say. "So he's gonna make her talk. He's gonna make her say what she knows about me an' what I know, an' what Travis told me an' what he didn't tell me. Is that it?"

"That's the idea as far as I can see," he says.

"All right," I tell him. "Go right ahead."

"What the hell?" he says. "Are you tellin' me to go ahead with this job?"

"That's O.K.," I tell him. "You go ahead with it. All you gotta do is this: You carry out the instructions that Clemensky gives you. If Capelli gets away with this kidnappin' act, you take the Vaughan baby along to the place that Clemensky tells you. When you get there you make some sorta excuse to get away for a few minutes, an' get me on a telephone. You get through to me somehow an' tell me where you are. You got that?"

He says: "I've got it. But you're takin' a helluva chance, aren't you? Supposin' Clemensky rubs this dame out?"

"Look," I tell him, "what are you bein' so goddam humane for? You mind your own business an' do what I tell you, see? I like it better that way. Now you know what to do. Just get off the line an' do it."

He says: "O.K." He says something else under his breath—something not very nice. Then he hangs up.

I come out an' go inta the Buttery Lounge. I stub out my cigarette an' do a little quiet thinkin' for a minute; then I go back inta the call-box an' call the Wilber Hotel. I ask is Mr. Capelli there? They say they'll try an' find him. I stick around two-three minutes; then Carl comes on the line.

"Hallo, Lemmy," he says. "Listen, I've been ringin' that dump of yours on Jermyn Street. They didn't know where you were. I was just gettin' worried."

"That's all right, Carl," I tell him. "You haven't got a thing to worry about. Now look, you know this set-up to-night?"

"I know it," he says. "Clemensky called through this afternoon an' I went along to see him. The idea is I get aboard some train, knock off the Vaughan dame, put her out of the train at a place where it slows down, an' the Clansing guy is gonna meet us in a car. After that we go some place—where I don't know."

"That's right," I tell him. "I got all this from Schrinkler."

He says: "That's fine. It looks as if that so-an'-so is playin' ball."

"That's right," I tell him. "He'll play ball just as long as it suits him. But I think he's bein' straight up to now. Look, Carl, you go ahead with it an' play it as long as you can an' don't have a show-down unless you have to. But don't let 'em do anything to that baby. She's precious, see?"

"O.K.," he says. "I'll take care of that. What are you gonna do about this?"

"I wouldn't know," I tell him. "I'll think up something, but I wanta let this thing develop a bit."

He laughs. "That's fine," he says. "I hope the development is gonna be O.K. for me an' the dame."

"You'll be O.K., Carl," I tell him. "Besides, even the best of dames have gotta take a chance sometimes. So long."

I hang up. I light another cigarette. I go back to the restaurant.

CHAPTER SEVEN
THE CLEMENSKY ANGLE

I

A LITTLE breeze is comin' up but it is a fine night. Piccadilly is a swell place in the moonlight. I take a look sideways at Gayda, who is walking along lookin' straight in front of her as if life was one big smell. Maybe if she wasn't holdin' my hand I would think this baby was annoyed about somethin'. Nobody says anythin'. I think to myself that I won't say anythin' until she does, an' for a woman she goes a helluva long time.

We're half-way towards Hyde Park Corner when she says: "She's very beautiful, isn't she, Sourpuss?"

"Meanin' who?" I ask her.

"Don't be damned silly," she snaps. "You know perfectly well who I mean. I suppose it's your guilty conscience makes you say 'meaning who.'"

"Look, honey," I tell her, "I haven't gotta guilty conscience. What do I haveta have a guilty conscience about?"

"I don't suppose you've got any conscience at all," she says. "But I could tell by the way this Pearl woman looks at you she's crazy about you. If I know anything of you you've been leading her on."

"Leadin' her on to what?" I say.

She gives a little laugh. "Oh, you wouldn't know, would you? You're one of those *nice* men—you can be trusted with a beautiful woman, can't you?"

"You oughta know," I tell her. I give her a big grin.

She makes a little hissin' noise. "That's *very* good," she says. "*I* ought to know. You hadn't known me for three minutes before you were kissing *me*!"

I get out my cigarette-case.

"Well, for cryin' out loud!" I tell her. "Me kissin' you. I like that one. Why dammit, you attacked me as soon as you set your eyes on me." I grin. "I didn't know I had so much sex appeal," I tell her.

"You know only too well about your sex appeal," she says. "And I'm afraid Pearl Mallory does too. Something's got to be done about that woman."

"Look, Gayda," I tell her. "You got me all wrong! I'm not the sorta guy who goes around makin' passes at women. I'm too busy, see?"

"You'd never be too busy for that," she says. "You just take that in your stride."

"All right," I say. "Let's look at it another way. I never did go for blondes in a big way. As a matter of fact I've always had a sort of anti . . . anti . . ."

"Antipathy you mean," she says.

"That's right," I tell her. "I have an antipathy to blondes owin' to some blonde momma tryin' to knife me some time in Saratoga."

She says seriously: "Sourpuss, I'm not a fool. You haven't got an antipathy to *any* sort of woman. You're an experimentalist where women are concerned. Provided a woman has something attractive about her you've just got to try and get away with something. All right. But I don't think it's fair to Pearl."

"What are you worryin' about?" I tell her. "Pearl can look after herself all right."

"I wonder!" she says. "You wouldn't like me to hate you, would you, Lemmy?"

I stop an' light my cigarette. "No," I say, "I wouldn't like that, Gayda. I wouldn't like that at all."

"Well," she says, "I could very easily, and not for the reason that you're thinking—not because I'm jealous."

I draw the cigarette smoke down inta my lungs. I say: "O.K. If you're not jealous you're givin' a damn good imitation of it. All right— for the sake of argument you're not jealous. Well, what's the reason?"

She says: "Pearl did you a good turn. She pretended to be Mrs. Travis when you wanted her to be. That was all right, but there's not the slightest reason why she should go on pretending to be Mrs. Travis, is there? And it might be dangerous for her—very danger- ous. But just because you want her around—just because you're keen on her—just because she's beautiful, you've given her the idea that she'll be doing something for her country by going on with this act. I suppose the poor girl doesn't realise that practically anything might happen to her."

I grin at her sideways. "Look," I tell her, "who do you think she's in the most danger from—these other guys or me?"

She says: "I don't know. I wouldn't trust you farther than I could throw a grand piano."

"All right," I say. "Take it easy. You don't have to trust me. Why should you trust me?"

She says: "I suppose I'm entitled to want to trust the man I'm going to marry."

"Oh no!" I tell her. "You don't haveta worry about a little thing like that. Who said you was gonna marry me? Didn't I tell you I was very hard to get?"

She says: "Damn your hide, Sourpuss, I'll tell you one thing—if I don't marry you nobody else is going to."

"Threatenin', hey?" I say. "Well, I like 'em that way. I like a dame with a will of her own."

"Just so you can make her do what *you* want?" she says.

"Oh no," I say. "Look, Gayda, I'm a gentle sorta cuss. The only thing that's wrong about me is I oughta been a Sunday school-teacher."

She says: "Like hell, Sourpuss . . . like hell!"

By now we have got to the hotel. She says: "Well, I suppose we have to say good-night. But I'm not too pleased with you. I think you're a bit of a heel."

I say: "It looks to me as if you think I'm a lot of a heel. Anyway, don't you worry. An' don't worry about Pearl. I'll be good to her. I'll treat her better than I've treated all the other broken women I've left behind me."

She says: "You can joke, Lemmy, but I'm serious."

"Right, you be serious," I tell her. "But don't be too serious. Now you run off to bed an' get some beauty-sleep. You'll feel better in the mornin'. Then you ring me up at the Regency an' maybe we'll fix to have lunch together."

She says: "All right. An' you needn't think I'm going to kiss you because I'm not."

"That suits me," I tell her. "I never did like the way you kiss. Somebody oughta give you some lessons."

She says: "You—" She puts her arms around my neck. She gives me a kiss that reminds me of nothin' so much as the porous plaster they usta stick on Grandpa in the olden days. When she has finished I have got so much lipstick stuck round my mouth that I look like a pansy!

She says: "All right. Now, you'd better clean that mouth of yours up and go. Perhaps I'll ring you up to-morrow and perhaps I won't."

"Oh yes, you will," I tell her. "When you wake up to-morrow, you'll wonder if I've gotta date with Pearl. She did look swell, didn't she? But then," I say, "black always did suit a blonde. She's got nice feet too. So long, Gayda."

I go off, but not so quickly that I can't hear the rude word she calls after me.

I wander back down Piccadilly, smokin' a cigarette, an' tryin' to put a few odd points together. Me—I don't think I'm doin' so well on this job. But what *can* I do? I know a coupla things an' I can guess a few more things. All I can do right now is to stick around an' wait for something to pop because something's *gotta* pop in a minute.

I turn down St. James's Street an' inta Jermyn Street. I go inta the hotel. I tell the night janitor that I'm expectin' a telephone-call any time from now on an' will he put it through to my room. I go upstairs, throw my hat in a corner, light a new cigarette an' give myself one outa the flask. Then I take my coat off an' lie down on the bed.

I lie there in the darkness smokin', lookin' up at the ceilin'. I'm thinkin' about Gayda an' Pearl. I am thinkin' that these two make a very swell combination. Maybe the guy who said how happy he could be with either if the other one wasn't there knew his asparagus tips. Maybe the mug was right after all!

It is nearly half-past one when the telephone goes. It is Gayda. "Sourpuss," she says, "something awful's happened. I don't know exactly what's the matter but Papa has been taken very ill. There was a telephone message waitin' for me here in my room."

"That's not so good," I tell her. "What're you gonna do, baby?"

"The only thing I can do is to go back," she says. "Luckily there's a train back in twenty minutes' time from Victoria—a fast train. So I'll go back on that."

I say: "Do that, honey. Maybe it's not so bad as you think. But I'm sorry."

She says in a miserable sorta tone: "So am I. And I'm sorry I was so angry with you to-night. I was going to ring you up to-morrow morning. I was going to ask you to take me to lunch. I can't help being jealous of you, you know. Besides, you can't really help it. . . ."

"I don't get you," I say. "I can't really help what?"

"Being like you are about women," she says. "I suppose really it's an inferiority complex with you. All your life you've been wanting a woman to fall for you—*any* sort of woman—and nothing's happened. So you're disappointed, and when some lucky circumstances throw really delightful girls like Pearl and me in your way you lose your head and go all funny. . . ."

I say: "Well, I'll be goddamed. . . ."

I can hear her laughing.

"You probably will be," she says. "One of these fine days some woman is going to make things tough for you, Lemmy. Like the one that Benzey was trying to tell us about. The one who tried to stab you with a corkscrew."

"She never did," I say. "She was a bit high an' she mistook me for a bottle of rye. What's the matter with you, Gayda? Still jealous?"

She says: "Sourpuss, I've told you. I'm very jealous of you."

"Look," I say, "don't you worry about a thing. An' you don't haveta talk to me like that. You might give me a swollen head."

"That's not possible," she says. "It couldn't be any more swollen than it is. Well, I've got to go now. Will you ring me up to-morrow afternoon at Mallows?"

"All right," I tell her. "I'll ring before if you like."

"No, ring in the afternoon. I'll have time to talk to you then. Good-night, Sourpuss."

I hang up the receiver. I switch on the light; light a cigarette an' have another one outa the flask. So it looks as if Clemensky has pulled it all right. That bozo's not such a mug after all. A cool guy this Clemensky—maybe a brainy guy too. Also he must have had somebody keepin' tabs on Gayda to get that message there at the right time. This is, of course, if Schrinkler is tellin' me the truth.

I sit on the edge of the bed an' start thinkin' about Schrinkler. It would be a scream if this heel was leadin' me up the garden path—if the stuff he's pulled on me about this kidnappin' business was phoney. It looks to me as if I'm sorta dependent on Carl Pardoe doin' his stuff, an' believe me I hope Carl will. I wouldn't be so pleased if somebody knocked Gayda Vaughan off.

I sit there blowin' smoke-rings an' thinkin' about her an' Pearl. She thinks I'm bein' a heel by gettin' Pearl to work with me. I reckon if Pearl knew I was allowin' Gayda to be kidnapped she'd think I was a heel too. Well, maybe I *am* a heel. I take a look in the mirror over the mantelpiece an' after a coupla minutes I come to the sincere conclusion that even if I am a heel I do not look like one. After which I qualify this with the thought that nobody has ever told me what a heel looks like anyway.

I have another shot outa the flask just to keep the old brain-pan workin'. It looks to me like most of this business at the moment is hingin' on Clemensky. Maybe I can do somethin' about that one. I pick up my hat an' go downstairs. I tell the night guy that if anybody wants me I'll be back in an hour—maybe. I go out.

II

Everything is very quiet around Mount Street. I believe I told you mugs that this Chez Clarence dump is on an upper floor in an apartment block near there. The moon has gone in an' it is plenty dark. I turn inta the apartment block. There is nobody around. I move along to the elevator, but it is not there. It is at one of the upper floors. I give a big sigh because walkin' up flights of stairs is not a habit of mine.

I have had time to do a lotta thinkin' by the time I get to the fourth floor. I walk down the passageway towards the entrance of the Club. The carpets are thick. I don't make any noise at all. Away at the end of the corridor is just a little blue light. I can just see. The foldin' doors that lead inta the Club hallway are shut. On one half of 'em a notice has been stuck. It is a typewritten notice. It says Chez Clarence will be closed until further notice by order of the Proprietor.

I stand there lookin' at the notice. I think this is not quite so good. I take out my cigarette-case, light a cigarette an' lean up against the wall. Where do we go from here?

After a bit I think it is a goddam shame that an attractive club like Chez Clarence should be shut up. I think maybe I will open it up again. The lock on the doors is the usual sorta double lock. I look at it for a few minutes. Then I take out my bill-fold. Inside I have got a piece of mica. I take it out, get out my pen-knife an' start to work on that lock. Two-three years ago a guy called Louie taught me how to open a lock with a piece of mica, an' his instructions musta been pretty good because inside six minutes I have got the entrance doors open. I go in, close 'em behind me, strike a light an' find the electric-light switch. I switch it on. I stand there in the hallway sniffin'. I can smell cigarette smoke—stale smoke maybe but English cigarette smoke all the same. Somebody has been around there not so long ago.

I walk over an' go inta the hat-check room. I switch the light on there. There is nothing. I go inta the baccarat room; the writing-room. There is not a thing. There is not even any amount of cigarette stubs in the ashtrays—just one or two. It looks as if the place hasn't been opened to-night. I come out back inta the hallway an' go inta the roulette room. On the other side is a door. I try it. It is locked.

I give a big sigh. I light myself a fresh cigarette an' start work on this door. While I am doin' it I am thinkin' about Clemensky. I am gettin' annoyed with this cuss. I got an idea that this bozo spells trouble. I get the door open, feel for the switch an' snap on the light.

Well, whatever trouble Clemensky has been makin' he's not gonna make any more. Right opposite me, set diagonally across the corner of the room, is a big desk. Clemensky is lyin' across it. His head is on the blotter, an' the blotter is stained so it looks black. There is a little trickle of blood runnin' over one side of the desk an' drippin' on the floor.

I go over an' take a look at him. Somebody has plugged him through the chest. I reckon they was standin' in front of the desk when they let him have it. Maybe they was sittin' on the desk talkin' to him. If that was so he ought not to have fallen forward; he oughta have gone backwards in the big chair. So I reckon whoever it was has given it to him has pushed him forward in order to make it easy to frisk him afterwards.

I take a look around. I can't find anything at all. Most of the drawers in the desk are empty. On one side of the room is a little cupboard. Hangin' up inside it are Clemensky's hat an' an evenin' overcoat.

I stub out my cigarette, switch the light off an' close the door. I hear the lock snap. I walk out inta the hallway, across the gamin'-room inta the writin'-room. I stick around there for a minute an' then I go back to the hallway, through the cloakroom an' inta the kitchen on the other side of the pass-door. I take a look around but I can't see anything. There is a cupboard alongside the door. One of those white metal things you see in most kitchens. I open it. Inside there is a clothes-hook, an' hangin' on this hook is a clothes-hanger an' a suit on it. An' the guy who has hung up that suit has taken trouble. The trousers hangin' across the shoulder-bar are in their proper creases an' the coat an' vest are put on the shoulder dead straight. I reckon that the guy is maybe fond of that suit.

I reckon I gotta do somethin' about this Clemensky business. I don't think I like it a lot. I go out of the kitchen an' ease across the hallway into the writin'-room. I open the door of the telephone-booth. I think it is about time I had a word with Herrick. Maybe he will not like all this business goin' on under his nose an' him knowin' nothing about it. I take up the receiver an' start to dial. Then I put the receiver back again.

I got an idea. That suit hangin' up in the kitchen!

Anyhow, there won't be any harm in lettin' Herrick stick around an' wait a while. This news'll keep. Maybe he won't be so pleased but there's something I wanta try.

I walk back inta the hallway. I stand there for a minute; then I go outside an' close the entrance doors behind me. I walk down the stairs. One way an' another it's a nice night. Outside a few spots of rain are fallin'. I walk back to the Regency, go up to my room, take my coat off an' lie down on the bed. I reckon all I can do now is to stick around an' think. It looks like I can't stop things happenin' so I'd better let 'em happen.

I lie there dozin' with one eye open waitin' for the telephone to ring, thinkin' about Clemensky. Maybe this guy wasn't so clever after all. Maybe he was just a sucker—like me! I grin to myself. I realise that in this case up to now I am just the big sucker stoogin' around an' lettin' every one get away with just what they want to. Well . . . maybe!

Anyway, Clemensky was a sucker too. This guy thought he was clever an' where's it got him? I think of him sittin' there at his desk with a nice big hole in his chest. I am also prepared to take six to four that whoever the guy was that put it there has got another one he'd like to put in me. I think maybe he will try before very long. Why not?

This don't worry me a lot. There have been a whole heap of guys wantin' to present me with a nice lead slug some time or other, but I'm still here an' most of them are not. At the same time, accordin' to the theory of chances an' the palooka who made up the percentage table in mathematics, if I go on long enough it's a certainty that one of the lead pills is goin' to arrive. Anyhow, I reckon I'll wait till the time comes.

I get around to thinkin' about Chez Clarence. Here is a nice set-up—an easy set-up—a place that was just suited for people to meet in; just another swell night-spot that could be used as a head-quarters for anything you like. One of those places where ninety-five per cent of the mugs who go there don't even know what's goin' on. But it's the other five per cent who matter. I go over the place in my mind, thinkin' about the different rooms I went into. Then I remember the suit hangin' in the clothes cupboard in the kitchen. Well, maybe I got something there.

I get up, light a cigarette an' go over to the telephone. I ring through to Blayne. The bell goes on ringin' a long time before he answers. I reckon the mug's asleep. After a bit he comes on the line.

"Look, Blayne," I tell him, "this is Lemmy. How is it with you?"

"It's O.K.," he says, "except I'm goddam bored with hangin' around Piccadilly in this Marine suit. Maybe I'll get some work to do some time."

"Don't worry," I tell him. "You got it. . . . Listen, there's a block of buildin's called the Clareville Apartments just off Mount Street. You get around there about half-past four. Plant yourself somewhere in the street an' stick around in a doorway or somewhere where you won't be seen. Maybe you'll see me around the neighbourhood some time. Maybe there'll be another guy. O.K. If you see a guy come outa the Clareville Apartments you tail him. Whatever happens you don't lose that baby. You got that?"

He says he's got it. I hang up an' go back to the bed. I lie there in the darkness smokin'.

At a quarter to four the telephone goes. It is my old friend Schrinkler. I say: "Hallo, Schrinkler. How's things goin'? How did the kidnap plot go off?"

He says: "It went off all right. But I'm tellin' you somethin', Copper, if I didn't like it before I don't like it now even some more."

"What're you scared about, Schrinkler?" I ask him. "Has something else happened?"

"Something else *ain't* happened," he says. "Look, everything goes all right, see? This Capelli guy gets the dame off the train like I told you. I'm stickin' around at a cross-roads at a place called Feresby. I gotta wait there, see, until Capelli shows up with the jane. When they show up I gotta come to a house near here. It's a place called Maitland Lodge, about five miles outa the village. All right. We gotta stick the dame in there an' we gotta wait until Clemensky shows up. That's the idea. Well, we come out here an' we got the dame. Everything's all right. But Clemensky don't show up. He oughta been here a long time ago. I don't like it. I'm gettin' worried."

"Not so good," I tell him. "I wonder what's happened to the guy?"

"Search me," he says. "But I don't get this. This guy Clemensky ain't the sorta bozo to make a plan an' then not go through with it. I wanta know what's happened to him."

"Yeah," I say, "I'd like to know too. Where're you speakin' from?"

"There's a phone in the house," he says.

"That's nice an' convenient," I tell him. "What's the number?" He gives it to me. "Tell me," I go on, "how's the Vaughan dame?"

"She's all right," says Schrinkler. "I reckon she's a thoroughbred that one. But she's told us plenty. Take it from me."

"I bet she has," I tell him. "I bet she's told you an' that heel Capelli where you both get off."

He says: "That's right. But words never hurt anybody. Well, where do we go from here?"

"Look," I tell him, "you blow, see, Schrinkler? Don't say anything to anybody—just get inta that car of yours an' scram. Come back to London. Give me a ring some time to-morrow afternoon, see?"

He says: "O.K. But what do I say to Capelli if he sees what I'm doin'?"

"Don't let him see what you're doin'," I tell him. "Just ease out nice an' quiet."

He sounds relieved. He says: "All right, but I still don't like it."

"Look, Schrinkler," I tell him, "you do what I tell you an' you'll be O.K. Get outa there an' ring me up to-morrow afternoon."

He says: "All right. But I wonder what Capelli's gonna do to the jane."

"That's my worry," I tell him. "Anyway, I told you the dame has got to take her chance."

I hang up. I reckon that's O.K.

I smoke another cigarette an' stick around for a bit. Then I go back to the telephone an' call this Feresby number that Schrinkler gave me. After a bit I hear Pardoe's voice on the line.

"Hey, Carl," I tell him. "This is Lemmy. How's it goin'?"

"Not so bad," he says. "But Schrinkler's taken a powder on me. Three-four minutes ago I saw him drive off. What's the guy up to now?"

"Don't worry," I tell him. "I just been talkin' to Schrinkler an' I told him to scram. How's the dame?"

"She's O.K.," he says. "But she don't like this kidnap stuff a bit. You should have heard what she told Schrinkler an' me. Say, Lemmy, that baby thinks something of you!"

"Yeah?" I say. "An' why?"

"She's done nothin' but tell us just what you'd do to us when you caught up with us," he says. "It looks as if she thinks you're the tops."

"The dame knows somethin'," I tell him. "Listen, Carl, how did this thing work out?"

"It was like shellin' peas," he says. "I got a tip off from Clemensky about the place that the train slowed down. After the train left Clapham Junction I eased along the corridor until I saw the carriage that the Vaughan *femme* was in; then I waited half an hour, like I was told. There was practically nobody on the train. Everything went just as he said. When we got to the place where the train slowed down I walked along the corridor an' stuck my head in the dame's carriage an' pulled the communication cord. Then I showed her a gun an' pulled a big act. I said if I had one crack out of her I was goin' to give it to her. She didn't seem to like that but she didn't say anything much. The train stopped. I took her out into the corridor an' helped her out on to the line. There was a helluva lot of shouting an' it was pitch dark. I got her away easily.

"I grabbed hold of her arm an' got her down the embankment on to the road. Schrinkler was waitin' in the car about fifty yards away, on the cross-roads, like Clemensky said.

"I pushed her into the car, got in an' we went off to this dump an' on the way she told us *all* about it. You should have heard that baby! There's nothin' wrong with *her* nerve, I'm tellin' you. An' that is all there was to it!"

"Nice work, Carl," I tell him.

"I'm glad you like it," he says. "An' where do we go from here?"

"Stick around until about eight o'clock," I say. "Then walk along to the nearest place an' hire a car. Drive the Vaughan baby down to the station an' put her on the train for Wilminton. You can show her that F.B.I. card of yours an' tell her we knew about the whole bag of tricks but we played it that way just to see what Clemensky was goin' to do with her."

"That'll be nice," he says. "Maybe she won't be so pleased about that."

"You should worry," I tell him. "Put it all on to me. Tell her I'll call her some time to-morrow an' explain everything."

Carl says O.K. an' hangs up. I reckon he's gonna have a nice time explainin' things to Gayda.

So that's that. I have a quick one outa the flask, grab my hat an' a Luger pistol outa the drawer, go downstairs an' walk around to Mount Street.

III

It is still good an' dark when I get round to the Clareville Apartments. I hang around on the other side of the street for a bit so as to give Blayne a chance to see where I'm goin'. I reckon he's hangin' around somewhere. Then I cross the road an' go in.

The elevator is still where it was before, up on the Chez Clarence floor. I go up the stairs, walk along the corridor an' listen outside the foldin' doors. But I can't hear anything. After a bit I open the doors like I did before an' go inside. I stand around in the hallway for two three minutes but there's nothin' stirrin'; then I snap on the light, go inta the kitchen an' look inta the clothes cupboard. The suit is still there. I look at the breast-pocket inside the coat. There is a New York tailor's tab sewn inside with the name of "A. Kraul" on it.

I close the cupboard, go back to the hallway, turn off the light an' strike a match so as to see my way back to the kitchen. I light a cigarette an' sit down. I reckon Clemensky was not such a smart boy. I reckon that guy was sufferin' from the thing that gets all the big shots down. They think they know everything an' they don't worry enough about the people they got workin' for them. I let my mind wander over this job from the start. Everything is easy an' then again everything is goddam difficult. It just depends which way you look at it.

I start thinkin' about Travis—the phoney one I mean. Here was another mug. This guy is a right royal sucker. He just believes anything that anybody tells him. Maybe they promised him some heavy sugar. Maybe he thought he was gonna be a millionaire. So he takes a chance. He takes the chance of gettin' himself on that boat an' waitin' for the real Travis to show up. He takes a chance on the voyage of gettin' bumped off or bein' found out or even of slippin' up over here when he arrived. He took all those chances an' what does it get him? All it gets him is three lead slugs in a telephone-booth. Travis was a sucker all right.

I sit there thinkin' an' maybe an hour goes by; then I hear some-thing. I snap off the kitchen light an' go back to my chair in the corner. I take the Luger outa my breast-pocket an' sit there waitin'.

After a minute I can hear some guy whistlin'. He is whistlin', "I don't want to walk without you, Baby." I think maybe he's right. The footsteps come near to the kitchen door; then it opens an' the light goes on.

Like I thought, it is the elevator guy. He is still in uniform an' his collar is still too big for him. His neck is thin an' his face is white—a sorta pasty colour. His red-rimmed eyes don't make him look any more handsome either. A nasty type, believe you me—the type that don't mind what he does or how he does it.

I say: "Good-mornin'. My guess is that you're A. Kraul."

He says: "Yes . . . so what then!" He sounds to me like a Broad-way guy tryin' to talk London English.

"Just nothin'," I tell him. "I've been stickin' around here waitin' for you to come back for your suit. It's a nice suit. The guy who made that suit for you made one for me once. I hope you paid him like I did."

He says: "Listen, what are you doing around here? This is private property."

"So's your Aunt Fanny!" I tell him. "Believe me, Kraul, this place is gonna be such public property before long you'd be surprised!"

He says: "Look, you're a smart fella, but I'm busy. I got a lot to do. What's all this about?"

"We'll come to that in a minute," I say. "In the meantime let me tell you something. You ain't busy an' you haven't got anything to do. All you gonna do is what I want you to do, see? I got one or two little things I wanta talk to you about."

He leans up against the wall. He puts his hand inta his coat-pocket an' fishes out a cigarette-case. He lights one. He is a cool guy this guy. He says: "What do I have to talk to you about, and who the hell are you anyway?"

"My name's Caution," I tell him. "I'm an agent of the F.B.I. I'm stickin' my nose inta a whole lotta things over here; some of them concern me an' some of 'em don't. But you're in no position to argue, Kraul. You're in a bad spot."

He says: "Yeah . . . so what? And what's the spot?"

"The spot is that you work here," I tell him. "An' this place is turnin' itself inta a regular sorta morgue. I suppose you wouldn't know anything about Clemensky?"

He says: "Look, what the hell do I have to know about Clemensky? Clemensky's the boss here. Maybe he'll want to know what you're doing kicking around this dump."

I say: "All right, sweetheart. You come for a little walk with me an' don't try anything; otherwise this gun might go off."

He says: "Getting tough, hey?"

"You'd be surprised," I tell him.

I take him outa the kitchen an' over to Clemensky's office.

I say: "I suppose you got a key, haven't you?"

He says yes. I tell him to open the door. He opens it. I prod him over the threshold with the gun barrel an' switch on the light. He stands there with his eyes poppin'. All the while I'm watchin' him. This guy is not registerin' any sorta excitement or anything like that. He's just a picture of surprise.

He says: "Jeez! What do you know about that?"

"A nice sight, ain't it?" I tell him. "It looks as if somebody has been catchin' up with somebody else. You wouldn't know who did that, I suppose?"

He shakes his head. "Search me!" he says. "I don't know a thing." He looks at Clemensky. "He owed me some dough too," he says.

I nod my head. "You're beginnin' to talk like Broadway now," I tell him. "Maybe you've forgotten to put that English act on." I light a cigarette. "This ain't gonna be so good for you, Kraul," I say.

He looks at me. He grins. "What does it matter to me?" he says. "The last time I saw Clemensky he was O.K. I can prove where I've been every minute since. If you think you're gonna hang anything on me you think some more. The only thing I'm worried about is that somebody has croaked this guy before he paid me what he owed me."

I grin. "You ain't the only one he owed dough to," I say. "So you don't know anything about this?"

He says: "Not a thing." He stands there nice an' easy, drawin' on his cigarette.

I say: "Well, that's that. Did you take the elevator when you left here last time?"

He says: "Sure I did. Clemensky had gone. I was the last one to leave the place. I was late so I didn't bother about changin'. I went down in the elevator an' left it on the ground floor."

"That's what I thought," I tell him. "Then Clemensky comes back, hey? He comes back here because somebody's telephoned him an' made a date to meet him here. Maybe that guy is somebody who's gotta key to the Club. Maybe they get here first. They go up in the elevator an' they're waitin' here in the Club for Clemensky to arrive. When he comes he presses the button downstairs an' gets the elevator down. He comes up in it. He leaves it on this floor to go down in, but he don't go down in it. Somebody gives it to him, an' *they* don't go down in the elevator because they don't wanta make any noise. They leave the elevator where it is an' go down by the stairway."

He says: "Ain't you the little Sherlock Holmes? All you gotta do now is to find this guy."

"That's right," I tell him. "Maybe that won't be easy, but we'll go on tryin'."

He says: "O.K. Is this conference over, because I got a lot to do?"

"No," I say. "You haven't got a goddam thing to do because, Kraul, there's something else I wanta ask you."

He says: "Yeah? An' what's that?"

"What did you do with Travis's body?" I ask him. "The guy you shot in the telephone booth."

He registers a bit this time but he soon gets hold of himself. He says:

"So I've been killin' some other people as well, have I?"

"You killed Travis all right," I say. "You was the only person here who *could* have killed Travis. While I was talkin' in the bar to Miss Vaughan an' the others, Travis went inta the telephone-booth to make a call. You was on duty at the front door. You saw him across the hallway. Somebody gave you the tip-off that the time had come for Travis or whatever his real name was to depart. So you gave it to him while he was in the phone-box. An' that was that!"

He says: "You oughta be writin' fiction. What had I gotta do with this guy Travis or whatever his name was? Why do I haveta kill him? You're nuts, Caution!"

I grin at him. "That's an easy one," I say. "You knew who Travis was. Clemensky knew who Travis was. Clemensky knew that Travis had brought those papers over. Clemensky knew where those papers were all right. Well, this Travis guy has done his job, hasn't he? He's only stickin' around now for the pay-off."

Kraul says: "I see. That sounds sweet to me. So somebody had him bumped so's not to pay him. That sounds good an' cock-eyed to me."

"No," I tell him, "that wasn't the reason. The reason was that I was gettin' around with Travis. When I brought him inta this Club maybe somebody knew that I'd just taken him down to the Carlton Hotel to have him identified by Mrs. Cara Travis. They knew that this guy was gonna start gettin' scared. They knew that if he found himself in a jam he'd probably talk an' talk plenty. So there wasn't any time to waste, was there? Travis has gotta be creased even if it means he's gonna be bumped in the Club call-box."

Kraul says: "Yeah, that's a nice story. Supposin' somebody had wanted to use the telephone."

"Well, nobody did," I say. "Maybe if I hadn't gone nosin' around an' seen a lighted cigarette stub on the carpet, you'd have got away with it. You're careless, Kraul; you'd better watch your step. It was tough for you that I went in an' found that guy."

He says: "Look, you're dreamin'. Just a long sweet pipe-dream. I think your brain's a little dusty."

"All right," I say. "Well, maybe you got an out here too, but you can tell it to the cops. I'm gonna turn you in."

He says: "That suits me. I'm not in anything that I can't get out of."

"That must be nice for you," I tell him. "Listen, if you don't wanta make things a bit harder for yourself you won't give me any hooey. Where did this guy Clemensky live?"

"In the Mayfield Apartments about four minutes from here. He's got a suite on the second floor."

"Is there a janitor there?" I ask him.

"Some old guy," he says, "but he's always high or asleep or something. He don't know a thing. He's never around."

"I get it," I say. "Look, you wouldn't have a key to that suite, I suppose?"

"How come I should have a key to Clemensky's place?" he says. "Who do you think I am? I just work here."

"Some worker!" I tell him. "Come on, let's get goin'.."

I shut the office door. We go back to the hallway. I open the foldin' doors an' let this Kraul guy go first. We walk down the passage towards the elevator. I open the gates an' he goes in. Then I do an act. I drop the Luger an' as I stop to pick it up I trip over. I fall full length in the corridor.

He does what I thought he'd do. He slams the elevator-gates an' presses the button. The elevator goes down.

I get up an' light a cigarette. I reckon this guy Kraul is pattin' himself on the back. I should worry about him.

Blayne will take care of that baby.

IV

The dawn is just breakin' when I leave the Chez Clarence. I walk along Mount Street an' find the Mayfield Apartments. I go in an' look around the hallway. But there's nobody there. The place is a quiet, high-class residential block—old-fashioned. But it looks good an' comfortable. In the hallway is an indicator. It says: *"Clemensky— Second Floor."*

I go up an' knock on the door. Nobody takes any notice. I knock two or three times more; then I start work on the door. It is an easy lock an' pretty soon I have got it open. I go inta the hallway an' close the door behind me. There are four rooms leadin' outa the hallway. I start with the one on the left—a bedroom. I go through it with a tooth-comb but I can't find a thing. Then I go inta the next room—a sittin'-room. It is a comfortable room with a big desk in the corner.

The desk is covered with papers. I go over an' take a look. Most of 'em seem to be bills an' papers relatin' to Chez Clarence. I try the drawers. They're all open except one—the bottom drawer on the right-hand side—a big drawer. I start work on it an' a coupla minutes afterwards I get it open. When I pull the drawer out I give a grin.

Inside is a big brown document case. There's a little plate on the front an' it says on it *"L. E. Travis."*

I take the case outa the drawer an' put it on the desk. I sit there lookin' at it an' wonder what I'm gonna find inside. I get a sorta kick outa sittin' there lookin' at this case. Maybe I'm tryin' to surprise myself like the children do.

After a bit I open it. Inside is a big sheaf of papers. I pull 'em out an' look at 'em. They are not the Mechanisation plans that Travis was supposed to bring over. There's no mistakin' what they are. They are the Travis divorce papers—the stuff that Wynn sent down at the last moment.

Well, it looks as if what I told Gayda was a good shot even if it did look like a guess. If Clemensky has got the document case an' the divorce papers the reasonable thing to believe is that he had the other ones too.

So there you are.

CHAPTER EIGHT
ROUTINE STUFF

I

IT IS twelve o'clock when I wake up. I get outa bed, light a cigarette an' start walkin' around the bedroom.

One thing that is stickin' outa foot is that these guys who are after these Mechanisation plans don't like each other much.

Figure it out for yourself. The guy who is put on the boat to wait for Travis has been bumped off. They've creased this guy because they reckon he was redundant; because they reckoned he was gettin' frightened; because they thought he might shoot his mouth. So they fix him an' they got nothing else to worry about.

O.K. Well, then the idea is that Clemensky has got the papers, because if Clemensky has got the document case an' the divorce papers it's a stone certainty he had the other ones as well. An' then Clemensky gets his. Somebody creases *him*.

I walk around the bedroom blowin' smoke-rings. I wonder how many other guys there were workin' in on this thing with the late lamented Clemensky. I know about Schrinkler an' I know about Kraul, although I'm not quite certain how Kraul is breakin' in the game. I don't know whether he is a big guy or a little guy. But I know one thing about Schrinkler—he is a big guy all right. Maybe you think

I've fallen for Schrinkler's line, but I haven't. That guy was a big shot an' a tough egg. Not the sorta guy to go out after chicken-feed. An' he played along with me too easily. He was too willin' to do what I wanted him to do.

Work it out for yourself. If he'd have liked to duck outa this business the first time I saw him he'd have been all right. What could I have done? Got him sent back to the United States, that's all. But he prefers to stay on. He stays on an' makes out he's playin' ball with me. Well, maybe he is but I don't think so. I got an idea that Schrinkler is gonna pull something in a minute. Something sweet!

I take a shower, ring for breakfast an' dress. I take one little tug at the flask, light a cigarette an' call through to Herrick at Scotland Yard.

"Listen, Herrick," I tell him when he comes on the line. "First of all I wanta tell you that there's no use in your blowin' off at me, see? Anything that's been happenin' around this city of yours is not *my* fault."

He says: "Lemmy, I don't like the sound of this. What's been going on?"

"Just a coupla murders," I tell him. "Maybe I oughta have told you about 'em before."

He says: "Well, why didn't you?"

"Candidly," I tell him, "I didn't wanta break the continuity. When the first one happened I had an idea that if you an' your boys started nosin' around things mighta been different an' I didn't want 'em to be different, see?"

He asks exactly what the situation is. There is a sorta tired note in Herrick's voice. Mark you, I am sorry for this guy. Every time I come over to this country an' start co-operatin' with him on some job, everything seems to go all screwy, an' there's always a corpse or two knockin' around just to give a background to the story, if you get me.

I tell him about the Travis killin' an' I tell him about Clemensky. Maybe he's gonna have a job findin' what's left of the phoney Travis. I don't even know where they parked this guy. But Clemensky is there all right, an' I tell Herrick he can pick him up any time he likes. He asks if I want these killin's kept quiet.

"It don't matter," I tell him, "not now. They've been kept quiet for long enough. It doesn't matter whether you make a noise about it or not. It won't affect the ultimate issue."

He says: "I don't like the sound of that, Lemmy. It sounds as if there's going to be some more trouble."

"There *has* to be," I tell him. "Look, why should I worry about a lotta thugs who get knocked off? I don't care how many of these palookas get themselves creased providin' I can put my finger on the head man eventually."

He says he wishes me luck. He says also that he'll be glad if I'll call through to him some time and let him know when somebody else is gonna be killed. I tell him I'll do my best. Then I make a coupla cracks an' hang up.

A swell guy Herrick!

I smoke another cigarette; then I ring through to the Carlton Hotel. I ask if there's a Mr. Benzey there. They tell me yes; he is in the American bar; will I hold on? After a minute Benzey comes on the line.

I say: "So directly my back's turned you're drinkin' yourself to death again. Whenever I wanta find you you're in a bar."

"Aw shucks!" he says. "Where else should I be? Besides, I wasn't even drinkin' . . . well, not much! I met a coupla interestin' guys here. We were talkin' about something big. . . ."

"I lay you six to four you was talkin' about Dieppe," I tell him.

"That's right," he says. "Look, one of these guys here saw me kill that German I was tellin' you about. Maybe you'd like to meet him some time."

"Why worry?" I tell him. "I'll take your word for it, an' anyway what's one Jerry more or less between pals?"

He says O.K. we'll let it go like that. I ask him about Pearl.

"Is that dame all right, Benzey? You know you're supposed to be keepin' your eye on her. I wouldn't have anything happen to her for a million dollars."

He says: "Yeah, she's all right. She's in her apartment playin' patience." He goes on: "Look, a funny thing happened early this mornin'."

"You don't say?" I say. "Such as . . .?"

"Some guy comes around here tryin' to see Pearl," says Benzey. "Well, the night clerk wasn't playin', see? I'd had a word with him. I told him that anybody who wanted to see Miss Mallory had to sorta see me first. So when this guy blows in, the night clerk gives me a tinkle, an' I come down an' see this bozo. I didn't like him much."

"D'you know what his name was?" I ask Benzey.

He says: "No, I didn't ask him. I just told him that Miss Mallory couldn't be disturbed. I said anything he wanted to talk to her about he could talk to me about."

"That's O.K., Benzey," I tell him. "I'd like to make a coupla guesses about this guy. Was he in a janitor's uniform with a collar that was too big for his neck? Had he got a thin white sorta face an' red-rimmed eyes—a guy who looked like a weasel—a nasty weasel?"

"That's the boyo," says Benzey. "What's he after?"

I grin to myself. "I wouldn't know," I say. "But if he shows up again you ring through to Herrick at Scotland Yard an' ask Herrick to wipe him up with my compliments."

Benzey says: "That's O.K. by me. But tell me something—what would a guy like that wanta see Pearl about?"

"You don't haveta be too curious, Benzey," I tell him. "I'll worry about that."

"O.K.," he says. "Go on, be the big brilliant guy. Don't tell me anything. It looks like I'm nothing but a stooge—a sorta St. Bernard hangin' around to see nobody gets at dames you want looked after."

"Which is more or less right," I tell him. "Look, pal, you go back to the bar an' have that other half an' talk some more about Dieppe. But before you do that call through to Pearl's apartment an' tell her not to go out till I've seen her. I wanta talk to that dame."

II

I get around to the Carlton at half-past two. I get the reception clerk to ring through to Pearl to say I'm on my way up. Benzey is still in the bar. It looks like he ain't exhausted this Dieppe business yet.

Pearl is at the desk in her sittin'-room when I arrive. She gets up an' comes across to me. By the way she is smilin' anybody would think she was pleased to see me.

She says: "Well, Lemmy, what's new?"

"Plenty," I tell her. "Maybe you'd be surprised to know that Gayda was kidnapped last night."

She leans up against the sideboard. She says: "My God! You don't really mean that, Lemmy?"

"An' how!" I tell her. "But don't worry. We got her out of it." I grin. "I got brains," I say.

"It's lucky you have," she says. She goes over to the table an' gets a cigarette-box. She gives me one. "Come and sit down," she says. "Tell me all about it."

"There ain't very much to tell, Pearl," I say. "The point is I want you to listen carefully to what I'm gonna say, because I don't want any slip-ups. Unless," I go on, "you wanta duck. If you wanta get outa this business all right. I shan't think any the worse of you. But I think I oughta warn you that if you're gonna stay in, it may be tough."

She gives me a little smile. She says: "You know I like seeing things through to their logical conclusion, Lemmy. Besides, it's amusing. Another thing, I like playing around with you. You make me laugh."

"That's nice for you," I tell her. "Maybe if somebody else was runnin' this job you'd like playin' around with *them* too."

She looks at me along her eyelashes. She says: "I don't say *that*. You know, Lemmy, I think you're rather fascinatin'."

I grin at her. "Now where have I heard that before?" I say.

She says: "Be serious, Lemmy. Do you really mean to tell me that Gayda is in danger? You know, she's a very beautiful woman and rather headstrong."

"You're tellin' me!" I say. "She's nearly as beautiful as you are. Tell me, Pearl, what would you say if I told you I was seriously thinkin' of marryin' Gayda?"

She looks a bit startled for a minute; then she says: "Do you really mean that?"

"Yeah," I say. "There's no law against it, is there?"

She says: "I think it'd be wonderful." She thinks for a minute. "I suppose she is your type."

She sounds a bit dubious to me.

"Exactly what's my type?" I tell her.

She says: "I don't know, but a woman would have to be pretty smart to keep up with you, Lemmy, but I think Gayda would be smart enough."

She is smilin' when she says this but somehow I don't believe it. The tone of her voice is a little flat, if you get me. Maybe you've heard one cat miaulin' about another cat. If you have you'll know what I mean.

She stubs out her cigarette. Then she says: "Tell me, Lemmy, what is it you want me to do?"

"Just this," I tell her. "I'm gonna get through to Gayda some time to-day. She's down at Wilminton. That baby's got a good nerve, but I bet she's a bit shaken after this kidnap job. I reckon any girl would be. Well, I'm a bit worried about Gayda."

She says: "Why, Lemmy? What's the trouble?"

"The trouble is this," I say. "The boys who have got those papers of Travis's seem to have an idea that she's playin' in with me. Maybe they think she's a sorta assistant, see? We do have women workin' with us sometimes, you know! Maybe they got an idea in their heads that they can use her to make a bargain with, see? Anyway, I want somebody to keep an eye on her. The idea was that I'd feel a great deal easier if you went down to Wilminton an' stucka round there. Two heads are better than one an' you're a cool sorta baby, Pearl. You don't fly off at a tangent like she does."

She nods her head. "Yes," she says, "I should think she was a little like that. You think my steadyin' influence might serve a good purpose, Lemmy?"

"That's the idea," I tell her.

She says: "Well, I'll do anything you say. If you like to arrange for me to go down there I'll do that willingly. Incidentally, I think it'd be rather nice. I like Gayda. I think she an' I would get on awfully well together."

I think to myself maybe yes an' maybe no, but I don't say anything. After a bit she says:

"When are you going to speak to Gayda?"

"Some time to-day," I tell her. "Stick around, Pearl, an' when I've talked to her, I'll get through to you."

She says: "Will Benzey be coming down?"

"I don't think so," I say. "I might want him up here. I suppose you're sorry about that?"

She says: "A little. I like Benzey. He's amusing. He makes me laugh."

"That's fine," I say. "It looks as if we all make you laugh."

She says: "What's the matter, Lemmy—jealous?"

"I should be jealous of Benzey," I tell her.

She says: "Well, you could be. Benzey's got something, you know."

"So's a gargoyle," I say. "Benzey looks fine. He's strong; he's as big as an elephant an' you know what he did in that raid in Dieppe. But when it comes to brains . . ."

She says in a soft sorta voice: "You know, Lemmy, there are other things besides brains."

"There may be," I say, "but I like a guy with an intellect."

She says: "Well, for all you know Benzey may have one."

"If he's got one he's been concealin' it very successfully," I tell her.

I get up. "Look, honey," I say. "I've gotta scram now. I'll be in touch with you later. So long!"

I scram.

III

I ring through to Wilminton at five o'clock. Gayda answers the telephone.

She says: "Well, what have you got to say to me? Tell me, were you a party to this kidnapping business, Sourpuss?"

"It's lucky for you I was," I tell her, "otherwise maybe you wouldn't have got out of it so easily. I knew it was comin' off but I wasn't worryin' because I had Carl Pardoe hangin' around lookin' after you." I laugh. "Those guys had an idea that he was a tough egg called Capelli. They thought Carl was workin' for them, see?"

She says: "Perhaps it's as well he was working for you."

I say: "Well, you got a thrill out of it, didn't you, Gayda? How did you like bein' kidnapped?"

She says: "I don't know. At first I didn't take it seriously, Sourpuss. Afterwards I got a little frightened. I didn't like the other man at all. He scared me."

"You mean Schrinkler?" I tell her. "Look, you don't wanta worry about him either. I've been puttin' in a lot of overtime on these guys. Schrinkler's playin' in with me too."

She laughs. She says: "You're pretty good, aren't you? You certainly know your stuff, Lemmy. The only thing I wonder about is if all these people were on your side why the kidnap had to take place at all."

"I thought you'd be wonderin' about that," I tell her. "Well, you see, I had to see what Clemensky was tryin' to pull. That was the boy who I was worryin' about."

She says: "Did you find out?"

"No, honeypot," I tell her. "But Clemensky did."

She says: "And just exactly what do you mean by that?"

"Somebody's rubbed Clemensky out," I tell her. "I went round to see that boyo after you rang through last night. I found him in his office at Chez Clarence. Somebody had shot him. That's not so good."

She says: "Isn't it? Why not?"

"I'd rather Clemensky was alive," I tell her. "I wanted that guy. Anyhow, his bein' killed proved one thing. You remember I told you that I reckoned that Clemensky was behind this job; that he got those papers off Travis. You remember that?"

She says: "Yes, Sourpuss, I remember."

"Well, I was right," I tell her. "I had a look over Clemensky's flat. I found Travis's—the *real* Travis's—document case."

"So you've got the papers?" she says.

"No," I tell her. "That's just it. The Mechanisation plans are gone. All I got was the document-case an' Lon Travis's divorce papers—all those reports that Wynn sent him about his wife—batches of 'em— an' much good they'll do me."

She says: "I see. That's not very good, is it, Lemmy?"

"It's not good an' it's not bad," I tell her. "Of course it could be better, but it shows me one thing. It shows me that these guys don't like each other very much. Work it out for yourself: The phoney Travis comes over here with the papers. He hands them over to Clemensky. Then he disappears. O.K. Then somebody else thinks that Clemensky has got the papers an' Clemensky gets rubbed out. The guy who fixed Clemensky opened the document-case, took out the Mechanisation plans an' didn't worry about the other stuff. So now somebody else has got 'em. The next job is to find out who that is."

She says: "This is terrible, Lemmy. These people mean business, don't they?"

"An' how!" I say. "But maybe I've got an idea in my head as to who the next contestant is. I'd lay a shade of odds that I know who's got those papers now."

She says: "Is it a secret or can I know?"

"You can know, babe," I tell her. "I've got an idea that Schrinkler is the boyo. I think he's been sittin' right on top of the heap—double-crossin' everybody."

She says: "So you think that, Lemmy."

"I think just that," I tell her. "Schrinkler hasn't double-crossed me up to date. He daren't do it. I was sittin' on the doorstep all the time right on top of him. But maybe now that Clemensky's outa the way, an' now that this kidnap business with you didn't come off, maybe Schrinkler is gonna take a different line. We'll see."

She says: "Lemmy, do you think Schrinkler killed Clemensky?"

"Why not?" I say. "He might have."

She says: "Well, you know, while I was down in that house and Schrinkler was there, he was waiting for Clemensky to come down. He was impatient. He was worried. According to you Clemensky was dead at that time."

"That's right," I say. "An' that certainly makes it look as if Schrinkler didn't do it. But you never know. He had time before the kidnap job started an' he mighta been puttin' on an act. It wouldn't have taken him long to drive that car of his down to wherever it was he picked you up, *after* he creased Clemensky."

She says: "No, I suppose not. Lemmy, tell me something. Why did Clemensky want to kidnap *me*?"

"That's an easy one," I tell her. "Look, work it out for yourself. You knew Travis, didn't you? An' it was you who took me up to Chez Clarence the night that Travis came in with me. Well, he was shot that night. He was shot in the Club, see? An' it ain't so difficult to see why. Clemensky thought I was gettin' next to Travis. He thought that Travis was stuck on you. Maybe he thought Travis had done a little talkin'. So he reckons he won't take any chances on the guy. So he had

Travis bumped. You gotta realise that it was only by accident that I found that baby. If I hadn't gone wanderin' around an' found him in the telephone-box nobody woulda known what had become of him."

She says: "I see. How terrible. It looks as if it isn't safe to be a friend of yours, Sourpuss."

"You're tellin' me, honey," I say. "I am a dangerous guy to know, but don't worry. I'll look after you."

She says: "That's all right. But who's going to look after *you*, Lemmy? I'm worrying about you. When am I going to see you? I want to talk to you. I want to talk to you about getting married."

"Look, honeybunch," I tell her. "Suppose we leave this marriage proposition until I get this job cleaned up. What's the good of you an' me gettin' tied up right in the middle of a schlmozzle like this. Most of the time we'd be duckin'. Let's leave it. Orange blossoms don't mix with gangsters like Clemensky."

She says: "I expect you're right, Lemmy. But I'm terribly disappointed."

"Me too," I tell her. "I'll get down an' see you as soon as I can."

She says: "Is there any reason why I shouldn't come up to town and see you?"

"I got a helluva reason, Gayda," I tell her, "an' that is Pearl Mallory."

"Oh yes?" she says. Her voice is a little bit cold. "And what's her trouble?"

"Look, babe," I tell her, "you cut out bein' jealous. There's nothin' on between Pearl an' me, see? We're just good friends an' I want you to be a friend to her too."

"Anything you say, Sourpuss," she says. "Well, what's the idea?"

"The idea is that I'm a little bit scared for her," I say. "Maybe somebody's gonna have a go at *her* in a minute. I got an idea that the elevator guy at Chez Clarence is workin' in with Schrinkler— a guy called Kraul. I got an idea it was Kraul who killed Travis, see? O.K. Well, I had a show-down with this baby last night, but he pulled a fast one on me an' got away. Early this mornin' he went down to the Carlton Hotel tryin' to see Pearl. Now get this: Kraul believed that Pearl was Mrs. Cara Travis, see—the real one. So what does he wanta see her for? I'm a bit sorry," I go on, "that I ever brought Pearl inta this, but I gotta make the best of a bad job, see? I wondered if you'd ask her to come down to Wilminton. I wondered if she could stay down there for a bit so that you could keep your eye on her."

She says: "Why not? I think that would be marvellous. She'd be good company too." There's a little pause; then she says: "Look, Lemmy, you don't *really* think that somebody would try an' kill Pearl, do you?"

"Why not?" I say. "They killed a coupla other guys an' they're not gonna hold off because she's a woman."

She says: "All right. Send her down here. I'll look after her, Lemmy."

"Thanks a lot, Gayda," I tell her. "You're swell. One of these fine days I'm gonna have enough time to tell you what I really think about you. I'll call through to Pearl an' tell her to get down as soon as she can."

She says: "Do that. It would be nice if she could get down for dinner to-night."

"O.K., honey," I tell her. "An' thanks a lot for everything you're doin'. I'll be seein' you."

I hang up. So that's that!

IV

At seven o'clock I go along to the Embassy an' have an hour with the big boy. I hand in Travis's document case an' the divorce-papers an' tell him the story. He gives me a big grin.

He says: "Well, all you got to do now is to find the Mechanisation plans and the individual who's got 'em. I'm glad that's your worry and not mine."

I say: "Thanks a lot, but I'm not worryin' too much about it either."

He asks me how I'm playin' along with Herrick on this job, an' I tell him that I'm tryin' not to worry Herrick too much an' that anyway if I want any co-operation I'll ask him for it. I slide over the fact that I have not told Herrick about these two killin's until a good time afterwards, because they got an old-fashioned idea in this country that they don't like corpses lyin' about too long. Anyhow the big boy seems fairly pleased, as he should be.

I go back to the Regency. While I am havin' dinner I am thinkin' to myself that by this time Pearl will be down at Wilminton. I sorta draw a picture of her an' Gayda havin' dinner together—wise-crackin' to each other across the table. A sweet pair, those babies!

At this moment a page-boy comes up an' tells me that Mr. Clansing is on the telephone. I go out to the hallway an' take the call in the booth. I got an idea that this is gonna be good.

I say: "Well, how's it goin'?"

He says: "Look, Caution, I wanta have a straight talk with you."

His voice sounds sorta flat an' hard. Maybe we're gonna have a slice of the real Schrinkler now.

"Oh yeah?" I say. "What are you gonna be serious about, sweetheart?"

He says: "Look, you're havin' a lotta trouble about this Travis business, aren't you? But I know what your big worry is."

"A thought-reader, hey?" I tell him. "All right, you tell me what's my big worry."

"I'm gonna make a coupla guesses," he says, "an' I think they're gonna be good. My first guess is that that guy Travis wasn't Travis at all. My second guess is that that boyo brought some Mechanisation papers—somethin' to do with tank warfare—some big stuff—over here with him. I got an idea that it's those papers you're after, hey, Caution?"

"All right," I tell him. "Suppose your idea's right. So what?"

He says: "Well, I think I can save you a lotta trouble."

"That's goddam nice of you, Schrinkler," I tell him. "You sound a bit fresh to me. Maybe you think you're sittin' pretty."

"Maybe I am," he says. "Maybe I'm sittin' right on top of the heap, hey?"

I say: "I've known guys who thought they were sittin' there to slide off."

"I'll take my chance of that," he says. "Look, I reckon you're worried more about those papers than you are about Travis or gettin' your hooks on me an' sendin' me back to the United States or anything else. Now why don't you talk sense an' tell me that I'm right."

I drop my cigarette stub on the floor of the call-box and put my foot on it.

"Well, maybe you are right, Schrinkler," I tell him. "I'm worried plenty about those papers. I gotta have 'em, see? An' you think you can help?"

"I don't think anything of the sort," he says. "I know I can help. The thing is what I'm gonna get for helpin'."

"I get it," I say. "So you think you're in a position where you can do a deal."

"I know I am," he says. "Look, I want some dough an' I also wanta know that both the U.S. cops an' the English cops are gonna lay off me. Well, if I get the dough an' a guarantee maybe I'll let you have those papers."

"I get it," I tell him. "A nice deal for you an' you think you're gonna get away with the murder thing too."

"Say, what the hell do you mean?" he says. "What murder thing?"

"Ain't you the little innocent cuss?" I tell him. "You wouldn't know that somebody ironed out Clemensky, would you?"

He says: "Jeez! So that's why he didn't turn up. Are you giving this to me straight, Caution?"

"I'm givin' it to you good an' straight," I tell him. "Somebody gave it to Clemensky in his own office an' I found Travis's document case with his divorce-papers in it in Clemensky's flat, so it looks like Clemensky had the Mechanisation papers too, doesn't it? An' if you're tryin' to do a deal about 'em—if you can put me on to them, it don't look so good for you, does it?"

He says: "Look, what does Clemensky matter? He don't matter to you an' he don't matter to me. That guy was askin' to get himself rubbed out anyway."

"Well, if he was askin' for it, he certainly got it," I say. "But let's come back to these papers. "What's the deal?"

He says: "The deal is this. If I get twenty-five grand you can have those papers. But I wanta know I'm gonna be O.K."

I think for a minute; then I say: "Well, I might even stretch a point an' find the dough. Where do I get in touch with you?"

He says: "Don't be a goddam fool, Caution. What sort of mug do you think I am? You're not goin' to see me until I've got that money, an' then maybe you're not gonna see me. I'm not walkin' inta one of your little set-ups, pal. I've heard about you."

"All right," I tell him. "What's the idea?"

"You think it over," he says. "You think of some way that you can pay over that dough an' guarantee that I'm gonna be O.K. I'll call through again. Maybe I'll come through to-morrow or the day after. I'm in no hurry. But you can take it from me that until you've straightened me out you're not gonna get your hooks on those papers. You got that?"

"I've got it," I tell him.

"O.K.," he says. "Well, if you're clever you'll get thinkin', because I mean business. An' I don't mean perhaps!"

I hear him hang up. I put back the receiver, take out a cigarette an' light it. I lean up against the side of the call-box smokin'. This guy Schrinkler thinks he's a clever guy.

I go back to the dinin'-room an' order myself some more coffee. While I'm drinkin' it I think about Schrinkler. Schrinkler is a tough egg an' he's gotta certain amount of brains in his head. But he thinks he's a clever guy all right. But so did Clemensky an' so did Travis. Well, somebody took care of those two an' maybe with a bit of luck I can take care of Schrinkler.

An' why not!

CHAPTER NINE
EXIT FOR KRAUL

I

I AM sittin' pretty. I got a full house with queens. I reckon I'm gonna scoop the pool. I take a look at the kitty. I reckon there is about four pounds seventeen on the table. They all throw in except Blayne. He says he'll see me. Maybe he thinks I'm bluffin'.

"O.K.," I tell him. "You put your money in, Blayne. But you'll be sorry."

He says: "Yeah!" He pays to see.

I put my cards down. Blayne grins. He lays his hand down an' the lousy so-an'-so has got a full-house with kings. He ropes in the dough.

"What d'ya know about that?" I tell him. "You must be unlucky in love. But I wish you'd had a bit more luck about that Kraul guy."

Blayne says: "What the hell! What could I do? Directly he comes inta Mount Street I'm on to him. He goes inta Piccadilly through Clarges Street an' just at the right time there is a cab passin' for him. He grabs it. O.K. Well, what do I do? There wasn't another cab in sight, an' I'm not good at runnin' at thirty miles an hour."

Pardoe, who is shufflin' the cards, says: "Yeah, it's only in fiction that there's always another cab for the dick."

Benzey pours himself out a stiff slug of whisky. He sinks it in one go. He says:

"I don't see what all the excitement is about this guy Kraul."

"You never see anything, sweetheart," I tell him. "You're so dumb it hurts. It's stickin' outa foot that Kraul killed the Travis guy, see? So Kraul's right in this. I wanta know what this guy's gonna do. He's gonna do something, ain't he?"

"Yeah?" says Benzey. "Why is he gonna do something? Why does he have to do somethin'? Who is this goddam Kraul anyhow?"

"This is the guy who came around to the Carlton to see Pearl," I tell him. "Don't that mean anything to you?"

"I'm no thought-reader," he says. "Maybe I ain't got so many brains as you have. Maybe I only have beauty an' physique an' a whole lot of allure."

He ducks as Pardoe takes a swipe at him.

"Listen, dumb-bell," I tell him. "An' try an' work it out for yourself. Kraul is tied in with Clemensky an' Schrinkler some way or another. Also it is a stone certainty that Kraul is the guy who bumped Travis. But he thinks he's got away with that. An' he certainly does not know that somebody creased Clemensky. That's why he goes back to Chez Clarence to get his suit that he didn't change into the night before. You can take it from me that Kraul is good an' surprised when he meets me there an' when I show him the remains of the late-lamented Clemensky. O.K. Well . . . I pull one on him. I let him get away because first of all I think that Blayne here is goin' to be on his tail, an' also because I want to see what the first thing is that this guy is goin' to do. Well, what does he do?"

Benzey says: "He goes rushin' around to the Carlton to see Pearl. But what the hell . . . ?"

"He don't know she's Pearl, nitwit," I tell him. "He thinks she's Mrs. Cara Travis. He thinks she's Mrs. Cara Travis because I have told him that Mrs. Travis is stayin' at the Carlton. Now maybe he hasn't ever met up with Mrs. Travis but he knows about her. An' he's not the only one. The phoney Travis hadn't ever met up with Cara Travis but *he* knew somethin' about her, didn't he? He knew enough to think he could make her play along with him."

"I get it," says Carl. "Kraul is playin' along on the same idea."

"Right," I say. "Kraul is in a spot. He knows we're after him for bumpin' Travis. He knows that I'm gonna get the cops here after him. So he wants help, don't he? He wants to make a getaway or to try an' pull somethin' else. So he goes rushin' around to the Carlton directly he thinks he's got a chance of seein' the dame."

"That's O.K.," says Carl. "But I still don't get the big idea."

Benzey says: "I don't get it either. Everybody's stoogin' around on this job an' nobody knows what he's doin' except Brilliance here. Brilliance knows but he never tells anybody."

Carl says: "Yeah, maybe he don't trust us." He slings me a wicked look. "On the other hand, maybe *he* don't know anything."

"O.K., you mugs," I tell 'em. "You stick around for a bit. Maybe I'm only guessin' but with a bit of luck some of my guesses are gonna come off."

Blayne says: "Well, it's all very interestin'. Where do we go from here, Lemmy?"

"My idea is this," I say. "I reckon I'm gonna send the three of you guys down to Wilminton. But don't stay at that inn that we stayed at. Stay at some small places on the other side of the town an' keep quiet."

Carl says: "Do you think something's goin' to pop down there, Lemmy?"

"Why not?" I tell him. "I think that maybe Clemensky gave Schrinkler a big idea before he handed in his paychecks."

Pardoe says: "Yeah? Such as what?"

"Look," I tell 'em, "I'll tell you guys a little fairy-story. Clemensky had the Mechanisation plans, so he kidnaps Gayda Vaughan, the idea bein' that he thought she was playin' in with me an' he wanted to find out all about it. Then, when he'd found it out maybe he was gonna bump the dame. Well, that was Schrinkler's idea. That's what he told me. But I don't believe it."

Pardoe says: "I get it. You think Clemensky was gonna hold this dame as a hostage?"

"Right," I say. "Clemensky's got the Mechanisation plans. Well, these things were obviously pinched to sell to the Jerries. But Clemensky is gettin' the breeze-up. Travis is bumped off an' there's likely to be a big smell about it flyin' around. He wants to look after himself. He wants to be safe. So he thinks maybe he can do a deal about those papers, an' in order to make himself safe he kidnaps Gayda. You got the idea?"

"I got it," says Carl. "He does a deal. He gets paid some dough for the papers an' he hands 'em over, but he still keeps the dame. When the deal is completed an' he knows he's safe, an' not until, he lets the dame go."

"Right," I say.

Benzey says: "For cryin' out loud! I got it. You think Schrinkler's gonna pull the same idea."

"Why not, you brainy guy?" I tell him. I throw my cards down. "Listen to me, you monkeys," I tell 'em. "Ain't it the obvious thing for Schrinkler to do? Look, he's the big guy now. Travis is dead. Clemensky's dead. Schrinkler's the head man. He's got the papers or he knows where they are. He wants to do a deal. He tells me on the telephone that I gotta think out some means by which he'll know he's safe before he does it. In other words he's not gonna be content with an appointment where somebody can pay the twenty-five grand an' take the Mechanisation plans. Schrinkler thinks we might pull a double-cross on him. An' why not?

"So I've got to think something up that'll let the guy know he's safe. Well, what can I think up? I reckon he thinks I'm gonna wait for him to ring me up in a few days. He reckons in the meantime, because I know where the papers are, because I know that they're not on their way to the Jerries, I'm not gonna do anything much. He's gonna sit around an' think. He'll start wonderin' what Clemensky's big idea was with Gayda. Then he'll get it. Then maybe he'll try the same idea himself."

Carl says: "I got to hand it to you, Lemmy. I think you're right."

"I'm goddam certain I'm right," I tell him. "Anyhow, I'm gonna stick around an' wait to hear what Schrinkler's got to say. In the meantime you guys know what to do. Blow down to Wilminton; stick around like I told you under cover. Directly you get yourself fixed in ring up my dump on Jermyn Street an' give me the addresses. You got that?"

They say they got it. I pick up my hat.

"Well, I'll be seein' you," I say.

Blayne says: "For cryin' out loud! Ain't it marvellous? Any time I play poker with this guy an' begin to win a little jack he fades out."

I grin at him. "I got brains, Blayne," I tell him. "That's why I'm a Chief Agent. You wanta study my system. So long, babies!" I fade.

It is just gettin' dark. Walkin' down Regent Street, thinkin' about this an' that, I wonder what the next move in this game is gonna be. I believe I have told you before that I am a guy who likes to sit in a corner an' let other people do the work, an' you can take it from me that it ain't a bad scheme in dealin' with the sorta skulduggery and mayhem that is goin' on over these Mechanisation plans.

But between you an' me an' the gate-post, the angle that I cannot get is this Kraul angle. Work it out for yourselves. Supposin' I am right in my guess that it was Kraul shot Travis. O.K. Well, if it was good enough for Clemensky to put Kraul on to doin' that job it was good enough for him to know what the general situation was. But Kraul didn't know. Kraul was good an' surprised when he saw Clemensky propped up against the desk dead. He wasn't puttin' on any act. He wasn't scared. He was just *surprised*. I wonder just how much Clemensky told this guy Kraul supposin' he told him anything.

But then again I mighta been wrong in that guess. It might not have been Kraul who shot Travis. There was another guy around Chez Clarence that night—big tough-lookin' guy—the one who was talkin' to Clemensky. He coulda done it.

I go into Oddenino's an' give myself a big one to keep the germs away. Then I come out, cross Piccadilly Circus an' go inta the Regency. When I get inside the doorway the hall porter gives me a letter. It is from Pearl. It says:

Dear Lemmy,

This is a line to let you know that Gayda and I are very happy down here. I might say that we miss you but you're swollen-headed enough as it is.

One thing is worrying me. By the last post I received a letter forwarded to me from the Carlton Hotel. You'll see it is from a man named Kraul. I don't know what it is about. Possibly you will. Anyhow here it is.

Perhaps when you've time you will call me.

Yours

Pearl.

I grin to myself. So the Kraul mug has started committin' himself to paper, has he? I put the letters in my pocket, go up to my room, have one outa the flask, light a cigarette an' read this Kraul letter. It is typed. It says:

Dear Mrs. Travis,

You won't know who I am, but I think it is about time that you and I got together and had a little talk. Maybe a little thinking will show you that we are both interested in the same sort of propositions that are flying around these days, and although I haven't met you before because there wasn't any reason why we should meet before, I reckon there is a good reason now. In fact there are two reasons.

The first of them is that something has happened to your husband and the second one is that something has happened to Clemensky. Possibly this name will mean something to you. If not, forget everything I've said.

But if it does you might come to the conclusion that it might be a good thing if you and I were to meet up some place and have a little talk. Maybe we could be of use to each other. In any event there wouldn't be any harm done.

I went along to the Carlton to try and get a word with you, but some guy said you wasn't seeing anybody, and I thought it might be the best thing to write you a letter.

It looks at the moment as if I'm in a spot. Maybe somebody is trying to hang something on me. Well, I'd hate to get into any sort of jam where I had to do some talking because that wouldn't do anybody any good.

If you'd be interested in having a little conference you might ring up Clerkenwell 76923 and maybe we could get together.

I don't have to tell you to destroy this letter, because although I don't know very much about you there's one thing I do know— you're no mug. Maybe I'll be seeing you.

Elvin T. Kraul.

I read the letter through again. I reckon that maybe this is gonna be a help to me. I light a fresh cigarette an' walk around the bedroom. After a bit I get the line I'm gonna play. I go downstairs an' ask the hall porter to get me through to Mallows an' to get Miss Pearl Mallory on the line.

While he is gettin' the number I stick around the hallway smokin'. It looks to me that I have got to get some of these dames workin' for me now. Five minutes go by; then he comes across an' tells me that Miss Mallory is on the line. I go inta the box.

I say: "Hallo, Pearl. How're things makin' out for you? An' thank you for sendin' me that letter."

She says: "Well, I hope you understand it, which is more than I do."

"I got an idea what it means," I say. "Anyhow, don't you worry your head about that, because there are two-three things you can do for me."

She says: "Well, I'll be glad to, Lemmy, if it's something I *can* do."

I say: "You can do this all right, but I want you to be careful about it. I want you to make sure you do it just the way I tell you to. Now listen, honey. At ten o'clock to-night I want you to call the number that Kraul mentioned in that letter—Clerkenwell 76923. When you get the number ask for Kraul. When he comes on the line tell him you're Cara Travis; tell him that you got his letter; ask him what he means by it. Ask him what he means by those cracks about your husband, Lon Travis, an' Clemensky. I want you to get him to talk, see? You got that?"

She says she's got it.

"All right," I tell her. "Well, you remember what he says an' ring me up here at twelve midnight an' talk to me. Will you do that, Pearl?"

She says yes, she'll do it. I ask her how she is an' how things are goin' down at Wilminton. I ask her about Gayda.

She says: "Gayda's all right, Lemmy. She's quietened down a lot. Incidentally, you know she's rather for you, don't you? She thinks you're marvellous."

I think to myself that maybe she sounds a little acid about this. I say: "Well, that's fine. Maybe you think I'm not?"

She says: "I don't know, Lemmy. I often wonder exactly what sort of person you are."

"What do you mean by that one?" I say. "Maybe you got some funny ideas about me, Pearl?"

She says: "Maybe I have. I can't see you marrying anybody, and I think it would be a great pity if you were to take Gayda for a ride."

I say: "Look, don't you think that baby can look after herself?"

She says: "Yes, I suppose she can. At the same time I should hate to think that you were amusing yourself."

"I'm not amusin' myself, Pearl," I tell her. "I got a job to do. Gayda happens to come inta the job. But that's no reason why I shouldn't be stuck on her, is it? What I'm tryin' to do at the moment is to look after her."

She says: "I wonder!"

"There's another mean crack," I tell her. "What d'you mean 'you wonder '?"

She says: "Well, I've got an idea in my head that you are just using Gayda and myself as sort of stooges in this case."

I laugh. "You mean like Benzey?" I say.

"That's right," she says, "rather like Benzey."

I say: "Well, that's O.K. But even if I wanta use a dame for a stooge I don't haveta make love to her."

She says: "Why not? I think you'd even do that if you thought it'd help."

I laugh. "You got me all wrong, Pearl," I tell her. "Anyway, I'm a martyr to duty. But you do what I told you about this Kraul guy, see?"

She says: "Very well, sir. I'll obey my orders. But when this business is over—if it ever is over—one of these fine days I'm going to tell you *exactly* what I think about you and your methods."

"You do that, Pearl," I tell her. "I'd like to listen. But look, there's one other little thing you can do for me."

She asks what it is.

"It's just this," I tell her: "I want you to have a quiet word with Vaughan—Gayda's Pa—see? You have a few words with him about that Clemensky kidnappin' business. You let him know that I was on to that job right away before it happened: that I wouldn't take a chance on Gayda. Tell him not to be too surprised at anything else that happens, but if it does just remember this: I'm lookin' after Gayda so he needn't get excited."

She hesitates for a minute; then she says: "All right, I'll tell him that. But listen to me, Lemmy; do you really think something is going to happen—you think Gayda is in danger?"

"Look, sweetheart," I tell her, "anybody connected with this business is in danger—everybody connected with me, see? Why shouldn't they be? Didn't somebody tell you there's a war on an' everybody's in it? Another thing, let me tell you this: It's stickin' outa foot that Gayda would be in the clear if she hadn't wanted to run around with me. But she did want to, see, an' anybody who wants to go runnin' around with me is liable to go runnin' inta some trouble."

She says: "So it seems, Lemmy. But Gayda didn't know that at the time, did she? Don't you think it would have been fairer for you to have told her that making your acquaintance was going to be a dangerous process for her? Don't you think you might have been decent enough to warn her in advance and let her decide whether she wanted to go on with it?"

I say: "Yeah . . . I mighta done that but I didn't think of it. Besides, I didn't know how things was gonna break. Another thing is that if I'd told Gayda about it at the start, if I'd have told her that knowin' me might get her in a jam she'd have been more keen than ever. She's that sorta baby. She's got a good nerve."

"Meaning that *I* haven't," she says.

"You said it—I didn't," I tell her. "But I am not particularly interested in your nerve right now, Pearl. What I'm askin' you to do don't take any nerve. Anybody could do it."

"Really," she says. She sounds as cold as ice. "Well . . . I'm glad I can do *something* anyway. Even if it is something that doesn't require any nerve."

"The trouble is you're not doin' it without a song an' dance," I tell her. "Goddam it, Pearl, look at all the palaver you're makin' over this. Be your age."

She says: "Damn your eyes, Lemmy, I will. But when this business is over I'll never talk to you again. You've got your nerve to talk to me like that. If I didn't feel that I was doing this for Uncle Sam, I'd see you somewhere."

"That's the talk, baby," I tell her. "You go on like that an' do your stuff an' maybe when this is all over, if you're very good, I might even give you a big kiss on the tip of your nose."

She don't say anything. She makes a noise like she was bein' slowly strangled.

"O.K.," I go on. "Now let's be serious. Look, Pearl, this job's gotta be played out. It's gotta be played out my way an' nothing's gonna stop it. I've got a job of work to do an' I'm gonna do it. That means you've got to do a job too an' so's Gayda. All I want you to do is to stop old man Vaughan from bellyachin' an' raisin' hell an' devils at a time I don't want him to. Because you gotta realise that if this boyo thinks Gayda's in danger maybe he's gonna ask for police protection for her, which is a thing I wouldn't like."

"Of course not," she says sorta acid. "I suppose that might stop things going the way you want them to go. It doesn't matter what happens to Gayda so long as you're all right."

"Look, acid-drop," I tell her, "if you wanta have it that way you have it that way. But if you're not gonna do what I tell you maybe I'll get Gayda to do it. *She* won't jib."

"So clever, aren't you?" she says. "I suppose you wouldn't think I was jealous of Gayda?"

"I don't think anything at all," I tell her. "All I want is action. Now you be a good girl. You call Kraul to-night like I told you an' you talk to old man Vaughan like an uncle. Tell him not to get scared; tell him I got everything under control an' I guarantee nothing is gonna happen to Gayda. All right. Are you goin' to ring me at twelve o'clock to-night an' give me the works?"

She says yes, she will. Then she says: "You know, I don't know if anybody's ever told you, but you're a heel."

"Maybe," I tell her. "Do I haveta weep because you think so?"

"I do think so," she says. "I think you're a heel." There's a pause. Then she says: "But even if I do think you're a heel I think you're a damned fascinating heel. Good-night. Mr. Caution. And blast your eyes!"

II

At five o'clock I get inta a cab an' go down to Scotland Yard. Herrick is sittin' at his desk smokin' that pipe of his. It smells like the same pipe that he was smokin' six years ago when I was over here on the Van Zelden case.

I say: "Well, Herrick, how's it goin'?"

"Not too bad, Lemmy," he says. "We had to do a little cleaning up at the Chez Clarence."

"I bet you did," I tell him. "Tell me something—did you find that guy Travis?"

"Yes," he says, "we found him. "He didn't look at all nice. He was in the basement. There's a sorta sub-basement under the lift-well and he was there under about two tons of coal."

I nod my head. "I get it," I say. "I suppose the coal-basement belongs to the Chez Clarence?"

"That's right," he says. "You know, Lemmy, I'd hate to interfere and I know sufficient about the job you're working on to know it's very important. But if it's possible we'd like an explanation of some of this business some time."

"I'm gonna give you the explanation of half of it right now," I tell him, "an' in the meantime will you be a good guy an' get them to check up an' tell me what the address of Clerkenwell 76923 is?"

He says he will. He makes a call an' tells some department to ring him back an' tell him. I sit myself down on the edge of his desk. I light a cigarette.

"Look, pal," I tell him, "this guy Travis was a phoney. He was put in on a boat comin' over from America to wait for the real Travis an' grab off the Mechanisation papers. All right. He got away with it.

He landed here with Travis's papers an' the other stuff. I reckon the Embassy told you about that?"

He nods his head.

"Well, without goin' inta a lotta details," I go on, "this Travis guy was killed by a fella called Elvin Kraul. Kraul was the only guy in Chez Clarence who coulda shot Travis. Travis had to be bumped off good an' quick. It was a job that somebody made their mind up about in a split second. O.K. Well, the only people in the Club who was there when he was shot was the man on the door—this Kraul—the girl in the hat-check room, Clemensky the proprietor, another pal of Clemensky's, a dame who was talkin' to me in the bar, the bar-tender an' Carl Pardoe—a special agent who was workin' with me. He was in the bar too.

"All right. At the time of the killin', the hat-check girl was in the cloakroom; Clemensky, Pardoe, the bar-tender, the dame an' myself were in the bar. Travis couldn't have been shot by the other guy because he was in the baccarat room an' he couldn't have shot Travis without walkin' across the hallway. The bar door was open an' he never walked across the hallway. So the only guy who coulda got inta the writin'-room to bump Travis in the telephone-box was Kraul. Maybe," I say, "there'll be some more evidence about Kraul a little bit later—maybe to-night."

He asks what the idea is.

"The idea is this," I tell him. "Kraul has got in touch with some dame that he thinks is Mrs. Travis. Some of these boyos think they got something on this dame. After he got away from me when he thought I was gonna pinch him, he sends a letter to this dame. He tells her to ring him up to-night at this Clerkenwell number I've just given you. That means to say that even if he doesn't know her he trusts her. All right. He's gotta talk to somebody. This Kraul needs help. He can't get outa this country an' he knows goddam well he'll be wiped up within a week or two. So he's gonna try an' pull something. Maybe we'll know more about that to-night."

He says: "Well, what do you want me to do?"

Right then the telephone-bell on his desk jangles. He talks for a minute; then he says:

"The Clerkenwell number you gave me is that of a newspaper shop name of Vayles. It's in a little place called Belden Court, Clerkenwell—not a particularly salubrious neighbourhood."

I nod my head: "Do you know of a saloon near there?" I tell him.

"Yes," he says, "there's a public-house near there on the corner of the main street about three minutes away called the 'Three Anchors '."

"O.K.," I say. "This is how we play it. You get a coupla police officers to meet me to-night at a quarter to ten at the Three Anchors. I reckon Kraul's going to the Vayles shop to get that telephone call. He's stickin' around somewhere in the neighbourhood. If he goes in there to get that call we wipe him up when he comes out. How's that?"

He says: "Yes, I expect there are two or three charges we can hold him on."

"I reckon there are a million," I say. "You got enough stuff under your Defence of the Realm for that guy. I lay you six to four his passport's a phoney one. I reckon when you check up on this boyo you'll find he's not an American at all, but some sorta guy who's been playin' in on this thing."

He says: "All right." He makes a coupla notes on his pad. He says he'll fix for a coupla police officers to meet me at the Three Anchors at nine forty-five that night.

I get up. I tell him that'll be fine.

"There's just one thing, Lemmy," he says. "You wouldn't shoot this Kraul or anything like that, would you? Just let the officers bring him in quietly."

"Sure," I tell him. "I wouldn't do anything really tough like that."

He gives me a big grin. "Like hell you wouldn't!" he says.

III

It is a nice dark night. The two cops an' I have been stickin' around the saloon bar at this Three Anchors dump, drinkin' double whiskies an' talkin' about everything we can think of. Nice guys these cops—quiet an' interestin'. I reckon that they wouldn't get excited too easily—not even about a cheap yegg like Kraul.

I look at my watch. It says three minutes to ten.

"O.K.," I tell the sergeant. "This is where we do it. I'll get across an' see what happens. You guys get on the corner in about five minutes' time an' come over when I whistle."

I ease through the saloon doors, along the street an' across the road. I keep in the shadow. A few yards along is a little alley an' half-way down this on the right-hand side is Vayles's shop. This dump is one of them little shops where you can buy anything from an evenin' newspaper to a stick of liquorice.

On the other side of the road is a doorway. I park myself there, just opposite the shop door, an' wait. I give myself a cigarette, keepin' my hand over the lighted end, an' give myself up to a whole lotta deep thought.

I am worryin' about this Kraul guy. I want this bozo outa the way an' I am only hopin' that he is goin' to be somewhere around to take the phone-call from Pearl. First of all maybe the call is goin' to tell me somethin', an' secondly I would rather this guy was wiped up. I reckon there is enough trouble flyin' about without havin' some more from this palooka.

Right in the middle of these deep thoughts a telephone-bell starts janglin' over the road. I look at my watch. It is dead on ten o'clock an' Pearl is keepin' to her time-table. I hope the rest of this business is goin' to work as easy. The bell goes on janglin' until I think that nobody's goin' to take any notice of it. Then it stops. A coupla minutes go by an' then the door of Vayles's shop opens an' a kid comes out. He turns right an' goes down towards the end of the alley away from the main street. I ease along on the other side of the road. The kid goes inta a house near the end of the alley. He is inside for a coupla minutes an' then he comes out an' runs back to the shop.

I go back to my doorway. A minute or two afterwards some guy comes from the other end of the alley. He is walkin' fast an' he is goin' towards the shop. When he gets opposite me I can just see by the bit of light that comes when the Vayles's shop door is opened. It is Kraul all right.

He goes inside. I slip across the road an' walk down on the other side, towards the house he came out of. I wait there for about five minutes an' then I hear him comin' towards me. I stand right up against the wall. As he goes past I stick out my foot an' he goes down like a sack of coke.

I put out my hand an' grab him by the back of his coat collar. I yank him up on to his feet an' as he turns around I hit him a sweet one on the point of the jaw.

He decides to contact the sidewalk again. When he gets up he is not feelin' so good. I stick him up against the wall. He stands there, rubbin' his ugly pan, lookin' at me like I was a rattlesnake.

"So you been doin' a little telephonin'?" I say. "Talkin' to some lady friend of yours, hey? Well, maybe it was thoughtful of you seein' that you won't probably be able to talk to that dame any more. Anyhow, who was she? Maybe it was Mrs. Cara Travis?"

He says: "You're a lousy guy, Caution. But you got brains. How the hell did you know who that was?"

I am watchin' him outa the corner of my eye. I can see that this mug is playin' for time, hopin' that he still might be able to make a getaway.

"You're too fond of writin' letters," I tell him. "You was mug enough to write a letter to Mrs. Cara Travis at the Carlton, wasn't you? Well . . . you threw out over that. I got my hooks on that letter—never mind how—an' all I had to do then was to keep this joint cased."

He says: "Smart guy, hey . . . well, you got nothin' on me."

"The cops here don't think that," I tell him. "They think somethin' different. They think they got a murder rap for you. They reckon you can't beat it either, Kraul. They got an open an' shut case that you killed Travis. It had to be you anyhow; there was nobody else there to do it."

"You're a goddam liar," he says. "There was another guy there. There was a guy called Canazzi—a pal of Schrinkler's."

"O.K.," I say. "You tell 'em an' see if they'll believe you. Anyhow, they'll want to ask this Canazzi about it. Where is the guy?"

"I don't know," he says. "He's with Schrinkler."

"An' where's Schrinkler?" I ask him.

He gives me a clever sorta grin.

"You'd like to know," he says. "You'd like to know plenty. Well, why the hell should I talk? If I'm gonna be the fall guy I'm gonna keep my trap shut."

"So you wanta do another deal," I say. "You're gonna tell me where Schrinkler is, if I make it easy for you over the Travis killin'?"

He puts his hands in his pockets. He is feelin' a little bit better.

He says: "Look, Caution—you're clever all right; but you ain't quite so good as you think. You don't know where Schrinkler is. An' you *gotta* know where he is, see? If you want them goddam papers that you're after you gotta know—an' you gotta be goddam good an' quick otherwise he won't even be anywhere where you can find him, see?"

"O.K.," I tell him. "An' you know where he is. All right, where is the guy?"

"I'm not talkin'," he says.

"You're not talkin' because you don't know," I tell him. "You been playin' a lot of fast hands, Kraul. You been bluffin'. You been bluffin' so much that you're very nearly takin' yourself for a ride. But if you're a wise guy you're goin' to talk all you know. Maybe you'll feel better when they get around to hangin' you."

He says: "O.K. You have it your way. If you turn me in you don't get Schrinkler. If you don't get Schrinkler you don't get them papers. You won't be feelin' so good then."

I give him a grin. "I'm gonna chance it, sweetheart," I tell him. "I'm gonna take a chance that I get Schrinkler an' anything else that's goin' without your help."

I grab him by the arm. I whistle. Away down at the end of the street I can hear the two plain-clothes cops comin'.

I start walkin' him along. He says: "You're a mug, Caution. If you're wise you're gonna do a deal. I can talk. I know plenty."

"You talk to yourself, Kraul," I say. "If you wanted to do a deal with me you oughta thought of that before you shot that mug Travis. But you thought you was the kingpin then, didn't you? You thought you were right on top of it. You thought you were goin' to get a sweet cut outa this an' now all you're gonna get is a nice hangin' party. An' I hope you enjoy it. It'll do you a lot of good."

I hand him over to the cops an' they take him away in a cab. I walk around for a bit until I get inta Holborn. I pick up a cab an' drive back to the Regency. When I get there the night guy hands me a telegram. It is from Gayda. It says:

"Think of me Sourpuss I'm crazy about you Gayda."

I grab a telegraph blank at the reception desk. I write her name an' address on it an' I put:

"*Me too—Sourpuss.*"

I tell the night guy to send it off in the mornin'. Then I go up to my room an' have one outa the flask.

I go to bed. I snap off the light an' lie there in the dark, lookin' at the ceilin'.

I am thinkin' that I could go places with a dame like Gayda. She is the sorta babe that a guy could go haywire over.

I think that with a bit of pushin' I could go haywire over her myself. An' why not?

I am just extendin' this line of thought when the telephone-bell goes. I jump off the bed an' look at the luminous dial of my wristwatch. It is two minutes past twelve. I reckon this is Pearl. I grin to myself. She may not be so stuck on me but she certainly keeps to her time-table.

It is her all right.

I say: "Well, baby, what did Kraul have to say?"

She says: "When he came on the telephone I asked if that were Mr. Kraul. He said yes, it was. Then I said I was Cara Travis; that I'd got his letter and what did he want? He said: 'You ought to know what I want. Look, I'm hot, see? The cops here are after me. Maybe you can make a coupla guesses why. Well, I'm still not scared. I reckon if I knew where Schrinkler was I could do a deal with that guy. He's got to have some place over here—somewhere I could hide out. You got that, sister?' I said I understood. Then he said: 'Well, what're you going to do about it?' I said I didn't know what to do. I should have to think. You see, I was in a difficult position," says Pearl. "I didn't know what to say. I didn't know what I was supposed to say."

"That's O.K.," I tell her. "You've done fine, Pearl. What did he say then?"

"He said I'd have to do some goddam quick thinking. He said he wasn't going to be the fall guy, and if he got in a spot that he couldn't get out of he was going to talk and talk plenty. He said the best thing I could do would be to meet him to-morrow. He suggested Piccadilly Circus subway at twelve o'clock. I asked him how I should know him.

He said: 'Don't you worry about knowing me, sister. I know you all right. I've seen your pictures in the papers plenty.'

"He said the best thing I could do in the meantime would be to contact Schrinkler and tell him that unless Schrinkler was going to stand by he was going to talk. Then he said this. He said: 'When you get on to Schrinkler you tell him I know all about Clemensky. You tell him there was only one person could have fixed Clemensky and that was Schrinkler. You tell him that if I'm going to take a murder rap for Travis he's going to take one for Clemensky, see?' "

"Fine," I say. "An' what did you say to that, Pearl?"

She says: "I said I'd think it over. I said I'd meet him and let him know. Then he said: 'You'd better think it over, sister, because if I *have* to talk I'll have to bring you in on this and maybe it won't be so good for you.' Then he hung up."

"Nice work, Pearl," I tell her. "One of these fine days I'm gonna give you a medal for what you've done."

"Oh yes!" she says sorta acid. "That's going to do me a lot of good, isn't it? I suppose the next thing I've got to do is to meet this Kraul. Maybe you're arranging for *me* to be kidnapped too!"

"Don't you worry, sweetheart," I tell her. "I wouldn't let a thing happen to you. Anyway, you don't haveta worry about the Kraul mug. At the present moment that boyo is twiddlin' his thumbs in a police cell some place."

She says: "I see. Well, having carried out my assignments for to-day perhaps I can go to bed now."

"You do that, Pearl," I tell her. "You go to bed an' put that pretty little blonde head of yours on the pillow an' dream about Lemmy. But maybe I don't haveta tell you to do that. Maybe you do it every night."

She says: "Listen, just keep quiet for a minute while I tell you exactly what I think about you, will you?"

I say: "Sure, I'd love to hear." I stand there restin' my elbow on the dressin'-table listenin' to her.

Boy, can she express herself!

CHAPTER TEN
A SPOT FOR GAYDA

I

I AM havin' my breakfast when Vaughan comes through inta the dinin'-room. He is steamed up all right. He looks like he could start something at any moment.

I point to the chair on the other side of my table an' he sits down. He don't waste any words either. He comes right to it. He says: "Look, Caution, I've trusted you and I didn't expect you to make a fool out of me."

"Take it easy, Vaughan," I tell him. "An' have a cup of coffee. Whatever the situation is, gettin' steamed up isn't gonna make it any better. Miss Mallory's been talkin' to you, hey?"

He says: "Yes. She spoke to me last night. I came up here as soon as I could. You know—this thing's got beyond a joke."

"It's never been a joke with me," I tell him. "Anyway, I thought Gayda was rather stuck on bein' engaged to an F.B.I. man?"

He says: "It's one thing being engaged to a man in the Federal Service and another thing being deliberately put into a dangerous situation."

"Just a minute," I tell him. "I'm not havin' that. If anybody put Gayda inta a dangerous spot it was anybody else but me."

He says: "How do you make that out?"

"I warned Gayda," I tell him. "I told her that if she played around with me she'd haveta take a chance. It's only reasonable for people to think that if she's hangin' around with me all the time she's workin' in with me."

"I don't agree with you," he says. "It's your business to look after her. Now she's mixed up in this thing you're trying to alibi yourself. It seems that some sort of attempt has already been made on Gayda and that you're expecting another one."

"That's it," I tell him. "An' there's precious little we can do about it."

He says: "I don't agree. If Gayda's in any sort of danger I'm going to the police."

"O.K.," I tell him. "You go to the police an' what happens? They'll give you a coupla plain-clothes dicks to hang around Gayda so that anybody who wants to pull anything is gonna lay-off for the time bein'. O.K. Nothing'll happen. Then after a while they'll think you're dreamin' an' take the dicks away. Then those other guys get goin' an' do what they were goin' to do. You take it from me, Mr. Vaughan, that police protection stuff is not gonna work."

He looks at me. His eyes are snappin'.

He says: "I think you've got a swell nerve. You can sit back there, feeding your face, an' talk about my daughter as if she didn't matter a damn. I thought you were keen on her?"

"You'd be surprised!" I tell him. "I'm *very* stuck on Gayda. But bein' crazy about her don't affect my common sense. Incidentally, you're not payin' very much of a compliment to me, are you? D'you think I'm the sorta mug who's gonna stick around an' let anything happen to her an' do nothing about it?"

He eases up a bit. He says: "Well, I certainly never thought you were that sort of man."

I give him a big grin an' offer him my cigarette-case. He takes a cigarette an' I light it for him. He's beginnin' to cool down.

"Look," I tell him. "I've got some very tough eggs—F.B.I. men— planted all around your dump. Directly anything happens I'm gonna know all about it. In fact I want it to happen, an' I want it to happen for her sake."

He says: "I don't understand that."

"Of course you don't," I tell him. "Now you listen to me. When I came up to your house the first time I was lookin' for Travis—or the guy you thought was Travis. An' this guy is tied up with these boys, see? Just because Gayda takes me along to the Chez Clarence an' because this Travis guy comes along too, this bunch have got an idea that Gayda's playin' in with me an' they think the best way to get at me is to get at her, see? So they try to pull a fast one. The guy Clemensky fixes to kidnap her. Well, what happens? What they didn't know was that one of the boys they got workin' in on that game was workin' for me too! I knew everything they was gonna do before they did it."

He says: "Well, I've got to admit that was clever all right."

"Look," I tell him, "don't you worry. You leave this thing to me. I'll look after Gayda all right."

He says: "That's all very well, but I think you've got the wrong slant on this, You're a man who's used to taking chances, but I'm not going to take a chance with Gayda."

I give him a big grin.

"Listen to you talkin'," I say. "You're not goin' to take a chance with Gayda! Don't make me laugh. You been takin' chances with Gayda ever since she come outa pigtails. She's one of those babies that are never happy unless they're takin' a chance. That's right an' you know it. I reckon Gayda's been gettin' in an' outa scrapes ever since she could speak words of more than one syllable. An' if she wasn't in this business she'd be up to her neck in something else an' you know it."

"I know one thing," he says, "and that is you're goddam plausible, Caution. Everything you say sounds like good common sense, but I'm still not satisfied."

"O.K. Well, what are you gonna do?" I ask him.

"I'm going to be tough with Gayda," he says. "I'll get her away some place—Ireland—or some other place where these people can't get at her. Once she's in their hands anything might happen. According to what Pearl Mallory said these people are pretty desperate. They'll stick at nothing."

"Maybe," I say. "Maybe they are desperate; maybe they're tough eggs. But I don't think very much of their brains. I don't think they're very clever."

"They were clever enough to get Gayda into their clutches once," he says. "She got out of that. That was a break. You were lucky enough to know what they were going to do, but I take it that you don't know what they're going to do next time?"

"That's right enough," I tell him. "All I can do is guess. But sometimes I'm a good guesser."

He says: "Look, what would you do if you were me; would you be content to chance your daughter's life on another man's guess—no matter how clever you thought he was?"

"No," I say, "I can't say I would. At the same time I think you're makin' a mountain out of a molehill, an' I think the thing for you to do is to stay put an' keep Gadya where she is. You move her off some place an' it might not be so good."

"Why not?" he asks.

"Well," I say, "she might be some place where I *couldn't* help her."

He says: "I wish to God I'd known about this from the start." He shrugs his shoulders. "You make it very difficult for me," he says. "You know, Gayda thinks the world of you. She'd probably refuse to go in any event. I'll have the devil of a job to get her to consent to leave Mallows."

I nod my head. "Well, that's up to you," I say. "You gotta do what you think best. But if you take a tip from me you'll lay off goin' to the police. That's not gonna help anyway."

He says: "No, maybe not. I think you're right there. If I go to them they'll probably have Gayda watched for a few weeks an' these other people won't act. I think I'll do my best to get her to leave Mallows. Anyway, she needs a holiday."

He gives me a grin. He is beginnin' to look better tempered about things. He says:

"You're a pair of determined cusses—both of you. I don't know which of you is the worst—you or she. You both want your own way an' you'll both do your best to get it." He laughs. "What a married couple you'll make," he says. He gets up. "Well, I'll be getting along, Lemmy," he says. "When are you coming down to Mallows? If you want to come down you'd better be quick because I'm going to do my best to get her to pack up and clear out right away."

"Well, you won't be goin' for a day or so," I tell him. "Maybe I'll come down to-morrow. But in the meantime don't get too annoyed with me. I'm doin' my best with a difficult situation."

He says: "Maybe, but I wish Gayda weren't concerned in it."

He says so long an' goes.

I sit back an' give myself another cigarette. It looks to me as if Pearl did her stuff all right. It also looks as if Vaughan is pretty scared for Gayda. I can understand that too. It's also a stone certainty that if he starts makin' preparations to move off with her, somehow Schrinkler is gonna get wind of it because I bet that boy's got somebody planted in the region of Mallows just to see what's goin' on. I get to thinkin' about what Vaughan said. Maybe Pearl is right about me. Maybe I'm bein' a bit tough about this. But what the hell! I gotta do my job. At least that's my story an' I'm gonna stick to it.

I stick around, read the papers an' take in a news-reel. About three o'clock Carl comes through. He is stayin' at a pub in some place called Chapfield about two miles on the other side of Mallows. He's got the boys planted in different places pretty well around the house. I make a note of the addresses and telephone-numbers. I tell Carl to keep his eyes skinned. Then I go upstairs, take one outa the flask, light a cigarette an' lie down.

Somebody once said that waitin' was the hardest part of any game, but I don't believe this guy.

You can always go to sleep.

II

At eight o'clock I give myself a swell dinner—at least as swell as Lord Woolton will let me have. Then I go over to Oddenino's Bar an' have a coupla quiet ones. It is a nice night an' while I'm walkin' across Piccadilly Circus I'm thinkin' about all the things I would like to be doin', that is if I ever get around to doin' the things I wanta do.

When I get back to the Regency, the hall porter tells me that there's an urgent telephone-call for me an' will I ring this number as soon as I come in. He gives me the number. It is Mallows.

I light a cigarette an' go inta the call-box. Three minutes later Pearl comes on the line. She don't sound so good.

"Lemmy," she says, "you've got to do something. Gayda's gone."

"What d'you mean she's gone?" I say. "D'you mean she's gone off with Vaughan? He was up here. He said he was gonna take her away to Ireland or something."

"No," she says, "I don't mean that. Mr. Vaughan hasn't come back here yet."

"O.K.," I tell her. "Now you take things easy, Pearl, an' don't get excited."

"I like your nerve," she says. "How do you expect me to feel? I tell you I'm certain Gayda's in terrible danger."

"So am I," I say. "I've been tellin' you that all along. But it's no good gettin' excited about it. Now take it easy an' relax. Tell me what's the matter."

She says: "I've been out with Gayda most of the day. When I came down to dinner to-night she didn't appear. A few minutes afterwards the butler brought me a note she'd left for me. I'll read it to you. . . .

Dear Pearl,

I know that everybody will be terribly angry with me for doing what I'm doing but it's fun, and maybe I'm going to steal a march on Sourpuss.

This morning somebody pushed a letter for me through the letter-box. It was from a man named Clansing. Clansing told me that he had been working with the people who had succeeded in stealing the papers that Sourpuss wants to get. Apparently this Clansing is a little bit scared. Also it seems he's quite prepared to do a deal—to give the papers to Sourpuss providing he gets some sort of guarantee about his own safety and some money.

He went on to say that if I would meet him this evening he was prepared to put me in a position wherein I could act as intermediary between him and Sourpuss. In other words, he guaranteed to return the papers to Sourpuss if I would arrange to hand him over the money when the time came and not disclose his whereabouts.

Well, what can I lose? Anyway, it's going to be fun if it's true and I don't see how it can be anything else. I'm perfectly certain this man Clansing is telling the truth. Besides, I think it would be wonderful if I could steal a march on Sourpuss and get those papers back for him.

Anyhow, I'm going to meet this Clansing. Tell Father not to be too scared. With luck I shall be back soon after dinner. If I'm not, well, it might be even more thrilling. Then I suggest you'd better get on to my delightful Sourpuss and tell him that he'll have to organise a rescue-party. But somehow I don't feel that will be necessary. I've always believed in my instinct and I believe that what Clansing says is the truth.

All my love to you, Pearl, darling,

Gayda.

I say: "Well, that's not so good, is it? So they pulled a fast one on her?"

Pearl says in a flat sorta voice: "Whatever they've done it's your fault."

"Now, be your age. Pearl," I tell her. "I wasn't expectin' anything like this."

"No?" she says. "Well, what were you expecting?"

"I was expectin' another kidnap," I say. "An' in order to kidnap the dame they got to get her away from Mallows. That's what I put you down there for, to keep an eye on her. Didn't I tell you to stick around an' not let her outa your sight? All right. Not only do I do that but I get some good guys around there watchin' that place. Nobody coulda got at Gayda without our knowin' something about it. At least that's what I thought. But I didn't think they'd pull one like this. Damn it, she's walked right into it. Clansing is Schrinkler, and Schrinkler, believe it or not, is some tough baby. That boy's gonna stop at nothing."

She says: "What *am* I to do, Lemmy? I don't know what to do. Mr. Vaughan's not here. Shall I go to the police?"

"Don't be silly, Pearl," I tell her. "That's not gonna do any good. Look, honey, I'll tell you what you better do. You get the quickest train an' come up here right away." I look at my watch. "It's nine-fifteen now. You oughta be here by eleven o'clock. I wanta talk to you about this. Maybe I can still get at this guy Schrinkler. Will you do that?"

She says: "Yes, I will if you think I ought to, although I don't see what I can do. What am I to do about Mr. Vaughan? Shall I leave a note?"

"Yeah," I say, "you'd better leave a note for Vaughan. You'd better tell him what's happened. Tell him not to get excited; tell him I'm handlin' it. An' you get up here as quick as you can."

She says: "Very well, Sourpuss. But I think you ought to know I hate you like hell."

"I should worry!" I tell her. "If a dame don't love me, I'd much prefer she hated me. All I can't stand is indifference. I'll be seein' you, sweetheart."

III

It is ten minutes past eleven when Pearl comes inta the little lounge at the side of the Regency hallway. She looks marvellous. Maybe I told you mugs before that this dame is certainly a looker.

I say: "Hallo, Pearl. Thanks for comin' up. Maybe you'd like a drink or some coffee or something."

She says she'd like some coffee. I go outside an' tell the night porter to fix it. Then I go back.

She says: "Lemmy, I'm fearfully worried about Gayda. I think this is terrible. I've a feeling that something awful's going to happen to her."

I shake my head. "Don't you believe it, Pearl," I say. "Look, you know that I wouldn't have put Gayda into anything that was really dangerous. She's gonna be all right."

She says: "How can you say that, Lemmy? These people are desperate. They'll do anything to her."

I take out my cigarette-case. I give her a cigarette an' take one myself. While I'm lightin' 'em I say:

"Use your brains, Pearl. This Schrinkler is no mug. He thinks he's got plenty to bargain with. He reckons that while he's got those Mechanisation papers he's safe, but that directly he hands 'em over he's not safe. He thinks that even if I do a deal with him an' agree to pay him the twenty-five grand he asked for those papers, directly I've got the papers I'm gonna have him pinched. That's sense, isn't it? Another thing, he knows he can't get outa this country. There's a war on an' the police here are pretty hot. All the ports would be watched. How's he gonna make it? But there's one way he can make it. If he's got Gayda as a hostage he reckons he's all right."

She says: "You mean to say that he'll want to do a deal with you now. He'll expect you to pay him the money and he'll hand over the papers but he won't let Gayda go till he's safe?"

"That's about it," I say.

She says: "My God, Lemmy, *are* you tough or are you! You're in love with this woman and you've deliberately put her in this position because you think it's going to help you get those papers back. Just think of Gayda's state of mind. She must be in an awful state. She must be terrified."

I say: "All right. Think of her state of mind. You know Gayda as well as I do. Gadya's tough an' she's out for adventure. Goddam it, she's probably likin' this like hell! She probably thinks it's a *big* adventure. She reckons she's gonna have something to talk about for the rest of her life."

She shrugs her shoulders. She says: "It's no good arguing with you. You're obstinate—so obstinate that sometimes I think you're stupid."

"Look, baby," I tell her. "You've called me a lot of things I haven't minded, but that's one thing you can't call me. I'm definitely not stupid."

"I think you're stupid—obstinate and stupid," she says. "All I'm concerned with is Gayda."

"Well, it's no good your bein' concerned," I say. "We know what the situation is an' we can't do anything to alter it."

I give her a grin.

"You don't think I'm just gonna stick around an' let Gayda stay put wherever they've got her?"

She says: "Do you know where Gayda is?"

I shake my head. "No," I tell her. "But I'm gonna find out somehow."

She says: "Well, I hope you're right, Lemmy. In the meantime, what do you want me to do?"

"I don't want you to do anything," I tell her.

She raises her eyebrows. "What do you mean?" she says. "You don't want me to do anything. Have you brought me up all this way to London just to tell me that you don't want me to do anything?"

"That's right," I tell her. "You got some place you can stay here in town, haven't you?"

"Of course," she says. "I've got my flat. But I still don't understand."

I grin. "Of course you don't," I say, "but the thing is I didn't want you hangin' around down at Mallows. There's too much breakin' around there. Maybe something's gonna happen around that part of the country now that Gayda's been kidnapped an' I didn't want you in it."

She looks at me. She looks surprised. She says:

"Aren't you amazing? You want me up here in case anything should happen down at Mallows. This consideration is too astounding, Lemmy."

I grin. "Maybe I'm not only thinkin' of you," I say. "Maybe I'm thinkin' of myself. But that's how it is. You go to your flat, Pearl, an' stick around there. Let me know what the address is. I'll get in touch with you in a day or so."

She says: "Very well. But I don't know that I'm awfully keen on your ideas, Lemmy."

"I gathered that," I tell her. "But believe it or not, baby, they work sometimes."

She says: "But they might not."

She writes the address down on a piece of paper I give her outa my note-book. She finishes her coffee. She says:

"Well, I suppose I'd better be going. If there's anything else you want. . . ."

I give her a sweet smile. "I want plenty," I tell her, "but if I was to tell you maybe you wouldn't be inclined to listen."

She says: "Probably not."

She gets up. She starts walkin' to the hallway.

I send the night porter out to get a cab.

I say: "Has anybody ever told you, Pearl, you've got a helluva mouth? I reckon you've got the prettiest mouth I've ever seen in my life."

She says: "I think it's very condescending of you to tell me. But then I expect you're an expert on mouths, aren't you?"

"I wouldn't go so far as to say that," I say. "But I know a pretty mouth when I see one."

She says: "I see. Well, as far as I'm concerned, so long as your interest ends there I'm quite satisfied."

The night guy comes in. He says there's a cab outside.

She says: "Well, good-night, Lemmy."

"Good-night, Pearl," I tell her. "An' thanks a lot. I'll be seein' you some time."

She says: "Maybe." She goes out. I got an idea that she is not so pleased with me.

I light a cigarette an' go up to my room. I snap on the light an' walk up an' down, tryin' to piece the odd bits an' pieces together. I reckon this jig-saw will begin to straighten itself out in a minute.

I am thinkin' about turnin' in when the telephone starts jang-lin'. For the first time in this goddam case I begin to feel a little bit excited. Maybe we're gonna get down to hard tacks now. Maybe this is gonna be Mister Schrinkler.

I am right. It's Schrinkler all right. He says:

"Hey, Caution, is that you?"

"Yeah," I tell him. "I was waitin' to hear from you. So you knocked off Gayda Vaughan. I suppose you think that's clever?"

He says: "Imitation is the most sincere form of flattery, isn't it? If it was good enough for Clemensky it's good enough for me."

I say: "It's all right if you like it. That was a nice idea bumpin' Clemensky an' then carryin' out his ideas."

He says: "Nuts to you! You talk big, Caution, but you don't know a thing. You couldn't *prove* I killed Clemensky."

"Look, Schrinkler," I tell him. "I'm not concerned with provin' anything. As for Clemensky I don't give a goddam rap whether he's dead or alive. At the present moment I'm not interested in murder. What I want is those Mechanisation papers."

"That's what I thought," he says. "Another thing," he goes on, "what's this big idea about me kidnappin' Gayda Vaughan?"

I say: "So you didn't kidnap her?"

"No," he says, "I didn't have to. I sent her a letter, see? I told her what the job was. I told her you wanted those papers. I said if she liked to meet me maybe we could fix something up. I said if she didn't it wouldn't be so good for you."

"I get it," I say. "So you did it that way. You told that dame that unless she played in with you you were gonna knock me off?"

"That's right," he says. "I thought that would be an artistic touch."

"Some artist," I tell him. "I reckon you're gonna come to an artis-tic end one of these fine days, Schrinkler."

He says: "Nuts to you! I don't want to hear your opinions. All I want to know from you is, are you gonna talk business or not?"

"O.K.," I tell him. "I'm talkin' business with you now because I *got* to talk business."

He says: "All right. First of all before we get to the money thing I'd like to ask you something. Have you done anything about this Gayda Vaughan business? Have you put the police on to it?"

"No," I tell him. "I'm not such a mug. You needn't worry about that. Nobody knows a thing about it. The Vaughan guy wanted to do something like that but I've stopped him."

"You were a wise guy, Caution," he says, "because if any cops start jumpin' around tryin' to stick their snouts inta this you know what I'll do to that dame."

"I can guess!" I tell him.

"All right," he says. "Here's the way it is. I'm ringin' you from London now, but directly I hang up I'm leavin'. I got a little place just outside Feresby. It's called 'Whitelands.' I'm goin' back there." I hear him laugh. "You can see how I trust you, Caution," he says. "I'm even givin' you my address. Maybe you'd like to come out there with some cops an' pick me up."

"Cut out the funny stuff," I tell him. "Let's get on with this deal."

He says: "O.K. I'll be back there inside of an hour. This is the way we play it. You come out. You oughta be able to do what I want you to do an' get out there inside three hours."

"Thanks a lot," I tell him. "An' what do I haveta do?"

"What you have to do is this," he says. "You knock up that Embassy of yours an' you get me a special passport. I wanta blow outa this dump to-morrow, see? I wanta get back to the States. Not only do I want an Embassy passport but I want a certified cheque on a Chicago bank for twenty-five grand. You got that?"

"I got it," I tell him.

"O.K.," he says. "I got an idea there's a boat sailin' to-morrow—a fast one. I'm goin' back on that boat. With a bit of luck I'll be in the States in six days. Then I cash the cheque, see? O.K. When that's done I'm gonna send you a cable. I'm gonna tell you where Gayda Vaughan is."

"I get it," I tell him. "Who's gonna be lookin' after her in the meantime?"

"You'd like to know, wouldn't you?" he says. "But look, there's a thing I oughta warn you about. The people who will be lookin' after that dame might get funny with her if they don't hear from me in seven or eight days' time. They'll wanta hear from me that I've got the dough an' I'm O.K. before they let her go. Well, that's how it is. Are we gonna deal, Caution?"

I look at my watch. I say: "O.K. I've got no option, have I? I'll be out with you about three o'clock to-morrow mornin'."

"O.K.," he says. "An' you'll have that passport an' that certified cheque?"

"I'll have 'em, you goddam heel," I tell him. "An' you know what I'd like to do with you. But I want those papers."

"You'll have 'em," he says. "You can have 'em to-morrow mornin'. Maybe I could get more for 'em somewhere else, but I'm a moderate guy. I'll be seein' you, Caution."

I hear the click of the receiver as he hangs up.

CHAPTER ELEVEN
THE DEAL WITH SCHRINKLER

I

SOMEWHERE around a clock strikes half-past one. I pour myself a shot of whisky outa the flask an' drink it. I put on ray overcoat an' hat, give myself a cigarette an' cross over to the doorway. I stop there. I got so used to runnin' around without a gun that I forgot the Luger.

I go over to the drawer, get it out an' put it in a side pocket of my overcoat; but I put it in the left-hand pocket because that is the pocket where the other guy never thinks you've got a gun. He always thinks you'll have it in the right-hand pocket, an' I am a guy who can shoot with my left hand just as well as I can with my right, which is useful sometimes.

I go downstairs. I ask the janitor if he has got an A.A. book. He gives me one. I look up this place called Feresby an' how to get there. I give the A.A. book back to the janitor an' tell this guy maybe I'll be back before mornin'. I tell him that if I'm not back by ten o'clock, or if I don't call through to him by then, he is to get through to Mr. Herrick at Whitehall 1212 an' tell him where I have gone an' that he might like to have a look an' see if I'm O.K. He'll know what I mean. I give the janitor the address at Feresby an' scram.

I walk around to the garage in Jermyn Street an' get out the car. It's not a bad sorta night—cold, but I don't mind that. There is a moon comin' up an' you can see pretty easily. Drivin' along smokin'

I get to thinkin' about this case an' all the things that have happened during the last three or four days. I wonder just what the grand finale's gonna be like. Maybe we're gonna have one an' maybe not. I have known sometimes before when I expected to have a grand finale an' all I got was a big fizzle an' I'm not a guy who likes anti-climaxes. I like explosions.

At a quarter to three I get to this dump. It is a nice little place—countryfied an' quiet. I stop at some place that looks like a railway station, go in an' find the porter. I ask him if he knows where White-lands is. He tells me. He says it's about a mile an' a half away on a turnin' off the main road.

Ten minutes later I get there. The road is a narrow dirt-road leadin' off the main road. It is a nice-lookin' little place set back in some ornamental sorta gardens.

I park the car by the side of the main gate, push open the gate an' walk up the gravel path. I notice that my feet are makin' a helluva noise, an' just for the moment the idea occurs to me that it wouldn't be so good if these guys was to try something funny with me *after* they've done this deal of theirs. What the hell! I shrug my shoulders. Life is like that an' I've been lucky before.

There is a bell-pull by the side of the door. I give it a jerk. Away back in the house I can hear a bell ringin'—one of those old-fashioned bells. I stand there on the porch an' light a cigarette.

The door opens. Somebody says: "Hallo, Caution. Come inside."

It is Schrinkler. He is standin' there just inside the hallway with the door half open. He is smilin'. He's lookin' at me like I was the honoured guest.

I say: "Well, I've come for the show-down, Schrinkler."

I go inta the hallway.

He says: "Yeah! Stick your hat on the peg. This ain't a bad little dump. An' come inside. I got some good whisky here."

I follow him inta the livin'-room. It is a big room an' there is a fire burnin'. A nice comfortable sorta room. I reckon Schrinkler knows how to look after himself.

I stand there with my hands in my overcoat pockets, watchin' him while he goes over to the sideboard an' pours out some whisky. A cool one, this Schrinkler. But then why not? He's been plenty tough for a long time. He's been one of those guys that get away with things. I reckon there are five or six States in America where the cops would like to get their hands on Schrinkler. I said would "like to." Maybe I told you before that this guy's been clever.

I go an' stand in front of the fireplace. After a minute he comes over to me. He's got a drink in each hand. He hands me one. He grins at me. He says: "Well, I hope there aren't any hard feelin's over this deal."

I take a drink. I say: "What d'you expect me to say? You don't think I *like* this, do you?"

He goes over to the big armchair one side of the fire. He sits down. He leans back an' looks at me, the whisky in his hand. He is quite happy. He is smilin'. He's on top of the job.

He says: "You don't haveta like it. You can't help it, can you? You see, I've been bankin' on one thing, Caution. You want those papers—bad."

"You're right there," I tell him. "I've got to have 'em."

He says: "Yeah!" He drinks the whisky. He puts the glass down on the floor by the side of the chair. He says: "Have you got that certified cheque?"

I nod my head. "I've got it," I say. "Where are the papers?"

He gives me another grin. He says: "Well, don't think I'm bein' funny or anything like that, but I've been thinkin' things out. I don't think I'm goin' to give you those papers to-night."

I look at him. I say: "What a lousy heel you are. You can't even do a deal."

He says: "Wait a minute. Don't get tough. I'm doin' a deal all right, but I got to look after myself, see? How do I know how you're playin' this? How do I know you haven't got some guys around here? Supposin' I gave you the papers now an' took the cheque, how do I know you're even gonna let me get away with this?"

I say: "Don't be a mug. Haven't you guarded yourself over that? Haven't you got the Vaughan dame?"

He says: "Yeah, I know. But I heard about you, Caution. You're a smart fella. Since I called you to-night I've been thinkin'. If you get those papers an' grab me you might be able to do a deal with me, mightn't you? You might threaten a lotta things if I didn't hand her over. You might promise a lotta things if I did. So I decided I wasn't gonna play it that way."

"I get it," I say. "Well, maybe you'll be good enough to tell me how you *have* decided to play it."

"Look," he says, "I'm not tryin' to be funny. I'm doin' what I said I was gonna do. You get a straight deal from me all right, Caution, and you get the papers. But this is how we're gonna do it. First of all I want that cheque an' that Embassy passport, see? Then to-morrow I'm gonna blow. In a week's time I oughta be back in the States. O.K. When I'm there an' I have got the cheque cashed I'll send you a cable. At the same time I'll send a cable somewhere else. The day after that Gayda Vaughan can go back home, an' when she goes back she'll take the papers with her. How d'you like that?"

"I don't like it a bit," I tell him. "It looks like we gotta give you twenty-five grand an' you're gonna get the cheque cashed. Then we've gotta trust you to let the dame go an' we've gotta trust you that she'll be given the papers to bring back. Why should I think you're gonna play ball?"

He says: "Look, I thought you were smart. Why don't you be your age, Caution. What's the good of those papers to me when I'm back in America. They're no goddam good at all, are they? I can't do any business with 'em over there. All right. Well, I'm the only person you got to worry about."

"Meanin' what?" I tell him.

"Meanin' everybody else in this job is finished bar me," he says. "Clemensky's out. Everybody's out. The only guy you got to worry about is me. You know goddam well I can't do anything with those papers in America. Besides, I'll tell you something. I'm goddam bored with this game."

"I'll say you are," I tell him. "You've done a nice bit of work for yourself in this job, Schrinkler. You been workin' your old racket. You got in on this business because Clemensky wanted a gorilla—a tough guy. He wanted somebody to knock Gayda Vaughan off. You were over here an' he fixed for you to do it for him. O.K. Well, you've been clever all right. You muscled-in on the job an' you've high-jacked the loot. Everybody else is in the cart but you."

He grins. He takes out a cigarette-case an' lights one. He draws the smoke down inta his lungs an' blows it out slowly.

He says: "Yeah. Maybe you're right. They all got what was comin' to 'em anyway. It looks like I'm sittin' on top of the job."

"I'm goddamed sorry but I've got to agree with you," I say. "The Travis guy got his. Kraul shot him. Then you fixed Clemensky. What are you gonna do about these guys? What're you doin' about that guy Kraul an' that other guy Canazzi?"

He says: "You should worry about Kraul. I don't give one goddam about him. He don't know anything. Kraul is a mug."

"He's a mug all right," I tell him. "He was pinched to-night. Maybe he'll do some talkin'."

He laughs. "Let him talk," he says. "He can't talk about me. You know, that Kraul guy was just a big bluff—just a trigger man. Nobody ever let him know a thing. So he can shoot his mouth as much as he likes."

I say: "Maybe he can. But maybe he can say a bit more than you think he can. I reckon Kraul's gonna shop you for that Clemensky job."

He says: "Yeah?" He don't look at all perturbed about this. "Well, let him," he says. "Why should I care?"

He yawns. "Well, what are you gonna do?" he says. "Are you gonna play ball or are you gonna be a mug an' try something funny."

"You're pretty sure of yourself, aren't you, Schrinkler?" I tell him.

"Why not?" he says. "I've been takin' chances all my life—big ones. It's the big chances that come off. I never go out for small-time stuff. That's where Clemensky made a mistake about me. He thought I was a small-time guy." He yawns again. He says: "All you gotta make up your mind about is this. Either you're gonna give me that certified cheque an' the passport, lay off till I'm back in the States an' take my word that you're gonna get Gayda Vaughan an' the papers, or else you're not. Supposin' you say no, what can you do? You can pinch me. Then you can start bringin' a lotta charges against me an' you gotta prove 'em. An' where's it gonna get you?

"If you get away with everything you wanta get away with, you still haven't got the papers an' you still haven't got Gayda Vaughan, an' I oughta tell you that that guy Canazzi is not a nice guy. If things didn't go right at his end, if he didn't hear from me when the time comes, he might not like it. He might get tough with that dame." He grins. "If he does," he says, "I wouldn't like to be her."

I throw my cigarette stub in the fire. I finish the drink an' put the glass on the mantelpiece behind me. I light another cigarette. I say: "It looks like I was a mug to come down here. Maybe I walked inta something. Maybe when you get that passport an' the cheque I'm not gonna get outa here."

He grins again. He says: "Maybe. But that ain't sense, is it? What do I wanta do a thing like that for? Where's it gonna get me? What good do I do myself by killin' *you*?"

I say: "Well, maybe there's some sense in that. It looks like you got me where you want me, Schrinkler."

He says: "Well, since you put it that way, that's how it is. So it seems there ain't a lot more to talk about." He gets up. He goes over to the sideboard an' pours himself another drink. He holds the glass up to the light an' looks at it. "Of course," he says, "I've been moderate over this. Twenty-five grand's not very much. I oughta have asked more. But then I always was a considerate guy."

"Like hell!" I tell him.

He says: "Well, I got plenty to do." He grins at me sideways. "I gotta get my packin' done. So maybe you'll hand over that passport an' the cheque."

"O.K.," I tell him. I open my overcoat, put my hand inside as if I was gonna take some papers outa my pocket. Then I put my left hand inta my overcoat pocket sorta casual. I bring out the Luger.

I say: "Come on, Schrinkler. I'm sorta bored with you. I've had enough of you."

He looks at me with his eyes poppin'.

He says: "For crissake!"

"Look," I tell him, "what the hell d'you think I am? You oughta know about me better than that. Did you think I was comin' out here to listen to some phoney proposition an' give you a certified cheque an' a passport to get outa this country? What the hell d'you think I am?"

He says: "Well, I'll be sugared! Look, Caution, don't be a bigger mug than you are. You gotta have those papers, haven't you?"

"You bet," I say. "An' somehow I'm gonna get 'em. But if you think I'm gonna be heisted by a cheap thug like you, you made a mistake. Get your hat, sweetheart, we're movin'."

He says: "O.K. I think you're a mug, but you have it your way."

He drinks the whisky, puts the glass down on the sideboard. Then he goes for his coat pocket. He has got the gun out an' is nearly set for a shot when I let him have it.

The Luger makes a noise like a cannon.

He flops back against the sideboard. He's got his left hand pressed to his stomach. He don't look so good. He stays there for a coupla seconds. His face is twisted. Then he tries to bring the hand with the gun in it up again. It looks as if he's plenty annoyed. So would you be if you were shot in the guts!

I say: "Take it easy, Schrinkler. You're all washed up. You're finished."

He says: "To hell—"

He crumples up. His knees sag. The gun drops outa his hand. He flops on to the carpet. I stand there in front of the fire waitin'. I stick around for two-three minutes. I can't hear a thing. Maybe there was nobody else in the place but him an' me. I stand there lookin' at him.

Maybe this is funny. Maybe the mug thought I was gonna fall for that tall story of his. Maybe he thought I was gonna let him get away with that passport an' certified cheque an' take his word that Gayda was comin' back some time with the papers. I reckon the late Mister Schrinkler was an optimist.

I light myself another cigarette. Then I go over this joint—out inta the hallway, up the stairs. There's nobody there. It is just a nice week-end sorta dump—nice an' restful for the nerves. I reckon Schrinkler never thought that he was gonna get his at this address.

I come downstairs again. There is a telephone in the hallway. I put the gun in my pocket an' get through to Carl Pardoe. When I have finished with him I go back to the livin'-room. I take a look at Schrinkler. Believe it or not, that guy is much better lookin' dead than he ever was alive.

I pour myself out a stiff one; then I sit in the big armchair an' drink it. I reckon that life is fulla surprises.

It looks like Schrinkler has found that out too. But maybe by now he knows all about a lotta things.

After a bit I go to sleep.

II

I wake up with a helluva start. Somebody is bangin' on the front door like hell. After a bit they stop bangin' an' give the bell a jingle. I reckon it's Carl an' he's been standin' there gettin' impatient or maybe wonderin' if some more of these tough eggs have got at me an' I'm all in one piece.

I cross over to the doorway. Schrinkler is still lyin' on the rug nice an' peaceful. I feel a lot happier about this guy since he's been dead.

I go outa the room, across the hallway an' open the door. An' am I surprised or am I? Standin' on the porch is Pearl. She is wearin' a fur coat an' looks like all the flowers in May. A nice-lookin' dame Pearl, but maybe I told you guys that before.

"Well . . . well," I say. "If this isn't a pleasant surprise. An' what can I do for you, Pearl? An' what are you doin' around here at this time of night? An' I thought I told you to stick around at your flat in London until I contacted you? What's been goin' on?"

"Nothing's been going on," she says. Her voice, which is usually nice an' low an' sorta husky, is as acid as hell. "But I don't know why you should think that I've got to do what *you* tell me."

"O.K.," I tell her. "So you don't want to do what I tell you. All right. Well, what're you doin' around here anyway? An' why did you come down here?"

She says: "After I left you I went to my flat. I telephoned through to Mallows. Mr. Vaughan had called through and the butler told him about Gayda. He's almost out of his wits."

"Well, what does he think he's goin' to do?" I ask her. "Bein' out of his wits won't help him or Gayda."

She stands there in the hallway lookin' at me like I was a nasty piece of cold boiled pork. She says:

"My God, you're tough, aren't you? Nothing means anything to you. You can't even understand it when Vaughan gets excited when his daughter's kidnapped. You're so bound up in your own ideas and schemes that you don't give a hoot what happens to any one else."

I grin at her. "Let's skip that, baby," I tell her. "Beefin' off at me won't help either. How did you know I was down here?"

"I went back to the Regency," she says. "The night porter gave me the address you'd left with him. I made up my mind to go back to Mallows at once and I thought I'd call in here on the way and see if there was anything you could—or would—do. That is if you're not *too* busy."

Her voice is good an' sarcastic.

"Another thing," she goes on. "Do I have to stand in this hallway? Isn't there somewhere I can sit down? I'm tired and cold and I'm worried sick about Gayda."

"I'd ask you to come inta the sittin'-room," I tell her, "but I got a corpse there. Still, if you stick around for a minute I'll get everything fixed an' then you can come in."

I leave her there in the hallway. I go back into the livin'-room, grab one of the loose rugs on the other side of the room an' put it over Schrinkler. Then I tell her to come in.

She stands in the doorway lookin' at the heap on the floor. She says: "What's that . . . who is it? Did you . . .?"

"Yeah," I tell her. "It *is* an' I *did*. That was Mister Schrinkler that was. A nice guy but he didn't know what was good for him."

She nods her head. She don't look so good. I go over to the side-board an' pour out some whisky an' a splash of soda. I give it to her. She sits down in the big chair. She says:

"Will you give me a cigarette, Lemmy?"

I give her one. She don't say anything for a bit. She just sits there, smokin'. Then she says: "What happened?"

"Schrinkler called through to the Regency after you'd gone," I tell her. "He'd got a big idea. He tried to pull one on me. The one I thought he was gonna pull."

She says: "About Gayda?"

"Right," I tell her. "He'd got Gayda. At least Canazzi—that side-kicker of his—has got her. The idea was that if I came out here an' brought an Embassy passport an' a certified cheque for twenty-five grand, the big boy on the floor here was gonna skip back to the States, cash the cheque an' when he knew he was O.K. he was gonna cable 'em to let Gayda go free. He was gonna give me the stuff I wanted—

the Mechanisation plans that Travis brought over—an' hold Gayda as a sorta hostage until he knew he was O.K."

She gives me a cold sorta look. She says: "Naturally, you didn't like that?"

"I didn't like it a bit," I tell her. "Any time I come down to doin' a deal with a guy like Schrinkler I hope somebody pushes me under a truck. But I didn't tell *him* that. I told him it was O.K. Anyway, I reckoned that there'd be a catch in it somewhere."

I take my glass over to the sideboard an' give myself another shot of Schrinkler's whisky. I haveta step over him to get it.

"When I got out here he pulled a fast one on me," I go on. "Or he tried to. The idea was then that he wasn't gonna give me the papers. They was gonna stick to them. All he wanted was the passport an' the cheque. He was goin' to clear out, an' when everything was O.K. he was goin' to cable for Gayda to be set free an' they was goin' to give *her* the papers to bring back. Well . . . I didn't like *that* either. I reckoned anyway that I'd had enough of this guy Schrinkler so I told him I was gonna take him in. Well, he didn't like it, see? He went for a gun so I let him have it an' there he is."

Pearl says in a quiet voice: "Yes, there he is, and what about Gayda?"

"I know," I tell her. "That is not quite so good, is it?"

She says: "My God . . . you can say it isn't quite so good. What's going to happen to that girl. They'll probably kill her. When this man Schrinkler doesn't show up, they'll know the game's up. They'll kill Gayda!"

"Why don't you take it easy?" I tell her. "Why do they have to kill Gayda? They can still do a deal. They've got the papers, haven't they?"

"Supposing they haven't," she says. "Supposing Schrinkler had them. Supposing he'd kept them. . . ."

"Not a chance," I tell her. "Schrinkler wouldn't be such a mug as to have those papers when I was around. You can bet your life that Canazzi has got those plans an' while he's got 'em he'll think he's safe. An' while he thinks he's safe Gayda'll be all right—"

"Until you start something else," she says. "Until you try another of your bright ideas." She looks at me as if I was a hamburger left over from last Friday. "There are moments when I detest you," she says.

"That's O.K. by me," I tell her. "I think you look swell when you're all steamed up like you are now. But then beautiful dames always look more beautiful when they're bad-tempered."

She looks at me along her eyelids. If looks could kill I reckon I would be stiffer than Schrinkler.

She says: "You're appalling. With Gayda in a situation that may mean death for her you can stand around and try to be smart. Either you haven't got any heart or you haven't got any brains."

"Maybe I got neither," I say. "Maybe I'm entirely filleted like a jellyfish. But that's as maybe, honeypot, an' it don't do for everybody to start bawlin' around the place an' goin' haywire any time somethin' serious happens. Me—I am a guy who likes to be nice an' cool an' stay that way."

She shrugs her shoulders.

Somebody starts ringin' the doorbell. Every time that goddam bell starts janglin' it gives me the willies. Maybe I'm gettin' a little nervy in my old age. I take a look at Pearl. She is lookin' into the fire an' there are a coupla big tears runnin' down her cheeks. A sweet baby, that one. An' the way she looks now I could eat her.

I go out inta the hallway an' open the door. Carl Pardoe an' Benzey are standin' on the porch. I tell 'em to come in.

Carl says: "Did anything break around here, Lemmy?"

"Plenty," I tell him. "I got Pearl Mallory inside an' a stiff under the carpet."

"Nice goin'," says Carl. "Would the stiff be Schrinkler?"

"Yeah," I say. "He got fresh so I hadta iron him out."

Benzey says: "Ain't he cute? He irons 'em out an' then puts 'em under the carpet. I suppose that's to preserve 'em."

We go inta the livin'-room. I introduce Carl to Pearl. Then I say:

"Look, Pearl, you aren't doin' any good around here, an' you're all washed up. You're tired an' you're worryin' yourself sick. You get outa here. Benzey's goin' to drive you back to Mallows. You better get back there an' wait for Vaughan to get back. He'll need somebody to keep him from doin' somethin' silly. You go back an' wait till he arrives; tell him to take it easy. Everything's gonna work out all right."

She gets up. "You're *too* comforting," she says. "I've never heard any one talk so much and do so little to help as you. Good-night, Mr. Pardoe."

She goes out. Benzey goes after her. He throws me an old-fashioned look over his shoulder.

Carl says: "D'you know what? I'll tell you something. My instinct an' my years of training as a detective tell me that that dame is not awfully fond of you right now."

"You're dead right," I tell him. "She hates my guts. She's worried about Gayda. Well . . . why shouldn't she . . .?"

Carl goes over an' lifts up the rug. He takes a look at Schrinkler an' then puts the rug back.

"The guy is definitely dead," he says. "So dead he don't even know it. Is that good or is it?"

I shrug my shoulders.

He says: "I reckon you aren't so pleased you had to crease him, are you, Lemmy?"

"What the hell!" I say. "He asked for it an' it was him or me."

"What about the papers?" he says. "I suppose the guy wouldn't have 'em cached around this dump some place?"

"No soap," I tell him. "He was tryin' another fast one. Canazzi's got the Mechanisation papers an' the girl."

Carl yawns. He says: "It's fun bein' a detective. Nothin' ever happens. At least not the way you want it. I can see a whole bundle of trouble for you. You got a corpse an' no Mechanisation papers. An' old man Vaughan is gonna tear your entrails out if this Canazzi guy don't return the girl right side up an' in good order. An' you ain't worryin'. That tells me something."

"Such as?" I ask him.

"Such as you got something up your sleeve," he says. "I know you. You're a cuss for nice little schemes that are so goddam woozy that every time somebody thinks they're gonna miss they come off. But I reckon you're overplayin' it this time. I reckon that Mister Caution has caught himself out."

He goes over to the sideboard an' pours himself a slug of Schrinkler's whisky. He drinks it very slowly an' then has another one.

He says: "Where do we go from here—or don't we?"

"Not for a bit," I say. "I reckon we gotta give Canazzi a little time to think, hey?"

Carl says: "Yeah. But definitely. Canazzi is stickin' around thinkin' that Schrinkler has maybe pulled this fast one on you. So he sticks around. He expects to hear something from Schrinkler. Because it is a bad egg to a barrel of diamonds that Schrinkler has fixed to call him on the phone when everything's O.K. When this don't happen Canazzi is gonna do one of two things."

"Such as what?" I ask him.

"Such as (*a*) he is comin' around here to see what's gone wrong with this bezuzus, or (*b*) he's gonna get himself a sharp knife an' cut little Gayda's throat."

I say: "Listen, for crissake don't talk like that. I'm a sensitive guy. Look, Carl, would it be goddam awful or would it if that guy wasta cut Gayda's throat?"

He says: "Yeah . . . it would be too bad for her. An' for a guy who's supposed to be stuck on that dame you're takin' it very nice an' easy. That bein' so I reckon you got it figured out that Canazzi is *not* going to carve that dame. You got it figured out that he's comin' around here."

"Nope," I tell him. "I have not got anything figured out. I have got sorta beyond figurin' anythin' out. But I reckon there's just a chance that this Canazzi guy is gonna show up here to find out what the hell has happened to Schrinkler."

"That suits me," says Carl. "An' when he comes what do we do with him? Do we fog him an' put him under the carpet with Schrinkler or do we persuade the boy to talk about where Gayda is?"

"We'll wait till the mug gets here," I say. "In the meantime I'm goin' to have a little sleep. You stick around an' keep your eyes skinned for any trouble that's blowin'."

He says: "O.K. What time would you like your early mornin' tea?"

"You call me in an hour, Carl," I say. "Unless anything breaks."

I flop down in the big chair an' doze off. I am sleepin' good an' hard when something wakes me. I sit up with a jerk. The room is in darkness an' I can hear a sorta gaspin' noise. Outside in the hallway the telephone-bell is janglin' like hell an' devils.

I slide over to the door good an' quick an' snap on the light. The gaspin' noise is comin' from Carl, who is sittin' in the other chair snorin' his head off. Some watchdog this guy!

I ease out inta the hallway an' grab the telephone. It is Benzey. He says: "Say, listen, I been ringin' you for ten minutes. I thought maybe you was dead or something."

"No," I say, "I'm still in one piece. What's breakin'?"

"You'd be surprised," he says. "Life is very amusin' around here. Just a little while ago Gayda blew in. Yeah . . . believe it or not—she make a break an' got away with it. She ditched Canazzi an' got back here. She walked about four-five miles through the rain. You oughta have seen that poor kid."

"Nice work," I tell him. "I'll be over as soon as I can make it."

"That ain't all," he says. "Is this Gayda good or is she! She—"

"Never mind about that," I tell him. "What's happened to Canazzi. Where did she leave him?"

"On the floor," he says. "She shot him with his own gun. You say what you like but I think that Gayda is cute."

"O.K.," I tell him. "Hold everything till I get there."

I hang up. I go back to the livin'-room an' give Carl a helluva dig. He wakes up. He says: "So what?"

"Gayda's back," I tell him with a big grin. "She shot Canazzi an' made a break. What did I tell you? I knew that dame would come out on top."

He gets up an' stretches. He says: "I can't make it out the way you get dames to do your work for you. How do you do it?"

"One of these days I'll tell you," I say. "Don't tell anybody but, believe it or not, I got a system!"

Chapter Twelve
SWEET DAME

I

There is a nasty cold drizzlin' rain. It is as dark as hell an' about as cheerful. When we turn inta the carriage-drive at Mallows I get to thinkin' about the first time I came to this dump—the night I met

Travis. There was a night for you! A swell moonlight night with love an' kisses an' what-have-you-got flyin' all over the place. Not like this night. No, sir!

Carl says: "I reckon you are not so pleased. I reckon this is not one of your big moments. Also I should not be at all surprised if the big boy does not want to tear your ears off when you weigh in with the report on this job."

I ask him why.

"Well," he says, "you got *one* guy pinched—Kraul. What does he matter? This Kraul guy is chicken-feed—small-time stuff. The guy is just a sorta amateur killer an' he don't know a goddam thing. He is a guy who stooged around for Clemensky. O.K. You got *him*. An' what else have you got? Just sweet nothin' at all. Travis is dead an' so he can't talk, an' Clemensky is dead an' he can't talk, an' now the only guy who coulda told you where those papers are is also no longer with us. Canazzi gettin' himself fogged has done you no good at all."

"You don't know, Carl," I tell him. "Maybe Gayda's got the papers."

"Like hell," says Carl. "I reckon they been kiddin' you along, these guys. I reckon Schrinkler was kiddin' you along. I reckon that even if you hadda handed that heel a passport an' the dough, an' even if he had got himself back to U.S., he wouldn't have handed the papers over to the dame. I reckon the stuff he gave you was all hooey. Directly he'd got away this Canazzi guy woulda slit Gayda's throat an' taken a powder with the papers."

"Yeah?" I say. "An' where would he have taken a powder to? Where does the guy go?"

"He woulda got away some place," says Carl. "These boys was organised. They got it on you this time, Lemmy."

"That's how it looks," I tell him. "But who cares? I can take it."

He grins. "That's swell," he says. "Because it looks like you'll have to."

"Yeah," I say. "An' everybody is gonna cheer. All you guys are goin' to laugh your heads off. Me . . . I reckon I'm in bad with everybody. Even the dames."

"That Pearl dame don't seem to like you a lot," he says. "An' that dame is a very swell number."

I don't say anything. Why should I? I stop the car an' go up the steps. I don't haveta ring. The door opens right away an' the butler guy is standin' there. I reckon the expression on this bozo's face would be the same if he was bein' trampled on by wild elephants. It would be goddam hard to play poker with this guy.

He says: "Come in, sir. Come in!"

I go inta the hall. Carl is right behind me. 1 am takin' off my coat when Pearl comes outa the passageway inta the hall. She is wearin' a close-fittin' blue velvet house-coat an' a strained expression. She don't look overjoyed at seein' me.

I say: "Well, Pearl, so all's well that ends well. . . ."

"I'm glad you think so," she says. She sounds like the cuttin' edge on a razor. "Would you like some coffee, Mr. Pardoe?"

He says yes. I say I would like some too. I light a cigarette.

"Look, Pearl," I tell her. "What the hell's the good of your bein' steamed up over this? Everything's O.K. now."

She says: "So everything's O.K.!" She sorta mimics my voice. "Isn't that too wonderful? The fact that Gayda has had to kill a man doesn't mean a thing to you. And you're supposed to be in love with her!" She shrugs her shoulders.

"Well, what can I do?" I ask her. "It ain't gonna help if I start doin' backfalls in the hallway, is it—or cryin' my eyes out? Where *is* Gayda?"

"She's in bed," she says. "Naturally she's suffered a terrible shock. But she's asked after you. She wants to see you." She shrugs her shoulders again. "She must be a glutton for punishment," she says.

"I can see I'm in for a lot of trouble," I say. "Is Vaughan here? Does he know about all this?"

"He knows," says Pearl. "We got him on the telephone. He's stay-ing at the Park Hotel. I told him that Gayda was all right. I asked him not to come back until to-morrow. I thought it would be better if he weren't here until Gayda is better. She has enough to put up with without having to hear her father tell you *exactly* what he thinks about you."

"All right," I tell her. "Just turn off the heat, willya? An' Where's Benzey?"

"He's asleep," she says. She turns away. She moves towards the staircase.

I say: "Just a minute. Pearl. How soon will I be able to talk to Gayda?"

She says: "I really can't see why you are in such a hurry. I hope she's asleep. I suppose you know it's not yet six o'clock."

"O.K.," I tell her. "Well, I'll be around."

She throws me a dirty look. She goes up the staircase.

I cross the hallway an' go inta the library. I throw my cigarette stub away an' light a fresh one.

Carl says: "Where do we go from here, Lemmy? I suppose there isn't very much we can do." He grins. "I suppose you'll be goin' up to see the big boy?"

"I'm in no hurry," I say. "In the meantime you better park here an' relax. Maybe I'll want you later."

I go out inta the hallway, up the staircase. I walk along the corridor. Away towards the other end I can see Pearl comin' out of one of the bedrooms, closin' the door quietly behind her.

I say: "Look, Pearl, maybe you're pretty fed up with me, but there's no need for you to go outa your way to show it like that. Maybe there's an explanation."

"You bet," she says. "You'll always have an explanation. Did any one ever tell you you were very plausible?"

I give her a big grin. "A lotta dames have told me that," I say.

"I expect they have," she says. "But I'm not one who falls for *that* line."

"Fine," I tell her. "That must be very nice for you. Which bedroom is Benzey usin'?"

She points towards the other end of the corridor.

"The second door on the right," she says, "I suppose you're going to cook up *another* scheme?"

"What's the use?" I tell her. "It looks to me as if this job's all over."

She says: "Yes, I believe the expression is 'all over bar the shouting'."

"That's right," I tell her. "Maybe we'll have some shoutin' in a minute."

"You're quite right," she says. "There'll be plenty of shouting when Mr. Vaughan gets here in the morning. You'd be wise if you weren't here."

"No soap," I say. "I never run away from guys. Well . . . I'll be seein' you."

I walk along to Benzey's bedroom an' stick my head inside the doorway. He is asleep. He's got his hands folded across his stomach, but he's not snorin'—not this time. He's makin' a sorta whistlin' noise—like some bird in pain. I give him a dig. He opens his eyes an' looks up at me. Then he sits up an' yawns.

He says: "For Pete's sake—can't I never get any sleep?"

"Listen, you human dynamo," I tell him. "This is where I want some action outa you. You just get up an' scram. Get outa this house, but make it a nice quiet job, see? Get the early train for London. There's one at six twenty-five. That means to say that you oughta be in town at seven-thirty. Telephone me at eight o'clock. You got that?"

He says he's got it. He says: "What do I haveta do?"

"I'll tell you when you call me," I say. "Now get goin'."

I go downstairs inta the library. Carl is sittin' in one of the big chairs by the fire. He is sound asleep. I flop down in the other one. I close my eyes. In about two minutes I'm asleep too.

II

It is eight o'clock when the butler wakes me up. He tells me I'm wanted on the telephone. I go out inta the hallway. I speak to Benzey. I tell him what he is to do an' I keep my voice very nice an' quiet. When I come back I wake Carl up.

"Look, Carl," I tell him. "This is gonna be funny. Just come with me, will ya?"

He says: "What's this?"

I say: "You'll see."

We go inta the hallway an' up the stairs. When I get to the top of the staircase Pearl is comin' outa one of the bedrooms. I walk down the corridor with Carl close behind me. As I go past her she says:

"You're not going to disturb Gayda, are you?"

"Yeah," I tell her. "I'm gonna disturb her plenty."

She says: "Is it necessary?"

"*I* think so," I say. "Incidentally, Pearl, maybe you'd like to string along too."

She says: "Surely there's nothing that you can have to say to Gayda that's important now. Why don't you let her sleep?"

"I don't feel like it," I say, I walk along the corridor. I knock on Gayda's door. Somebody says: "Come in."

I open the door an' step inta the room. Just over my shoulder I can see Carl, with Pearl behind him.

Gayda is propped up against the pillows. There are dark circles under her eyes. She looks sorta strained an' nervy.

I say: "Well, Gayda, it's too bad you hadta kill Canazzi."

She says in a weak voice: "Oh, Sourpuss . . . Sourpuss. . . . It was terrible! I've often wondered what it was like to kill a man." She gives a little sob. "Now I know."

"You didn't know before, did you, pal?" I tell her. "Didn't you know when you killed Clemensky?"

I hear a gasp from Pearl. I turn around. Carl is lookin' at me with his eyes poppin'.

"Ladies an' gentlemen," I say, "let me present you to the heroine in this job—*Mrs. Cara Travis.*"

I look at the dame in the bed. All of a sudden she looks a million years old.

She says: "You must be mad!"

"Like hell I am," I tell her. "You know, Cara, I've been wise to you from the start. The first night I came up here lookin' for Travis you made a big mistake. You shouldn't have tried to rub me out."

Pearl says: "But . . ."

"Pipe down, sweetheart," I tell her.

Gayda says: "Don't take any notice of him. Pearl. I think he's a little mental."

"That's a sweet one from you," I tell her. "Ain't it marvellous," I go on, "the more beautiful they are the worse they are! Look at her—three times a killer. She got Travis shot; she killed Clemensky; she puts Schrinkler inta a spot where he's got to get his; then she kills Canazzi."

I grin at her. "That's O.K.," I say. "But what I don't forgive you for, baby, is for thinkin' that I was such a mug that I wasn't wise to you."

She laughs. She's got her nerve back all right. She puts her hands behind her head. She leans back there smilin' at me. She looks sweet.

She says: "You're terribly clever, aren't you, Sourpuss? I've always heard that about you."

"Clever enough for you," I tell her. "Maybe you'd like to hear how clever I am. All right. When I came up here on that first night you had to think quickly, didn't you? Here was somebody lookin' for Travis an' you knew he wasn't Travis. You got scared. You wasn't certain as to whether anybody had an idea as to who you were; whether they knew that Miss Gayda Vaughan was Mrs. Cara Travis—the real Travis's wife—the woman he wanted to divorce.

"So you pulled a fast one. You made up your mind quickly. You told me that Travis was cock-eyed. You said you'd get the butler to give him some black coffee so as to get him fit to talk to me. You also told me that there was a pistol-shootin' competition goin' on downstairs. In other words, you'd made up your mind what you were gonna do you were alibi-ing yourself before you did it.

"Then you took me out in the moonlight an' played a very pretty little love scene, an' when you went back inta the house you took a shot at me with a gun with a silencer on it. It wasn't a bad shot either. Of course that was an accident, wasn't it? That was one of the cock-eyed guys in the pistol-shootin' competition? That was the first bad break.

"An' you weren't quite certain; you weren't quite certain as to whether I was really Pleyell or who I was. But one thing you did know. If I was Pleyell I was gonna know that the phoney Travis *was* phoney. So after I'd had a talk with him an' didn't do anything about it, you came to the conclusion I wasn't Pleyell. Then you wondered what the hell I was playin' at. You made up your mind that you'd gotta work fast."

She says: "You're really rather marvellous, Sourpuss. It must be your intelligence that I'm so keen on. I'm still crazy about you."

"I bet you are," I tell her. "You're gonna be even more crazy about me when I'm through."

She says: "Go on, Sourpuss. You're fearfully interesting. Tell me some more about what I did."

"The next idea was to get the phoney Travis outa the way. He'd done his job. An' you'd got Travis's document case. In that case were the Mechanisation plans an' the Travis divorce papers.

"So you asked me to meet you an' go to Chez Clarence to do a little gamblin'. What you wanted to do was to see Clemensky right under my nose—Clemensky who was in this job with you—Clemensky who was the only guy who knew *you* were Mrs. Cara Travis. You wanted to get the money from him to pay the stooge Travis off an' get him outa the way. Well, you got it. That was the eight thousand pounds you were supposed to win from Clemensky.

"An' it was tough on that guy Travis. If I hadn't played it the way I did maybe you'd have let him get away with his eight thousand pounds.

"But I was a bit too fast for you. When I went with you to Chez Clarence I telephoned somebody. I telephoned a woman. I told you it was Mrs. Cara Travis an' you didn't feel so good about that, did you? You wondered what the hell I was gettin' some dame to front as Mrs. Cara Travis for. But you soon knew. When I got back to the Chez Clarence bringin' Travis with me, you knew that I'd taken him round to see her; you knew that I was after an identification. Now you were goddam certain that I *knew* he wasn't Travis.

"Then you got a bit scared, didn't you. You wondered what was gonna happen next. But one thing you was certain of. You were certain that I didn't know you were Cara Travis, which is where you made a big mistake."

She says: "That's another interesting point, Sourpuss. Tell me how did you know—supposing that I am Cara Travis?"

"There was a guy chasin' after you for fifteen-sixteen months in the States," I say, "a private detective by the name of Lolly—one of the guys who was tryin' to get that divorce evidence on you that your husband wanted. I had a meeting with that guy before Travis sailed for England. He gave me a description of you. After the first night I knew it had to be you. Anyhow, you soon proved it."

"Did I?" she says.

"You did," I go on. "When I brought Travis back to the Chez Clarence you knew he *had* to be fixed. You thought he might get scared an' talk. So you told Clemensky that he'd gotta be straightened out. While I was talkin' to you in the bar with Carl Pardoe here, Kraul, the man on the door, watched Travis go inta the telephone-box. He went in there an' shot him. An' that was that! I went inta that room two-three minutes later an' found him there."

Gayda gives a little yawn. She says: "So I had Travis killed and then I suppose everything was all right?"

"Not quite," I tell her. "But it was a lot easier for you because he was outa the way."

"Your next trouble was Clemensky. He wasn't feelin' so good. You'd had eight thousand pounds off him to give to Travis an' you'd still got it. An' *you* had all the papers. Now I reckon Clemensky was a guy who was put over here to look after the money side of this job an' he was beginnin' to get a little bit scared of you. You were sittin' right on top of it. You'd got eight thousand pounds an' you'd got the papers. Clemensky knew you were tough an' clever. So he decides to pull a fast one on you. He wants to have a little talk with you; he wants to make you talk sense. He wants to get back that eight thousand pounds that you didn't give Travis. But more than anything else he wants those Mechanisation papers. Once he's got those he knows you've gotta play ball."

I walk over to the table by the side of the bed an' stub out my cigarette. Pardoe is leanin' against the mantelpiece. There is a little grin about his mouth. I reckon Carl is comin' to the conclusion that I'm not such a mug after all. Pearl is standin' at the bottom of the bed. She is lookin' at Gayda. She looks scared. She looks as if she is sayin' something nasty. Well, maybe she is.

"The trouble with all you guys is always the same," I say. "You don't trust each other. I know that. All you saps have been workin' for *me* all the way along." I grin at her. "Only I wasn't mug enough to let you know it.

"Now we come to the next mug—Schrinkler. Schrinkler's over here workin' with Clemensky because Clemensky wants a tough egg around an' Schrinkler is certainly that. But I'm already on to Schrinkler an' he is supposed to be playin' in with me. Clemensky fixes with Schrinkler to kidnap you. They were goin' to hold you until such time as you coughed up those papers. But what you didn't know was that Schrinkler wised me up about that kidnappin' business an' I put Carl Pardoe in to take care of you. But I coulda saved myself the trouble because you knew all about it. Schrinkler not only double-crossed me;

he double-crossed Clemensky. *He told you all about it.* Schrinkler was workin' in with you. An' why not. He was that sorta guy!

"You told him you'd got the papers an' he looked on you as bein' the head man in this job. He was lookin' after himself.

"So now you gotta fix Clemensky. When I took you back to your hotel in Knightsbridge that night you knew goddam well there was goin' to be a message for you sayin' your father was ill. You knew all about it. You knew you were supposed to go back to Mallows on that train. You knew you were goin' to be taken off that train an' taken to some dump of Clemensky's. Schrinkler had told you the whole thing.

"So what did you do? Or maybe you'd like to tell me?"

She say in a soft voice: "No, Sourpuss, I'd hate to. I'd hate to interrupt this little fairy story. You tell me."

"All right," I say. "I'll tell you. After I'd left you at your hotel you nipped out an' you got down to the Chez Clarence. You had a key. You knew you'd find Clemensky there. He was there all right. He was in his office waitin' to be phoned by Schrinkler to say the snatch was O.K.

"An' *was* he surprised!

"Well, you shot Clemensky. Then you thought you'd be really clever. You'd got Travis's document case with you. You took Clemensky's key off him. You went round to his apartment. You planted Travis's document case with the divorce papers in it in Clemensky's apartment. I found 'em there. That was supposed to prove something to me. That was supposed to prove to me *that Clemensky had the papers*; that he'd taken the Mechanisation papers outa the case an' left the other stuff there because he wasn't worryin' about it. Maybe you remember me tellin' you about that. You thought I'd fallen for that, didn't you, sweetheart?

"Then you scrammed back to your hotel. You telephoned through to me at the Regency an' told me the story about Vaughan bein' ill an' that you were catchin' that train back. You had to go through with that kidnap plot because you didn't know then that Carl Pardoe—who you thought was Capelli—was workin' in with me, an' also you didn't want him an' Schrinkler to know you had bumped Clemensky.

"Well, you got outa that business all right an' came back to Mallows.

"All right. So now Clemensky's dead an' you've still got the papers an' Travis is dead, so he can't talk. You're not worryin' about Kraul. Anyhow, he can't do any harm because he don't know a thing. He was just a stooge. He don't know you've got anything to do with this business. An' now Clemensky is outa the way. Clemensky was the only one who knew who you were. But now you've got a new partner in this game. You've got Schrinkler. You're wonderin' how you can fix Schrinkler.

"Well, you get a big idea. You put it up to Schrinkler an' bein' a mug he falls for it. The idea is that *he* kidnaps you. He kidnaps you to hold you as a hostage while he gets away. Now this is clever because by this time Schrinkler is gettin' a little bit scared of this business. He wants to get out of it. This way he gets out. All he wants is jack. He don't give a damn about those Mechanisation papers. In fact he's rather scared of them. They look too hot for him. So you tell him you've got it all fixed. He's to write you a letter tellin' you he's Clansing, an' you, bein' a brave adventurous sorta girl, are goin' to fall for it just to help me.

"Then you go off with Canazzi—another mug—an' Schrinkler rings me up an' gives me a proposition, the idea bein' that I give him a passport to get outa this country an' a twenty-five grand cheque, an' the mug thinks I'm so keen on gettin' those Mechanisation papers back that I'll do it.

"Well, you didn't care what I did. If I fell for this line of Schrinkler's an' gave him the passport an' the dough he woulda got outa the country. You were goin' to fix Canazzi anyway because Schrinkler was through with the deal; he'd got his pay-off an' he was finished. Then all you had to do was to fix this escape from Canazzi after bein' forced to shoot him in order to get away. An' there you are!"

She says: "Sourpuss, you really *are* marvellous. So you knew I was going to kill Canazzi too."

Carl says: "I gotta hand it to you, Lemmy."

"You *had* to kill Canazzi," I tell her. "You don't mean to tell me that you were goin' to split what you got from sellin' those Mechanisation papers with that punk? I suppose he took you off to some other house in the neighbourhood. Maybe you were gonna say you shot him defendin' your honour. Like hell!" I say. "I reckon you had a gun when you went off with Canazzi. You waited two-three hours to give me time to have my interview with Schrinkler. Then you let Canazzi have it an' wandered back here through the rain. A nice act, sweetheart."

She says: "Well, it all seems very simple, doesn't it, Lemmy? None of it seems to have worried you very much."

"Not very much," I tell her. "Everybody around thought I was the big mug, of course, including Pearl here. You'd be surprised to know how sympathetic she's been with you."

I sling a wicked look at Pearl. "Maybe you know now why I sent you down here to Mallows," I tell her, "just to keep an eye on things. You've been doin' better work than you know, Pearl."

She don't say anything. She's still lookin' at Gayda with wide eyes.

"She's a nice little thing," I go on, "ain't she? Here's a dame who fixes to have the phoney Travis killed an' who shot two men—Clemensky an' Canazzi. She was pretty certain too that something would happen between Schrinkler an' myself. I reckon she knew I wasn't gonna fall for that mug's line. I reckon she knew I'd try an' take Schrinkler in an' that the tough egg would start something an' there'd be a gun-fight."

"Yeah," say's Carl, "an' then one of two things woulda happened. Either Schrinkler gets killed or you get killed."

"Right," I say. "An' it don't matter to her which. Whatever happens she's sittin' on top of the heap. All she has to do is to fix Canazzi.

"An' then everything is all set. The next thing is to sell the Mechanisation plans to the Germans—a job that I reckon Clemensky fixed a long time ago."

The dame in the bed looks at Pearl. She is smilin'—not a very nice smile. She says:

"He's wonderful, isn't he?"

Pearl says in that soft voice of hers: "I'm beginning to think so."

I go on: "You see, from the start we knew something, Cara. We knew why Travis wanted to divorce you. He'd suspected you for a long time. That was the real reason why he wanted to get away from you. He knew you were playin' in with some very funny people and with America at war he didn't trust you. Maybe he told somebody that."

She says in a hard voice: "Who did he tell?"

"He told Lolly, the private detective," I tell her, "the dick who was trailin' around after you for fifteen months."

She gives another little yawn. She says: "Well, it's all very interesting. And so I killed all these poeple an' I have these papers and I was going to sell them to the Germans. It sounds like a fairy story, doesn't it? *How* was I going to sell them?"

"That's an easy one," I tell her. "That phoney father of yours, Vaughan, thought of a bright idea. He was scared about you. He wanted to get you away from all these guys, He was goin' to take you to Ireland—another nice set-up. I bet he was all set this mornin' with his travel permits an' everything fixed to take his little daughter over to Ireland, where she'd be nice an' safe. Well," I go on, "South Ireland's a neutral country, ain't it? There are Germans over there. That's where the deal was gonna be done."

Pearl says: "My God! So that's what they were going to do."

"Yeah, Pearl," I tell her. "That's what they were going to do. I bet Vaughan had a surprise when Benzey an' Herrick walked inta the Park Hotel an' pinched him this morning."

Carl lights a cigarette. He says: "Nice work, Lemmy—a nice showdown."

The dame in the bed says: "It's all very *interesting*, Sourpuss. But there's just one small point."

"Never mind about it bein' interestin'," I tell her. "The question is, is it true?"

She says sorta casual: "Well, supposing I admit for the sake of argument that some of it *might* be true, I'm still on top of this job, aren't I?"

I nod my head. "Yeah," I tell her. "Meanin' you still got those Mechanisation papers?"

"Meanin' just that," she says. "I know the value of those papers, Sourpuss. I know the U.S. and British Governments *must* have them. You see . . . I can *still* do a deal."

"Yeah?" I tell her. "So you can still do a deal? All right. How d'you propose to do it?"

She says: "Well, I've got to protect myself, haven't I? I've got a suggestion to make. You said we were going to I Ireland to negotiate those papers. I suggest that I go there. Eire's a neutral country.

I should be safe there. When I get there, Sourpuss, I'll let you know where the Mechanisation papers are."

She lies back on the frilled pillows smilin' at me. Little Cara has got her nerve all right.

"That sounds to me like Schrinkler talkin' again," I tell her. "How would I know I was gonna get the papers?"

She shrugs her pretty shoulders. "I'm afraid you'll have to take a chance on that, Sourpuss dear," she says.

I draw the cigarette smoke down inta my lungs. I blow a coupla smoke-rings. I don't say anything for a bit; then I say:

"You know, Cara, I've been wonderin' what I'm gonna do about you. I can do one of two things. I can hand you over to the cops here an' let them deal with you, or I can let you go to Ireland."

Pearl says: "My God, Lemmy, you're not going to let her go?"

"Why not?" I tell her. "Maybe you've heard about these Germans. They're not nice gays. They hate to be taken for a ride."

Pearl says: "I don't understand."

"Can't you see how it is?" I say. "Right now over in Ireland are two or three of these Nazi guys waitin' to take delivery of these Mechanisation papers. They are probably goin' to pay plenty too. But supposin' they didn't get the plans. Supposin' this dame went over there an' handed them a lot of hooey. Supposin' the papers she handed over to them was just a lot of mush. What d'you think those boys would do to her?"

The dame in the bed says: "That's a nice supposition, Lemmy. But, you see, I *have* got the papers."

"You got nothing, sweetheart," I tell her. "I've got 'em. I've had 'em for a long time."

She jerks up in bed. Her eyes are like slits. She says in an odd sorta voice:

"What the hell do you mean? I tell you *I've* got those papers."

"No, you haven't, sweetheart," I say. "You gave 'em to me on a plate. You see, you fell for that stuff that I told you about Clemensky. I told you that I reckoned that Clemensky would have those papers. You wanted to prove to me that he'd got 'em. Well, there was only one way you could do that. You did it. You planted Travis's document case with the divorce papers in it in Clemensky's apartment. You took the Mechanisation papers out. You kept those."

She says: "I *kept* them and I've *got* them."

"Nuts," I tell her. "Those plans are a lotta hooey. Any expert who took a look at 'em would know that. The real Mechanisation plans were in code in the divorce papers—in the two years' 'reports' of the agents who'd been followin' you around. An' how d'you like that, sweetheart?"

She falls back on to the pillows. She makes a hissin' noise between her teeth. She looks like a ghost.

"You see, Cara," I say, "when Travis brought those papers over we knew somebody was gonna get at 'em. We also knew that Travis had had several firms of agents watchin' you for fifteen months tryin' to get evidence for divorce. Well, we thought of a swell idea. We faked up a whole bundle of supposed private detective reports. It was a nice job. Those reports contained in code the whole of the Mechanisation plans. The idea was that if anybody was after those documents they'd pinch the wrong lot.

"Well, it came off. You had those plans. You had the case an' both sets of papers, an' you were mug enough to give me back the case an' the set of papers I wanted. An' how do you like that, sweetheart?"

She don't say anything. Her head flops forward. Her mouth is hangin' open.

Pearl says: "My God . . . she's fainted."

Carl says: "An' why not? Wouldn't you?"

III

Blayne says: "There's a helluva lot in this jackpot. It's been up an' down twice. That means there's nearly fifteen pounds in the kitty. I'm gettin' heart disease."

Benzey pours himself out a shot. He says: "I reckon Brilliance here is gonna win this jackpot. Brilliance always gets away with everythin'. But maybe you guys know that."

Carl says: "What's eatin' you, Benzey? You're O.K. You got appeal. The trouble with you is that you ain't got enough of it."

He deals the cards. I look at mine an' get a thrill. I got three kings. I open the jackpot an' discard one card to bluff these guys I got only two pairs. Blayne draws one card also.

Everybody else goes out. Blayne an' I do a little bettin'. The kitty is up to over twenty pounds when he sees me. I throw 'em down. Blayne grins an' puts his hand down. Believe it or not, that guy has got three aces!

He puts on a helluva grin an' grabs the kitty. Just then the telephone starts janglin'. Carl goes outside to answer it. After a minute he comes back. He says:

"It's some dame. She wants you, Lemmy. Also this dame has a very nice voice—sorta arch, if you get me."

"All the dames I know have got nice voices," I say.

I go outside to the telephone.

Somebody says: "Is this Mr. Caution?"

I say yes it is.

The dame says: "Well . . . I've a message for you. Miss Mallory asked me to telephone you and ask you—"

"How did Miss Mallory know I was around here at Carl Pardoe's place?" I ask. "There's only one guys knows this address."

The dame says: "She must have got it from the Embassy musn't she?"

I get it. "Oh yeah?" I say. "So it's you, Pearl?"

"Yes," she says. "It's me, I'm in town. At my apartment. I wanted to congratulate you, Lemmy. I think you were swell."

"Crooks are always mugs," I tell her. "If they wasn't they wouldn't be crooks. Anyhow, Pearl, *you* were swell *all* the time. You helped plenty."

"I didn't do a thing," she says. "You see—there are only two things I can do really well—they are driving a car and making coffee."

"I don't believe you," I tell her. "I don't believe you can drive a car any an' I certainly do *not* believe you can make coffee."

She says: "Oh, really! You wouldn't like to make a bet on that, I suppose."

I say: "I'll bet you half a dozen hats to a cigar you can't do either of those things. But if you take the bet it's got to be decided under conditions that I make."

She says: "Very well . . . I'll agree to that. It's a bet."

"O.K.," I tell her. "Well, you drive the car around here. You better park at the bottom of the mews. Then you sound your horn three times. I'll come down an' you can take me around to your flat an' make the coffee. Then I'll tell you if you've won."

She says: "I knew there was a catch in this."

"Don't you do it if you don't want to," I tell her. "Maybe you're afraid of losin'."

She says: "It isn't that, Lemmy. But it's late. It's after eleven o'clock and I was wondering . . ."

"What were you wonderin'?" I ask her.

"Well . . ." she says. "I was wondering just how much I can trust you."

"You can't," I tell her. "Where dames are concerned I am a very untrustworthy guy. An' when the dame is as beautiful as you are an' her voice is as soft an' low an' husky as yours an' her nature is as swell as yours, an' she has such allure, sex appeal, *oomph* an' what-have-you-got generally, well, then, I am so untrustworthy that it's just nobody's business."

She says: "That's what I thought."

She gives a little sigh. Then she says: "How do I get around to that place?"

THE END